WELCOME TO THE NEIGHBORHOOD

"What I'm sayin' is, if you stick your hand on my coat, you might not get it back."

"Whoa!" Leather Vest mocked, and threw his hands up, pretending to be terrified. "I believe we've got us a rattlesnake here, Rafe. Better jump back before he bites ya." He took an exaggerated step back then to Rafe's amusement before the smile of contempt returned to his face, and he focused his gaze upon Adam as he issued his warning. "Now I'm gonna teach you a little respect, and show you what happens to jokers who threaten me." He reached for one of his pistols.

Before he could pull it, Adam threw the glass of beer in his eyes, at the same time grasping his rifle by the barrel. Swinging it like a club, he cracked Rafe on the side of his head before the startled bully could pull his revolver halfway out of his holster. In almost one continuous move, he spun around to face Leather Vest, who was sputtering and spitting, trying to wipe the beer out of his eyes. One quick thrust with the butt of his rifle smashed Leather Vest's nose and dropped him to the fl

OUTLAW PASS

Charles G. West

BERKLEY
New York

BERKLEY
An imprint of Penguin Random House LLC
penguinrandomhouse.com

ISBN: 9780451234957

Signet mass-market edition / October 2011
Berkley mass-market edition / April 2021

Printed in the United States of America
10

For Ronda

Chapter 1

"Mose said you were lookin' for me," Adam Blaine said when he met his father coming from the barn. "If you're still worryin' about those missin' cows over on the north range, I found 'em this mornin' holed up in a ravine near the creek."

"No," Nathan Blaine replied. "I figured you'd find 'em. I knew they wouldn't be far. Mose always blames the Indians when we've got cattle missin'. I keep tellin' him that if there's one or two missin', then it might be hungry Injuns cuttin' out some of the stock—but not when we're talkin' about twenty or thirty at a time."

Adam smiled, picturing the worried face of the old Indian scout. Mose Stebbins had come to work for Adam's father when his eyesight began to fail him and he no longer trusted himself to lead a cavalry scouting party. The old man had gone on many a hunting trip with him in the mountains to the north and the Absarokas to the south. Now his eyes were no longer sharp enough to be accurate on shots of any distance. Never one to admit to this weakness, he always tended to give Adam the longer shot, saying the young man needed the practice. "I counted thirty-two head," Adam said, "all bunched up together."

"I figured," his father repeated. "That ain't why I sent Mose to find you, though." He waited for Adam to step down from the saddle. "I think it's time you went to look for your brother."

"Yessir," Adam replied without emotion. Jake, three years his junior, had been away from home for over a year. That in itself was not cause for concern for Adam and his father. Jake had sent a message that he was planning to leave Bannack and head for home that very day. Now, two weeks later, Jake had failed to show up from what should have been a five-day ride at most. There was no concern on his father's part for the first week. Jake was always his free-spirited son, prone to drift with the wind, and Nathan was not surprised when he didn't show when he was supposed to. Never content to work at raising cattle, Jake had hurried off to join the horde of other dreamers when news of a major gold discovery in Bannack reached their little settlement on the Yellowstone. Adam had to smile when he remembered Jake's promise on the day he left. "I'll find enough gold to buy all the stock we need to make the Triple-B the biggest cattle spread in the Gallatin Valley."

His father had responded with the statement that the Triple-B was already the biggest. "But if you have to chase your tail in a circle around Bannack, go to hell on. When you run outta grub, come on home."

Nathan's claim was not an exaggeration. The Triple-B *was* the largest, but it was because it was the only cattle ranch in the valley. He had built it up from its simple start as a small herd he had driven up from his home in Briscoe County, Texas. The old man was now fully aware that his was a situation that was bound to change, and soon. More and more settlers were showing up on the trail that led from Fort Laramie to the gold strikes in Bannack and the more recent one in Virginia City. These were not the folks that worried Nathan; they were just passing through. It was the people looking for space to build new homes who concerned him, and the fertile land of the Gallatin Valley was a strong attraction to many of these farm families. Nathan knew the fences would be coming, and his free range would be shrinking with each new arrival. John Bozeman, along with Daniel Rouse and William Beall, was already rumored to be thinking about laying out a town. For now, there was room for everybody, but how long would that be the case? These were the issues he would deal with in the not too distant future. His concern on this day, however, was for his son, and what trouble he might have gotten himself into in the mining camps. In sharp contrast to Jake, Adam was as steady as a granite cliff. Taller by a couple of inches on a powerful frame, Adam was truly Jake's big brother, and Nathan was confident that his elder son would ensure the continued success of his ranch long after he was gone. Adam had been getting his younger brother out of scrapes since they were boys, so it was not unusual that Nathan was sending him to find Jake once again.

It was all the same to Adam. Unlike his brother, he never crowded his mind with thoughts of country he had never seen, or places he had not been. To him, life was what you made it, with whatever tools or weapons were at your disposal. He didn't fault Jake for being a dreamer. That's just the way Jake was. In fact, Adam sometimes envied his younger brother's longing to see the valley beyond the next mountain, or to follow the river to its beginning. Jake often teased his brother about his emotionless approach to each new day and the work that was waiting to be done. But he knew and appreciated the fact that the rock that was Adam was always there to lean on. Mose said Adam was soulful, born without a funny bone, but Nathan suspected his son's serious approach to just about everything was due to his mother's early death and the subsequent burden that had fallen upon him to look after his younger brother while doing a man's share of the ranch work. It was Adam who had convinced his father to let Jake follow the prospectors to the gold fields. "He'll get it out of his system pretty quick," Adam had predicted, "when he finds out all his hard work won't result in much more than a little grub money." As it turned out, however, Jake had evidently stuck with it longer than Adam had figured. And according to the message he sent, he was coming home with a little more than "grub money." Adam wasn't surprised in one respect, however, knowing how important it was to Jake to prove that he was his own man, and was not dependent upon his father or Adam to make his mark. Still, it was hard to picture Jake with a pick or shovel in his hand. No matter what he did, though, Jake was always going to be Jake, wild, sometimes to the extent of recklessness, and that was more than likely the reason for his failure to arrive when he said he would. Maybe he had encountered a saloon along the way that had tempted him to risk some of his fortune on cards and women. It wouldn't be the first time. *I wouldn't be surprised*, Adam thought. *Well, I'll go see if I can find him.*

"I figured you'd be ridin' Bucky," Nathan Blaine remarked when he walked into the barn where Adam was securing his saddlebags on a red roan named Brownie. Bucky was Adam's favorite horse and almost always his first choice when considering a ride of any length.

In response to his father's comment, Adam turned to gaze at the big bay gelding in the corral. "I decided it'd be best to let Bucky rest for a few days," he said. "He's tryin' to get a split hoof on his left front, and I'm hopin' it'll heal on its own, given a little time. Tell Mose and Doc not to work him till I get back."

"I will," Nathan responded. "Here," he said, and handed Adam a roll of bills. "You might need some extra money in case you have to bail your brother out of jail or somethin'." Then he gave him a small pouch. "There's three gold double eagles in here. That ain't but sixty dollars, but you might need it in case they won't take any paper money in that damn place." Adam nodded, took the money, and put it away in his saddlebag. Nathan stepped back then while his son climbed up in the saddle. "You be careful, Adam."

"I will, Pa," Adam said, and slid his Henry rifle into the saddle scabbard. With no further words of parting than this, Adam wheeled the roan and set him on a southwest course toward the Yellowstone. His father spun on his heel and returned to the house, confident that Adam would find his brother. Passing the back corner of the corral, Adam saw Mose and Doc replacing a broken rail. He pulled up when he was hailed by Mose, who walked out to meet him.

"Boy," Mose addressed him—he always called him boy. Adam figured the old man would always think of him and Jake as the two scrappy little fellows in their childhood. "You be damn careful, you hear? There's a lot of wild, godless outlaws preyin' on the hardworkin' folks around them diggin's. You mind your back."

"I will, Mose. I'll find Jake and be back here before you know I'm gone."

Mose remained there for several minutes, hands on hips, watching Adam until he turned Brownie toward the river. Of Nathan Blaine's two sons, he admitted to himself, Adam was his favorite. Maybe it was because Adam had always been interested in learning everything Mose offered to teach him, whether it was stalking and killing an elk or knowing a horse's mind. Unlike Jake, who openly flaunted his self-reliance, Adam seemed secure in a quiet confidence that he was prepared to handle whatever confronted him. In spite of their differences, Mose had to concede that the two brothers were close. He attributed that to Adam's maturity and the fact that he had more or less watched over his younger brother since their mother died. Mose's thoughts were interrupted by the sound of Nathan Blaine calling for him from the house. *I don't know how long this place would survive without me to take care of everything,* he thought as he turned and started toward the back door of the house.

Adam arrived at the bank of the Madison River at the end of the second day's travel, his first day having been shortened considerably by his late departure from the Triple-B. He made his camp a hundred yards up a stream that emptied into the river where the light from his fire might not be noticed by anyone passing by. After an uneventful night, he was out of his blanket at first light and saddling the roan, preparing to ride for ten or twelve miles along the river before stopping to rest his horse and have his breakfast. Following an already well-traveled road, the roan maintained a steady pace, so much so that Adam decided to push on until Brownie showed signs of getting tired. Consequently, it was close to noon when he decided the horse had earned a good rest.

While he sat by his small fire, drinking a cup of coffee and gnawing on a strip of jerky, he idly watched the red roan as it nosed around in a patch of green lilies at the water's edge. There had never been any reason for him to travel to Alder Gulch, so all he knew about Virginia City, Nevada City, and the other towns along that gulch was what he had heard—that they were wide-open and lawless towns with thousands of new people streaming in every day. Based on these stories, he had halfway expected to meet other travelers on the road along the Madison, but so far, he was the only traffic. Back in the saddle, he continued his journey.

Leaving the river, he followed the road up into the hills for another nine or ten miles before sundown once again called for him to make camp. Virginia City couldn't be more than another half day's ride, he figured, and Bannack was supposed to be about sixty miles beyond Virginia City. And although Jake was supposed to be in Bannack, Adam planned to start looking for his brother in the saloons and bawdy

houses in Alder Gulch and Daylight Gulch before
moving on to Bannack. If he was lucky, he might find
him holed up there, delayed by a run of luck at the
poker table, or a *fancy lady* who happened to catch his
eye. He shook his head and sighed, much like a harried
parent thinking about a rambunctious child, as he
guided the roan toward a stand of cottonwood trees
that suggested the presence of some form of water.
Sure enough, he found a small stream cutting a shallow gully between the trees. In short order, he had his
horse taken care of and a fire glowing cheerfully. With
his coffeepot bubbling on the edge of the fire, he broke
out his frying pan and started to prepare some more of
the jerky he had brought. It was then he noticed the
ears perking up on the roan grazing nearby, followed a
few seconds later by an inquisitive nicker. Knowing it
could be anything out in the darkness that caused the
horse to inquire, a mountain lion or a bear, he nevertheless casually rolled away from the firelight, drawing his rifle from the saddle behind him as he did.
"Hello the camp," a call came a few minutes later. "Saw
your fire back there. Mind if we come in? There's just
the two of us."

Adam's first thought was that he hadn't hidden his
camp very well, but there was nothing to remedy that
now. "Come on in," he called back while edging his
way a little farther from the firelight until his back was
against the trunk of a cottonwood.

In a few moments, two riders approached the fire,
slow-walking their horses through the trees beside
the stream and leading a packhorse. Pulling up in the
small clearing, they looked right and left before sighting Adam sitting with his back to the tree. "Howdy,"

one of the men said. "Don't blame you for bein' careful. There's a helluva lot of road agents ridin' these trails around here. We all have to be careful."

"That's what I hear," Adam replied, and got to his feet, his rifle still in hand. "You're welcome to some coffee. I don't have much food to offer but some jerky I was fixin' to fry when you rode up."

"'Preciate it," the rider said. "Me and Jim here would love some of that coffee, but we've got plenty of fresh-kilt deer meat that needs to be et before it starts to turn. Jim shot a young buck a few hours ago right when it was crossin' the river. So if you'll furnish the coffee, we'll furnish the meat."

"That sounds like a fair deal to me," Adam said, still watching his visitors with a cautious eye.

The two dismounted then. "My name's Rob Hawkins," the one doing all the talking said. "My partner here is Jim Highsmith. We're headin' to Virginia City. Which way are you headin'?"

"Adam Blaine," Adam said. "I'm goin' the same way you are."

"You headin' to the diggin's to try your luck at prospectin'?" Highsmith asked, speaking for the first time.

"Nope," Adam replied. "I'm lookin' for my brother. He's the prospector in the family. I don't know much about it, to tell you the truth." He continued to watch the men carefully as they tied their horses near the stream, taking special note that they left their rifles in the saddle boots. In a show of equal trust, he walked back over to his saddle on the ground and slipped his rifle back in the sling.

The gesture did not go unnoticed by his guests. Rob smiled and unbuckled his gun belt. "Why don't we just hang our handguns on our saddles, so we don't have to keep an eye on each other, and cook up some of this meat?" His remark served to clear the tension from the air, and all three chuckled as Jim and Adam followed his example. "Matter of fact, I might pull off my boots and pants. They still ain't dry." He went on to relate the encounter with the deer at the river. "If Jim had waited till the damn deer climbed up on the bank, I wouldn'ta had to go in the river after him. I swear, he shot him when he was right in the middle, and he was about to wash downstream with the current."

Jim shrugged and replied in defense of his actions, "How was I to know if he was gonna come on across or turn and go to the other bank? You'da got your ass wet either way."

"Oughta made you go in after him," Rob groused. "You were the one that shot him."

Adam recharged his coffeepot to accommodate the new arrivals while Rob carved off some of the fresh venison. There was no need to conserve. The meat wouldn't keep much longer with the weather as warm as it was, so everyone ate their fill. By the time a state of satisfaction was reached, the three men felt at ease with one another, and the talk turned to prospecting. Rob, sitting by the fire in his underwear, complained that he and Jim were too late in arriving at the diggings, but decided they had nothing better to do. "There's always some little spot that nobody found, and that might be the place we hit it big."

"Maybe so," Adam said. "You sound like my brother. The only difference is my brother ain't much for hard work. He'll likely look for some way to have somebody

else do the diggin'." He studied his two visitors without
the sense of suspicion he had applied at first. They were
an interesting pair. Rob was tall and lanky, and his face
wore an expression of carefree indifference. His partner, Jim, was a study in contrast. He was short and
stocky, his face reflecting a sense of constant worry. He
walked with a slight limp, the result of having been
born with one leg considerably shorter than the other,
according to him. Before the evening was over, Adam
invited them to unsaddle their horses and ride on in to
Virginia City with him in the morning.

The conversation eventually got around to the many
rumors of gangs of road agents that preyed upon the
trails between the gold fields and Salt Lake City, and
the lack of law enforcement to protect stagecoaches
and freighters. "Bannack, Virginia City, and all the other
little towns along those gulches are wide open for outlaws," Rob said. "And since you say you ain't ever been
to any of them places, you'd best beware of who you
talk to, especially if you're carryin' any money on you."

"Well, I reckon I don't have anythin' to worry about,"
Adam lied, "'cause I'm dead broke. But I 'preciate the
warnin'. Like I said, I'm just lookin' for my brother, and
as soon as I find him, the outlaws are welcome to Alder
Gulch and Daylight Gulch, too."

"Still ain't a bad idea to sleep with your six-shooter
handy, though," Rob said, and that's what all three did
when it was time to turn in.

The night passed without incident and Adam, long
accustomed to short nights working with cattle, was
out of his blanket and reviving the fire before his two

visitors were awake. "Damn, Adam," Rob commented upon awakening to the aroma of fresh coffee, "I might trade ol' Highsmith in for you."

Sitting up then and scratching his head vigorously, Jim replied. "Hell, I'm the one that shot us a deer. You'd starve to death if I left the huntin' up to you."

Adam had to laugh. They were a pair, all right. He was going to miss them. On his own, he would already have been in the saddle, but he waited for his new acquaintances, who were evidently not endowed with his workmanlike urgency to get started. Since it was no more than a half day's ride to Virginia City, however, that estimate confirmed by Rob and Jim the night before, he figured he could afford to dawdle a bit on the trail. Once they were on the way, he learned that they were as familiar with the territory as they had claimed, for they left the main road and led him on a less-traveled trail over the hills that shaved a good two miles off the trip.

"Well, there she is," Rob announced when they topped a high hill after leaving the game trail where it again intercepted the road. Below them were the buildings of Virginia City, structures of all kinds: log stores, some with board facades, tents, brush wickiups. There were even some houses that had incorporated stone, evidently quarried from the hills surrounding the gulch. And there was new construction still going on, on every vacant piece of ground, which was in extremely short supply. The timber on the surrounding hills had all been clear-cut to provide lumber for the saloons, hotels, and bawdy houses. Adam was amazed. He had heard of the population explosion that had taken place along the approximate fifteen miles of the gulch, but nothing he had heard could have prepared him for the scene below him. The gulch was like an open anthill, with thousands of people working away at their claims. Some labored with picks and shovels, digging for bedrock, while others wheeled loads of dirt to sluice boxes. The narrow street was jammed with sixteen-, even twenty-horse bull trains, pulling as many as four wagons hitched together. They were competing with mule trains and packhorses to navigate the muddy streets.

The thought struck Adam that there couldn't possibly be enough gold in the gulch to accommodate all these people. Watching his reaction to the chaotic scene below them, Rob guessed what he might be thinking. "Ain't gonna be easy findin' your brother, is it?"

"Reckon not," Adam replied thoughtfully. "I didn't figure it was gonna be."

"Trouble is," Jim interjected, "this here is just Virginia City. There's half a dozen or more places along Alder and Daylight gulches that's already big enough to have a name—Junction, Adobetown, Highland, Summit, and a few others."

"You say he started out from Bannack?" Rob asked. When Adam nodded, Rob suggested that his brother might still be there.

"Maybe," Adam said. "But if he did leave Bannack, he mighta stopped on the way, so I expect I'd best look around here before I move on to Bannack just to be sure." The odds were against his ever finding Jake in the writhing mass of humanity below him, but he had no choice. He reached over to each side to shake hands with his new friends. They were not going into Virginia City, planning instead to join some friends farther up

Daylight Gulch. "You two take care of yourselves," he said in parting, "and good luck prospectin'."

"Good luck to you," Rob returned. "Hope you find your brother." Jim saluted with a finger to the brim of his hat, and the two continued along the ridge while Adam turned the roan down the hill.

Chapter 2

Unlike his younger brother, Adam was not comfortable in the noisy cauldron of a boomtown. As he guided Brownie through the clogged thoroughfare called Wallace Street, he was often forced to pull the roan up sharply to avoid running over a drunk staggering from one of the saloons, or a collision with a bull train. As unaccustomed to the turmoil and noise as his master, the roan was not able to adapt and soon became skittish and jumpy. Adam decided he had better stable the horse and canvass the town on foot. The best choice turned out to be a livery stable at the upper end of the street.

"Howdy, neighbor," a wiry little man with a shiny bald head and a long flowing gray beard called out in greeting when Adam dismounted at the stable door. "What can I do for you?"

"I need to board my horse for a night or two," Adam replied. "He ain't used to so much noise and confusion, and I think he'd be better off in a stall."

"Well, I reckon my place is about as quiet as anywhere else in town," the stable owner said. "Three dollars a night in advance."

"Three dollars?" Adam exclaimed. "That's a little high, ain't it?"

"You *are* new in town, ain'tcha? Hell, I'm the cheapest around—three dollars a night—in advance," he emphasized.

It was plain to Adam that his money would soon run out at that rate, so one night was all he was willing to splurge on the red roan; then he would camp outside town. "We'll go for one night," he said, then hesitated before asking, "How much for a ration of oats?"

The bald man smiled. "Dollar extra."

"Damn!" Adam exclaimed. "A dollar for a quarter's worth of oats."

"I give a fair measure."

Adam shook his head in disbelief. "I reckon there ain't no banks in town to rob, so an outlaw has to go into the livery stable business to get by."

The owner was not amused. "Like I said, mister, you're sure as hell new in town." He shrugged. "But them's the rates. Ain't gonna be any cheaper anywhere else. All the same to me if you leave your horse here or not."

Adam stroked Brownie's neck and said, "Well, boy, you can go in style for one night, but don't go gettin' used to it." He reached in his pocket and brought out his money. He had peeled off only a couple of bills when the stable owner stopped him.

"Whoa! I don't deal in no paper money. Dust is the currency hereabouts. Nobody deals for paper."

Adam didn't respond at once, remembering then what his father had said when he gave him the double eagles. The old man was right on that call. After a few seconds' pause, he went to his saddlebags and retrieved the small pouch. Taking out one of the coins, he handed it to the bald man and said, "This is a twenty-dollar gold piece, so you damn sure better have sixteen dollars' worth of gold dust for change."

The owner took the coin, turned it over two or three times inspecting it before placing it in his teeth to test it. "I reckon it's genuine," he conceded. "I can give you dust for it."

Adam followed him into a storeroom where a set of scales sat on a shelf. The man pulled a pouch from inside his trousers and weighed out a small pile of dust. "There you go," he said, "sixteen dollars."

Adam could not be certain the man had used the proper weight to measure the gold dust, but he looked at it closely as if he did know. "How do I know that's pure gold dust?"

"It's as pure as you'll fine. Don't matter how pure it is as long as it's worth sixteen dollars—and that's what it's worth."

"I'll be using it to buy some supplies, so if it ain't sixteen dollars' worth, I'm comin' back to shoot your ass," Adam stated.

There was something in the broad-shouldered young man's eyes that convinced the stable owner that he didn't waste words in idle boasting. "Listen, young feller," he hastened to reply, his tone much less indifferent than before, "ever'thin's high in this town. You ask around, anybody'll tell you Jack Samson's an honest man. I'll tell you what I'll do. Since you're new in town, I'll give your horse a double order of oats and no extra charge. How's that?"

"The horse will appreciate it," Adam answered, although his deadpanned expression did not change. "You by any chance know a man named Jake Blaine?"

Samson shook his head. "I can't say as I do," he replied.

Adam hardly expected him to remember Jake by name even if he had seen him, but he figured it wouldn't hurt to ask. With Samson watching, he pulled the saddle off Brownie. Then Jack led the horse into an empty stall. Adam followed him in and threw his saddle in a corner of the stall. "My saddlebags be all right here?" he asked. When Samson said nobody would disturb them there, Adam put the pouch with the two remaining double eagles in his pocket, drew his rifle from the saddle sling, and left the stable to begin his search of the saloons.

It took very little time to verify the difficulty he had anticipated in looking for Jake. In every saloon he entered, the response was a variation of a similar reply. "Hell, mister, I ain't got the time or the inclination to know every prospector and drunk that comes in here. I just sell 'em whiskey and beer. I don't *wanna* know their names." When he had canvassed all the saloons in Virginia City, he tried his luck in the stores with the same lack of success. As a last result, he inquired at the hotels on the possibility that, if Jake had actually struck it rich, he might have sprung for a room. That was not the case, however. There was no Jake Blaine on any hotel registries. At the end of the evening, he stopped back at an establishment called O'Grady's, the first saloon he had visited, to have a glass of beer while he thought about what he should do next.

The bartender recognized him as having been in earlier that evening asking about someone. "You find that feller you were lookin' for?" he asked when he set the glass of beer on the bar before Adam. "What was his name?"

"Jake Blaine," Adam replied. "No, I ain't found him yet." He took a step to the side when a man pushed into the bar beside him. Adam took another step to the side to give him more room, but was stopped when a second man moved in to box him in. Not sure if it was intentional or not, he stepped back away from the bar, still holding the glass of beer in his hand. A quick look right and left told him there was plenty of space on either side, and no reason to crowd him, so he took a moment for a closer look at the two. Nothing unusual, he decided, two men who looked pretty much like most of the men in the saloon, so he moved down the bar a few paces to drink his beer.

"What's the matter, big'un," one of the men slurred, "was we crampin' your style too much?"

Why, he couldn't imagine, but it was obvious now that the crowding by the two was intentional. "As a matter of fact, you were," Adam answered, "but there's plenty of room at the bar, so I'll move out of your way." He could see that he wasn't going to be allowed to avoid a confrontation, judging by the malicious grins in place on each face. What he couldn't understand was why they had picked him out to hassle.

The one who had spoken to him, a man of average height, wearing a fancy hand-tooled leather vest and two revolvers with their handles forward, gave his partner a sideways glance and said, "You hear that, Rafe? He said we was crampin' his style." Turning a contemptuous gaze toward Adam, he said, "I hear you been askin' a lot of questions around town about somebody you're lookin' for."

"I reckon that's right," Adam replied. "I'm lookin' for somebody. Does that bother you for some reason?" He took a sip of his beer and let his free hand casually drop down next to the barrel of his rifle, propped against the bar beside him.

Leather Vest's sneer widened as he continued to lock his eyes on Adam's. "He wants to know if it bothers us, Rafe." Rafe nodded with a cruel grin still in place. "I'll tell you what bothers me," Leather Vest continued. "You smell like a lawman to me—come in town askin' ever'body if they've seen some feller around. We got a sheriff in this town, and we ain't got no use for no federal marshal to come nosin' around where they got no business. So why don't you tell me if you're a damn marshal and who the hell you're lookin' for?"

Adam glanced at the bartender, who had stopped polishing a shot glass, and now stood watching his reactions. He was also aware that the entire barroom had suddenly become silent as every eye was upon him, waiting for his reaction. Hoping to quickly defuse a tense situation, Adam smiled and replied. "I ain't a marshal. The man I'm lookin' for is my brother. He's been missin' for a while and I came to find him, so I reckon there's nothin' to worry you."

"Is that so?" Leather Vest said, not willing to let the matter drop, and encouraged by Adam's apparent reluctance to cause trouble. "Just lookin' for your brother, huh?" He winked at his companion and continued his obvious intent to intimidate the stranger. "So you're sayin' that if I was to pull your coat aside, I wouldn't find no marshal's badge pinned on your shirt. Is that right?" He took a step closer, and his partner moved to position himself at Adam's left.

Having reached the limit of his patience with the two troublemakers, Adam resigned himself to what appeared to be inevitable. With another glance at the bartender, he decided the altercation would be confined to the two men and himself, with the bartender merely an interested spectator. With his hand still loosely grasping the glass of beer as it rested on the bar, he gazed into Leather Vest's eyes and replied, "What I'm sayin' is, if you stick your hand on my coat, you might not get it back."

"Whoa!" Leather Vest mocked, and threw his hands up, pretending to be terrified. "I believe we've got us a rattlesnake here, Rafe. Better jump back before he bites ya." He took an exaggerated step back then to Rafe's amusement before the smile of contempt returned to his face, and he focused his gaze upon Adam as he issued his warning. "Now I'm gonna teach you a little respect, and show you what happens to jokers who threaten me." He reached for one of his pistols.

Before he could pull it, Adam threw the glass of beer in his eyes, at the same time grasping his rifle by the barrel. Swinging it like a club, he cracked Rafe beside his head before the startled bully could pull his revolver halfway out of his holster. In almost one continuous move, he spun around to face Leather Vest, who was sputtering and spitting, trying to wipe the beer out of his eyes. One quick thrust with the butt of his rifle smashed Leather Vest's nose and dropped him to the floor on top of Rafe. Checking to make sure the two were temporarily incapable of further action, he pulled their weapons from their holsters and threw them over in a corner behind the bar. With a quick glance in the bartender's direction, he said, "I'd appreciate it if you

just let those pistols lie where they are for a few minutes." The bartender nodded. There was the hint of
a grin on his face. Adam cast a precautionary glance
around the crowded barroom, then walked delibe-
ately toward the door.

As he disappeared out the doorway, a slight, graying
man moved up to the bar across from the bartender. He
looked down at Rafe and his partner as they both struggled to clear their heads enough to sit up. Then, looking
back at the bartender, he grinned and commented, "He
moves pretty damn quick for a big man, don't he?"

Outside the saloon, Adam turned in the direction of
the stable. He had not taken five steps before he heard
someone come out the door behind him. Thinking the
two he had just fought with must have recovered, he
whirled around with his rifle in position to fire, only to
discover the frail, gray-haired man, his hands raised in
surrender. "Hold on, mister!" the little man gasped.
Seeing immediately that the man meant him no harm,
Adam dropped the rifle to his side. "I didn't mean to
startle you. My name's Earl Foster. I own the dry goods
store two doors down."

"I beg your pardon, sir," Adam said. "I reckon I'm
still a little jumpy."

"I don't wonder," Earl said. "Mind if I walk with you
a piece?"

"Why, I reckon not," Adam said, unable to think of
a reason to tell him no, and somewhat curious as to
why the man wanted to.

Earl fell in step beside Adam as he walked along the
short length of board walkway in front of a couple of
stores. "This is my place," he said when they were passing the second door, "dry goods, most anything you

want in the line of clothes, sheets, towels, household items of all kinds." Still puzzled, Adam was about to ask him what he wanted when Earl continued. "First of all, let me tell you how much I enjoyed watching you put Frank Fancher and Rafe Tolbert in their proper place. Somebody's been needing to do that for a long time. But I want to warn you to be damn careful if you're planning to be in town long."

"I can't see any good reason why they came after me in the first place," Adam said. "Is that the way strangers are treated in this town? If it is, it seems to me it'd be a full-time job for those two, with as many folks as there are pourin' into this gulch every day."

"No," Earl responded. "That's just it. There's a lot of fine folks in Virginia City, honest, hardworking folks. You being a stranger, you wouldn't know it by running into that pair in the saloon. You see, the reason they started hassling you is that you've been looking all over town for somebody, and they thought you might be a U.S. marshal."

"I told them I wasn't a lawman. I'm lookin' for my brother," Adam protested.

"Yeah, but they don't believe that, and they don't want any marshals sticking their noses in their business."

"What's their business?" Adam asked.

"Robbery and murder," Earl answered simply.

Surprised by the candid reply, Adam said, "I heard there was a sheriff in Virginia City."

"There is," Earl replied, "somebody that calls himself the sheriff, and some of us think he's the biggest crook of them all. But don't tell anybody I said so. I don't want my place burned down."

Adam found the little man's story hard to believe.

"In a town this size?" he responded. "There must be thousands of people livin' here. Why don't you run the sheriff outta town and elect a new one?"

"It ain't that simple. Nobody elected Henry Plummer sheriff in the first place. He kinda appointed himself sheriff. There are an awful lot of decent folks here now, and we're trying our best to build a respectable town, but the outlaws came in with the prospectors and there was no law and order. The closest capital city of any size is Lewiston in Idaho, seven hundred miles away, and that's about the only place where they've got law and order. Oh, sure, we've got a sheriff, and he talks a good game, meeting with the business owners and the miners on a regular basis. There's a lot of gold in this gulch, but the trouble is trying to get it out after you've struck it rich. You see, it ain't just a few, like Fancher and Tolbert. There's hundreds of 'em, and some folks believe Plummer's the one calling the shots, just like he did in Bannack. The sheriff in Bannack is one of his men. Everybody knows those two you tangled with in the saloon are members of the gang holding up stagecoaches and freight wagons on every road out of here, but nobody can prove it. They don't usually leave witnesses, or they wear masks. And there isn't a gold shipment that leaves here that they don't know about ahead of time."

The news was not entirely new to Adam. He had heard that road agents preyed on the trails between towns along the gulch, as well as the road to Salt Lake City, but he was amazed to hear they were as many as Earl claimed. He was immediately struck by an alarming thought. What if this had something to do with Jake's failure to arrive home from Bannack? He looked at Earl. "Between here and Bannack?"

Earl understood the question. "Sure," he answered. "Bannack's about played out except for the bigger mining companies, but gold coming from here to buy supplies in Bannack is still hit regular. That's why army troops are sent to guard any large shipments from one of the bigger mines out to Salt Lake City." He studied Adam's thoughtful expression for a few moments before commenting again. "I thought you needed to know the situation around here. You might have made more enemies tonight than those two in the saloon."

Adam's concentration was on his brother and the fear that Jake might never have gotten out of Bannack. He felt an urgency now to get there as soon as possible. Jake was as good with a gun as anyone, and faster than most when it came to getting off a shot. But that didn't guarantee anything when the odds were too heavily stacked against you. To Earl, he said, "I appreciate your warnin', but I'm not hangin' around to make more enemies. I'm leavin' for Bannack at first light. Maybe I can keep from gettin' shot till then. What about this feller, Samson, that owns the stables?" Adam asked then. "Is he on the sheriff's list of road agents?"

"No, Jack's not in with Plummer's crowd. He'll deal fair with you," Earl replied.

After Earl gave Adam directions to the road to Bannack, they parted company, Earl to his room in the rear of his store, and Adam heading to the stables to check on his horse. "You watch your back," Earl called out as he stepped off the boardwalk and disappeared between the buildings.

This seemed to be the standard advice everybody offered. "I will," Adam replied, "and thanks again."

He decided against staying in the hotel that night for two reasons. The first was the inflated costs for everything in the town; the second was a matter of caution. In light of his altercation with the two outlaws in the saloon, and his subsequent talk with Earl Foster, he decided it a prudent idea to sleep in the stable with his horse. That way, he'd be ready to ride before sunup, he hoped before the acquaintances he had made the night before decided to look for him.

He returned to the barn to find Samson already gone for the night and the stable door barred on the inside. Walking around the barn, he discovered a small shack behind it, which was obviously the stable owner's house. Judging by the light in the window, he figured that Samson was probably eating his supper. Adam considered disturbing him to inquire about sleeping in the stall with his horse, but only for a moment. *I'm paying him enough for Brownie's board*, he thought. *To hell with it.* He continued his walk around the barn, looking for a means of entrance, but the only other door he found was at the back, and it had a padlock on it. Back to the front of the building after finding no likely way to get inside, he looked up at the hayloft door. It was closed, but didn't appear to be barred. "I could reach that if I had my horse," he murmured. "Too bad he's inside the damn barn." Then a rain barrel at the corner of the building caught his eye. He studied it for a few moments, shifting his gaze back and forth between the barrel and the hayloft door, estimating the distance. It was worth a try, he decided.

After taking a look around to make sure no one of the noisy crowd of saloon patrons down the street had noticed him lurking around the stables, he went to the rain barrel and quickly pushed it over on its side, dumping its full contents on the ground. From the impression left in the soil, he guessed that it had been in place for quite some time, causing him to hope the bottom had not become too rotten to support his weight. When all the water had emptied, he rolled the barrel over to the stable doors and stood it upside down beneath the hayloft. *I don't know . . . ,* he thought as he cautiously climbed upon the weathered bottom of the barrel. *If this damn bottom is rotten, I'll end up in the barrel.* On his knees, he rose very gingerly to his feet with no indication of failure other than a creaking, cracking sound of the weathered bottom.

Standing as tall as he could on tiptoes, he found that the sill of the hayloft door was still inches above his reach. "Damn!" he swore in frustration. A sudden increase in the creaking from the barrel bottom informed him that he had to do something quickly. Looking up at the door above him, he determined that there was a few inches' gap between the bottom of the door and the doorsill. With no more time to decide, he flexed his knees and jumped just as the barrel bottom broke in two. He managed to catch hold of the sill, but was now dangling by his fingertips, and wondering if the whole endeavor was worth it to save a few dollars.

By sliding his hands, one at a time, under the edge of one of the double doors, he succeeded in pushing it open. Feeling the toll on his arms from hanging there, he wondered if he had enough strength left to pull himself up, but at this point, he determined that he had no choice. With a maximum of exertion, and by walking his boots up the face of the barn, he was able to scramble up into the hayloft. The noise of his frantic clambering should have been enough to alert anyone in the house behind the stables, but had evidently not. Safely up in the loft, he sat down in the hay for a few moments to catch his breath. "I ain't ever gonna tell anybody I did this," he said.

On his feet then, he made his way back through the dark loft to find the ladder, and climbed down. There was barely enough light in the stable for him to see, but he was able to make his way to the front doors without stumbling on anything. Lifting the bar, he opened the doors, took a quick look up and down the street, then rolled the broken barrel back to its original position at the corner of the building. Barring the doors again, he went back to the stall where Brownie stood waiting. Intent upon getting a few hours of sleep before leaving for Bannack, he prepared his bed.

Lying on his saddle blanket, spread on the hay, he was soon asleep, oblivious of the gentle sounds of the red roan standing over him, or the distant sounds of the saloons near the lower end of the street. Morning came sooner than he expected, and he awoke with a start to discover thin slivers of light peeking through the cracks in the sides of the stable. "Damn," he cursed, for he had intended to be on his way before first light. Moving as rapidly as he could, he threw his saddle on the roan and led him to the front door. He had just removed the bar from the doors when he heard Samson come in the back door. "What the hell—" Samson started before Adam interrupted him.

"Good mornin'," Adam called out cheerfully. "Thought I'd pick up my horse and get an early start."

"How the hell did you get in here?" Samson wanted to know.

Adam looked at him as if surprised he should ask. "Why, through the front door. I figured you'd left it unbarred in case I came by early. I appreciate it."

"Not barred?" Samson replied, confused. "You tellin' me the doors were not locked?"

"Why, I reckon not. How else would I have gotten in? You musta forgot to slip the bar on. Sounds like the kinda thing I might do." He pointed Brownie's head toward the open door. "Well, no harm done, and I best be movin' along." He nudged the roan with his heels and was out the door, leaving a thoroughly confused stable owner behind scratching his head.

Chapter 3

Climbing up out of Virginia City, he set out along the
hills that formed Alder Gulch, intent upon striking the
road leading west toward Bannack. It was late enough
in the summer for a brisk chill in the early morning,
but it looked promising for a good day to travel. The
air was fresh and a welcome change from that of Jack
Samson's stable. Adam would have enjoyed the ride
had it not been for the serious concern for Jake that
weighed heavily on his mind. He hadn't ridden far,
however, when the lack of breakfast reminded him
that there had been no supper, either. So when he came
to a tiny stream making its way down toward Alder
Creek through a grove of nut pine and juniper, he
decided to remedy the problem. He soon had a fire
going and his coffeepot working up a strong brew. In
short order, he had a pan full of jerky frying. The roan
decided upon a breakfast of violets, which grew in
wild profusion on the hills, and of which he had a
choice of white, blue, or yellow. "You'd better eat fast,"

he told the horse, "'cause I ain't plannin' to be here long. I'll give you a longer rest later."

After his brief breakfast stop, he rode along a high ridge, dotted with pines and dwarf cedars. Judging by the cleared patches and the many stumps, he could see that it had once been a thickly wooded hillside. It was now evidently home to any number of animals, for he saw striped badgers everywhere as he descended the slope, causing him to watch carefully as he guided Brownie toward the road he could now see in the distance below him. Earl's directions were easy to follow, and he was sure it was the road he was looking for. Descending a particularly steep section of the slope, Brownie started to slide and braced his front legs to keep from going head over heels, causing Adam to lean back, almost touching the horse's croup. Brownie maintained his balance just fine, but just then a badger, seeing the horse and rider sliding down toward it, bolted for cover. It was barely a few feet from Brownie's front hooves when it bolted. The startled horse reacted by trying to sidestep the frightened varmint, throwing Adam off balance in the saddle. As soon as it happened, Adam knew it was a tragic piece of bad luck, for he clearly heard the loud snap of Brownie's cannon bone in his right front leg when it found the badger hole. Man and horse tumbled down the hillside and Adam was thrown from the saddle, narrowly escaping being crushed by Brownie.

When he finally managed to collect himself at the bottom of the slope, he scrambled to his feet cursing his luck, for he knew Brownie's leg was broken. A dozen yards above him, he saw the injured horse trying to get to his feet, but unable to. Adam hurried to reach the suffering roan, knowing already there was only one way he could help him, but hating like hell to do it. When he reached Brownie, the horse was lying still, somehow sensing that it was all over for him. The leg was as badly broken as Adam had feared, with a clean break in the cannon bone, just above the fetlock joint. Brownie's eyes were wild and wide open as Adam gently stroked his face and neck. After a few seconds, Adam pulled his .44 from his holster and quickly relieved the suffering horse of its misery.

He stood there for a long moment, looking down at the roan. "You were a damn good horse," he said in way of eulogy. "It ain't no fittin' way for you to go." Looking around him then, he was forced to take stock of this unexpected situation. "You left me in a helluva fix," he added. He was going to have to find another horse somewhere, but the prospects of that being anywhere close to where he now stood were pretty slim. "Well," he sighed, "I'd better save what I can. No use to sit here all day waitin' for somethin' to happen." He eyed the road stretching out before him. It was sixty miles to Bannack. "It's gonna be a helluva walk if I don't find someplace to buy a horse."

It took a great deal of effort to pull his saddle off Brownie's carcass, even with the help of a sizable pine limb he used for leverage, but he was finally able to free the stirrup and cinch from beneath the carcass. Next, he stood looking at the supplies he had packed, wishing he had brought a packhorse as his father had suggested. There was no way he could carry everything with him, so he resigned himself to keeping his saddle and bridle, his weapons and ammunition, as well as some jerky in his saddlebags. He left his coffeepot and frying pan, plus anything else he thought he could do without, hidden in a pile of rocks, knowing he would most likely never return for them. Hefting his saddle on his shoulder, he started walking down the road to Bannack, his mind occupied with the predicament he now found himself in. He had not gone more than a hundred yards when he suddenly stopped, dumped his saddle on the ground, and walked back to the pile of rocks to retrieve his battered old coffeepot and a sack of coffee beans. "Hell," he swore, "I can't do without these."

It didn't take long to work up a sweat when the noonday sun found him toiling under his heavy load some six miles from the place where Brownie's carcass was no doubt already being visited by a party of buzzards. Ready for a rest, he took advantage of a small stream that the road crossed before climbing up between two ridges ahead. The thought had already entered his mind that there might not be any ranches between this little stream and Bannack, but he had no time to dwell on it, for in the distance behind him his salvation appeared in the form of a bright yellow stagecoach. He wasted no time in picking up his belongings and hurrying back to the edge of the road where he could be seen in plenty of time. He took his hat off and waved it back and forth just in case the driver was too nearsighted to see him.

"Uh-oh," Mutt Jeffries murmured to himself when he caught sight of the lone figure flagging him down in the distance. With his having been stopped before by masked road agents, his first thought was naturally one of suspicion. There were a couple of things about this one, however, that made him unsure. He was toting a saddle on his shoulder and he wasn't wearing a mask. In addition, the place where the man stood was not one Mutt would have picked to bushwhack a stage. There were two ways to speculate on the situation. He could be an unlucky traveler who had lost his horse, or he could be planning to pick up his horse somewhere up ahead where the rest of his gang of outlaws were waiting. And the fact that he wore no mask might be because they planned to leave no witnesses.

He thought about the four thousand dollars in gold dust hidden in a lockbox under his feet that was supposed to go to a mining equipment company in Salt Lake City. It would not be the first time someone had tipped the outlaws off. It had happened many times before. Then he thought about the passengers inside the coach. In addition to Henry Murphy, the owner of the equipment company, there was a man named Potter, his wife, and Bonnie Wells, a former dance hall lady who had been escorted to the stage by one of Sheriff Plummer's deputies. Mutt's decision to stop for the man on foot might jeopardize the safety of his passengers. He had to consider that. As he neared the man, still waving his hat, he noted his sweat-soaked shirt and thought to himself, *Hell, that man's been walking for a fair piece with that load on his back*. The thought flashed through his mind that he had noticed a couple of buzzards circling a few miles back. He couldn't in good conscience leave a man on foot out here. "Ho, back!" he yelled to his horses, and drew back hard on the reins.

Not sure the coach was going to stop, Adam watched as the team of six horses thundered past him and the stage finally came to a halt about thirty yards beyond. As soon as the coach was stopped, Henry Murphy, immediately concerned, opened the door and stuck his head and shoulders out, fearing that his gold dust under the boot was in danger. "Driver!" he shouted. "Why are we stopping?"

"Just pickin' up another passenger," Mutt replied, hoping he had made the right judgment. By the time Murphy had time to formulate his objection, Adam had hustled into earshot and Murphy decided to hold his tongue. "Havin' a little trouble?" Mutt asked when Adam caught up to him.

"Sure am," Adam replied. "My horse stepped in a badger hole back there a ways and I had to put him down. I was headin' for Bannack."

"Well, that's where I'm goin'," Mutt said. "If you've got the fare, throw your gear in the rear boot and climb aboard. If you ain't, I'll give you a lift to Haney's. That's about three miles up the road from here where we stop for dinner and change the horses."

"I reckon I've got the fare," Adam said. "I'll go all the way to Bannack."

"Hustle it up," Mutt said. "I've got a schedule to meet. You can pay me when we get to Haney's."

Adam untied the straps securing the waterproofed leather hood on the rear boot, but there was little room for his saddle and saddlebags among the items of express parcels and mail without extensive reorganizing, so he threw his saddle on top of the coach with the rest of the luggage. He was still squaring it away when Mutt urged the horses forward and the stage lurched into top speed again. If Adam had not quickly grabbed the luggage rail, he might have landed right back in the road. He crawled up to settle himself in the driver's box beside Mutt. The grizzled driver gave him a cursory glance before commenting, "I gotta make good time on these flat stretches, 'cause there's plenty of hills between here and Bannack."

"When do you figure on gettin' to Bannack?" Adam asked.

"Probably about eight or nine o'clock tonight," Mutt replied, then turned his head to take a longer look at his new passenger. "If I don't have to stop to pick up no more stranded pilgrims," he added with a grin. "My name's Mutt Jeffries. Welcome aboard."

"Adam Blaine," Adam returned. "I'm glad you came along when you did. I ain't sure I coulda carried my saddle all the way to Bannack."

Mutt chuckled. "It'da been a long walk, all right. Looks like you already worked up a good sweat, but you mighta been able to buy you another horse up ahead at Haney's. You are in luck, though, 'cause if I had left Virginia City when I was supposed to, I'da already been past this section of the road." He didn't share the reason he had been delayed—waiting for the gold now occupying the compartment beneath his feet.

It was a short ride to the ranch that served as a swing station and passenger rest stop as Mutt held his team to a ground-eating pace of five miles an hour. Swinging his horses into the yard of a log ranch house, he pulled the coach up in front of the door. As he and Adam climbed down, he announced loudly to his passengers, "I'll be pulling outta here in forty-five minutes. Go on inside and Miz Haney'll feed you. She can show you ladies where to go if you need to wash up. You gents can take a little walk behind the barn yonder." He grabbed the handle, opened the coach door, and stood holding it while his passengers stepped out. "Howdy, Walter." He nodded to Walter Haney when the owner drove a fresh team of horses up beside the coach and waited while his son unhitched the tired horses.

"Mutt," Haney returned. "You're runnin' a little behind, ain'tcha?"

"Yeah, I reckon," Mutt allowed, "a little."

"Not many passengers," Haney commented as he watched them step down to settle their feet on solid ground after twelve miles of rocking to and fro in the coach. "Frances will probably have too much food."

"I'll do my part to see that not too much of it goes to waste," Mutt replied. He turned then to settle up with Adam, who was waiting to pay his fare.

"Don't suppose you take paper money," Adam started.

"Hell, yeah," Mutt interrupted. "I ain't got no scale to weigh dust. There's a few places where paper spends good as gold back in Virginia City."

That suited Adam just fine, bothered not in the least by Mutt's implication that his ticket money would not necessarily find its way into the stage company's coffers. The transaction completed, he left to join the other men behind the barn. Standing several yards apart, Frank Potter and Henry Murphy etched two dark patterns on the wall of the barn. Adam nodded to them as he found a place to do his business. Potter nodded in acknowledgment, but Murphy looked straight ahead without responding. Hurrying to finish, he rounded the corner of the barn in time to intercept Mutt, who was on his way to join the relief party.

"Just a word, driver," Murphy said as Mutt started to walk past him. He glanced behind him to make sure he could not be heard behind the barn. "Do you know anything about that man you picked up back there?"

"Well, nossir," Mutt replied, "only that he lost his horse and he wants to go to Bannack."

"Don't you find it a little bit suspicious that he happened to show up on the road like that—right out of nowhere?" When Mutt hesitated and shrugged his shoulders, Murphy reminded him that he had a lot to be concerned about. "You can certainly see that I, more than the other passengers, have a great deal at stake here. And I don't think we should take any unnecessary risks with strangers along the way. I think I'm within my rights to ask you to tell the man he'll have to leave us here."

Mutt was confounded for a moment, not sure how to respond to Murphy's demand. "Well, I don't know, Mr. Murphy." He hesitated. "He seems like a nice enough young feller—and he's paid his fare to Bannack. I don't see how I can kick him off just because he don't look right to you. I mean, that's the business of the stage line—to carry folks to wherever they wanna go, as long as they pay their fare."

"You can tell him he'll have to wait for the next stage," Murphy suggested.

"Hell, Mr. Murphy," Mutt replied, rankled a bit by Murphy's demand. "There won't be another stage comin' this way for four days. I ain't seen no good reason to suspect this feller has any idea about what's under the front boot than any of the other passengers."

"So you're refusing to honor my request," Murphy stated, more than a little testy.

"I reckon that's right," Mutt replied.

"Very well," Murphy said, fully angry. "Your superiors will certainly hear of your position on this, and if anything happens to my shipment before we reach Bannack, you'll be called upon to explain your actions."

Mutt's dander was completely up by this time. "Well, that's fine as hell by me, so if you ain't got no more complaints, I'll go take a leak. If you're lookin' to get somethin' to eat, you'd best be about it, 'cause I aim to pull outta here when I said I would." The matter closed as far as he was concerned, he rounded the corner of the barn and almost collided with Adam on his way to the house. "I hope to hell you ain't in with them road agents," he mumbled, too low for Adam to hear.

"What?" Adam asked, but Mutt just shook his head and kept walking. Adam walked back to the coach, where Walter Haney was just completing the hitching of the new team of horses. "Mind if I wash some of this dust off in the horse trough over there?"

"Help yourself," Haney replied. "Best not take too long, though, if you're hungry. Ol' Mutt'll leave you standin' here." He chuckled after the comment.

"'Preciate it," Adam replied, and headed for the trough and the pump that supplied it with water. He had accumulated a good bit of dust as well as a few minor scratches he had been unaware of until splashing himself with water, a result of his tumble down that rocky slope when Brownie fell. When he had finished, he followed the others, who were already inside the house.

Before sitting down at the table, Adam paused briefly to nod to the other passengers, who were already well into the spread provided by Frances Haney. He received a polite nod from the Potters, and a frank silent appraisal from the woman seated on the other side of the table from them. Murphy, seated at the end, made no show of acknowledgment, but fixed him with an accusing gaze for a long moment before returning his attention to his plate. Busy piling food on his plate, Mutt sat at the other end of the table, his mind too focused on the victuals to notice Adam. The cool reception was not lost on Adam, but failed to cause him concern, although he did wonder what there was about him that generated their disapproval. Primary in his mind was to find his brother. What these strangers thought about him mattered none at all.

The meal was void of conversation for quite some time with no sound save that of knife and fork on china. Accustomed to livelier guests as a rule, Frances Haney was finally compelled to comment as she came around with the coffeepot. "I declare, you're the quietest folks I believe we've ever had in here. Is anything wrong?"

Her question caused a twitter from Ethel Potter, who looked up from her plate to suggest, "I guess we must all be too hungry to talk." She looked around at everyone and smiled. When her gaze lit upon Adam, she paused. "I should say welcome to our new passenger," she said. "I'm Ethel Potter. This is my husband, Frank. We're on our way to Salt Lake City."

Adam nodded and said, "My name's Adam Blaine. Pleased to meet you, ma'am." He looked up then to get introductions from the others, but all he received was a nod from Frank Potter and a stare from the single woman beside him. After a moment, he shrugged and returned his attention to his plate. The silence at the table returned until Henry Murphy finished his dinner and shoved his plate away from him.

"I was wondering, Mr. Blaine," Murphy started, "what line of work you're in."

Adam looked up to meet Murphy's eye, remembering the gruff-looking man's indifference to him before. "Cattle," he answered, "cattle and horses."

Murphy raised his eyebrows slightly as if surprised. "I'd have thought you would be interested in gold," he said. "Most men around here are after gold, one way or another."

"I expect that's right," Adam said. "But that just ain't my line."

Murphy continued. "That's why there are so many road agents preying on innocent folks on every trail around here when most of the time it's just poor hardworking people trying to get from one town to another. Take this coach, for instance. There's nothing of real value on this run, certainly not enough to warrant a gang of outlaws to hold us up."

"It doesn't seem to slow 'em down any," Frank Potter interjected, disagreeing with Murphy's statement. "Shoot, they'll rob you of anything you've got. Doesn't matter if it's worth anything or not."

Adam glanced from one man to the other, wondering what prompted the discussion. He decided after a moment's reflection that Murphy probably had something to lose, and in a clumsy sort of way, he was probing him, searching for clues that he might be one such outlaw. "Well, Mr. Murphy, maybe we'll be lucky and won't be held up," he said, reached for another biscuit, and returned his concentration to his plate.

"I sincerely hope you're right, Mr. Blaine," Murphy said. "It would be a grievous sin to cause harm to these innocent passengers." He pushed back from the table and stood up to leave.

The Potters got to their feet, as well, ready to return to the coach. "All this talk about outlaws is enough to upset your stomach," Ethel commented to her husband.

"I reckon you're right," Frank replied. "But like Mr. Murphy said, we ain't got any money, so it'd be a waste of time trying to rob us."

Adam didn't bother to look up, but he sensed that Potter's statement seemed to have been dropped for his benefit. He had to smile to himself, thinking, *I should have spruced up a little more, so these folks wouldn't worry themselves about me.* He almost laughed aloud when the next question was posed to him.

Eating in seeming indifference to the dinnertime topic of discussion, Bonnie Wells took the last sip from her coffee and leaned close to Adam. "Are you in one of those gangs of outlaws? 'Cause, if you are, I'd just as soon know it now, and I'll get off this damn stagecoach. And you and me can negotiate how much I've got that's worth stealing right here. You can take it out in trade."

With his fork stalled halfway between his plate and his mouth, Adam turned to take a close look at the woman. He had never bothered to before, and even under casual scrutiny, it was fairly obvious that she had traveled a lot of these rugged roads from one gold strike to the next. It was hard to say for sure, but he guessed she might have been a handsome woman at one time in her life. The roads had taken their toll on her, however, and the generous application of powder and paint was sorely challenged to cover the lines etched in her face. The tired eyes searching his told him that she was serious about her query. "Lady," he said, "if I was an outlaw, your proposition would truly interest me, but you've got nothin' to fear from me. I'm just tryin' to get to Bannack to look for my brother."

"Well, I reckon that's a relief," she said. Then with a tired smile she added, "We could still negotiate something when we get to Bannack, if you're of a mind to."

"Now, that's a right tempting proposition," he replied, with no desire to insult the woman. "But I reckon I just don't have that on my mind right at the moment."

"Hmph," she grunted, "I thought all men had that on their mind most of the time." With that, she got up and casually strolled out the door.

Adam glanced up to find Mutt grinning at him. "That there is Miss Bonnie Wells," he announced grandly. "She might tell you different, but I suspect Sheriff Plummer invited her to take my stagecoach outta town. There was too many fellers wakin' up with their pockets empty after an evenin' with Bonnie. One feller was found in the alley behind the Silver Dollar with his throat cut. Nobody could say that Bonnie done it, but the last time anybody saw him alive he was followin' Bonnie upstairs to her room." He took another biscuit from the plate and put it in his pocket. "Just thought you'd be interested," he said as he got to his feet. "Reckon it's time to get goin'."

"'Preciate the information," Adam said, and followed Mutt out the door. "Ain't likely to happen to me, though."

"Mighty good vittles," Mutt sang out to Frances Haney as they walked past her, "just like always."

"That goes for me, too, ma'am," Adam said.

They found the other four passengers standing together by the coach door, obviously engaged in a discussion of some kind. It seemed that Murphy was doing most of the talking, but the conversation met a sudden death as Mutt and Adam approached. "I got a fair idea what they're talkin' about," Mutt commented. "It's liable to be a bit chilly inside the coach. You might wanna ride up top with me again."

"Suits me," Adam said with a touch of chagrin, knowing that he was being tried for the crime of being a stranger. Without hesitation, he climbed up to the driver's box to take his place, saving Murphy the bother of suggesting it to Mutt.

Chapter 4

The sun was settling close upon the Rocky Mountains to the west of them when the first sign of trouble appeared. With the Beaverhead River far behind them, Mutt was about to feel confident that the trip was going to be without incident. Approaching a long, narrow draw, he called upon the horses for more speed, anxious to emerge quickly from the confining walls of the canyon. As soon as he saw the three riders appear at the head of the draw, however, he knew his luck had run out. Just as he feared, when he looked behind him, three more riders appeared to box the stage in. "Uh-oh," he mumbled low, "this don't look too good."

Alert to the situation at the same time as Mutt, Adam reached behind him and pulled his rifle from his saddle. Cranking a cartridge into the chamber, he then put the weapon between them with the barrel resting at his feet. His actions caused Mutt to warn him. "Take it easy, man. You're liable to get us all kilt. They're all wearin' masks, so they're just after the gold under the boot. If we don't do nothin' foolish, they'll just take it and go."

"How do they know what's in the boot?"

"They always know when any sizable amount is on the stage," Mutt replied. "And folks is beginnin' to figure the sheriff is the one that tips 'em off."

"Why don't the citizens of Virginia City and Bannack do somethin' about it?" Adam asked, finding the situation hard to understand in spite of the explanation offered by Earl Foster the night before.

"They've already started doin' somethin'," Mutt said. "Vigilantes. There's already been a half dozen outlaws hung, but there's too many of 'em." He gave Adam a warning frown and repeated, "Best thing now is to just let 'em take what they want, and leastways they won't hurt nobody."

"All right," Adam replied, and sat patiently as Mutt pulled the coach to a stop several yards short of the three outlaws awaiting them in the middle of the narrow road. As Mutt had said, they were masked, two of them with full cloth hoods with eyeholes, the other with a bandanna hiding all but his eyes. Adam could already feel the anger moving rapidly throughout his body as he witnessed the casual manner in which the road agents sat their horses, as if they were tax collectors, waiting to steal from those who had worked to earn their possessions.

"Don't do nothin' foolish," Mutt warned again, sensing Adam's anger. "This ain't the first time I've been held up. Just do what they say and you'll live to make it to Bannack."

With pistols out and aimed at Mutt and Adam, the outlaws moved up beside the driver's box. One, a large man wearing a black hat pulled down over his cloth mask, was obviously the boss. He took a quick glance in the coach before speaking to Mutt. "Mutt Jeffries, I do believe," he announced almost cheerfully. "It's been a little while since I stopped you. Nice seein' you again."

"Yeah," Mutt replied sarcastically, "it's a real pleasure."

Mutt's response brought a brief chuckle from the outlaw before he ordered, "All right, everybody out of the coach!" He kept his pistol trained on Adam and Mutt. "You two just sit right where you are." He waited then while his other three companions rode up behind the coach and dismounted. "Get 'em outta there," he barked at one of the two beside him when there had been some hesitation from the passengers to disembark. His men snatched the doors open and rudely herded the terrified passengers out. Black Hat returned his focus to Mutt. "What'cha got in that compartment under your feet, Mutt?"

"I don't know if there's anythin' in there," Mutt lied. "That ain't my department. I just drive the horses."

Again, a chuckle from Black Hat. "Now, Mutt, you know better'n tryin' to tell me shit like that. 'Spose you unlock it and we'll take a little look?"

"I can't," Mutt replied. "I ain't got no key for that lock."

"Is that a fact?" Black Hat replied, enjoying the little game being played. "I guess this just ain't our lucky day, boys. Ol' Mutt here ain't got no key." He gave Adam a hard looking-over then, which told Adam the man was deciding if he was a special guard for the gold that he obviously knew to be under the boot. "I don't suppose you've got the key to that box, have you?"

"Nope," Adam replied stoically.

"I expect you'd best hand me that pistol you're

wearin','" Black Hat said, "handle first." Adam realized then that the outlaw could not see the rifle resting against his leg, so he drew the .44 from his holster and tossed it down. "I said hand it to me," Black Hat spat in a flash of anger as the weapon fell to the ground at his horse's hooves. He soon recovered his casual mood, however. "Now, I wonder who might have a key to that box with four thousand dollars' worth of gold in it." Unnoticed by anyone, Henry Murphy blanched when the exact sum was mentioned, but a moment later his trembling was evident to all. Thoroughly enjoying the position Murphy was in, Black Hat continued. "Whaddaya think, boys? I'm willin' to bet the ol' gent there in the fancy suit might have a key that fits that lock."

"Might at that," one of his men replied. They had already begun stripping the passengers of anything they found of value. "He ain't got but a few dollars in his wallet and a gold watch—about the only things I found so far." Murphy stood with all his pockets turned inside out. Next to him, Frank Potter stood, quaking with fear, his pockets inside out as well.

"We don't have any money," Frank's wife spoke up. "Why don't you leave us alone?"

"You just keep your mouth shut," she was told, "or I'm gonna shut it for you." The outlaw snatched her purse from her and dumped the contents on the ground. Potter made a move to come to his wife's defense and promptly received a sharp rap across his face with the barrel of the outlaw's pistol.

"There's no cause for that." The remark came from Adam, still seated in the driver's box beside Mutt.

Black Hat cocked his head sharply upon hearing it.

"I'll get to you in a minute," he said. Turning back to the man searching Murphy, he said, "Unbutton his britches and pull 'em down." Mortified, Murphy stood trembling as his trousers were dropped to his ankles, revealing the money belt he wore under them. "Well, lookee here," Black Hat taunted. "If I had a key to that much gold, that's where I'd hide it. Relieve the man of his burden." Looking back at Mutt then, he said, "All right, Mutt, you and your friend climb down offa that seat now."

Before there was time to comply, they were distracted by a minor drama taking place between one of the outlaws and Bonnie Wells. "What you got hid under that skirt?" he goaded. "You wearin' a money belt, too?" Although his face was concealed by a red bandanna with his hat pulled low on his forehead, it was obvious he was a young man.

"You know what's under that skirt, you son of a bitch," Bonnie replied fearlessly. "You've paid for it plenty of times."

"Ha!" he responded. "Not hardly. I ain't never been that hard up, or that drunk. Now, you might as well hand over your money. I know you got it hid on you somewhere." He grabbed her by the throat and slammed her up against the coach.

Not at all intimidated, but angered by his aggression, she reached up and jerked the bandanna from his face. "Why don't you let us all get a look at you, Billy Crabtree? You think I didn't know that was you?"

"Oh, shit!" Mutt murmured almost too softly to be heard, for her act of defiance could very well spell execution for the rest of them. Billy Crabtree grabbed his bandanna and tried frantically to replace it over his face while looking plaintively back at Black Hat, knowing he had made a huge mistake.

"Well, now, Billy," Black Hat said, his tone soft and patient. "It looks like we've got us a little problem, don't it? You've gone and let these folks identify you. When they get to Bannack, they'll most likely tell everybody, and those damn vigilantes will be lookin' to run you down. I reckon you'd better head for someplace way the hell away from here, and you better not waste any time doin' it."

Confused and panicky from this unexpected turn of events, Billy pleaded for redemption. "I couldn't help it, Jesse. I didn't know the bitch was gonna grab for it."

Obviously angry, but still maintaining his patient manner, Black Hat remarked, "Well, now you've told 'em my name, too. Why the hell don't you just tell 'em everybody else's and be done with it?"

"I didn't mean to, Jesse," Billy begged, his self-control draining by the second. "We can kill 'em all," he cried. "Then nobody will know. We've done it before! We'll start with her!" He grabbed Bonnie's throat again and pointed his pistol at her head. "Whaddaya say, Jesse? No witnesses."

"You can have what's under my skirt, Billy." Bonnie managed to choke the words out in spite of the strength of his grip. She reached under her skirt, but there was no purse in her hand when she pulled it out again. By the time Billy realized it was a derringer, he was already on his way to hell, shot in the heart. In reflex, he was able to pull the trigger on his .44, but Bonnie had ducked and the bullet embedded harmlessly in the side of the coach.

The sudden gunfire triggered an explosive response that, even though it lasted no more than a minute, had everybody running for cover. In the ensuing chaos, the horses bolted, those pulling the stage, as well as those the outlaws rode. All Mutt could say for sure was that he heard Adam's Henry rifle barking out round after round as he tried to control his frightened team as they tried to gallop away. On the ground an instant after Bonnie's shot, Adam pulled Ethel out of the way of one of the outlaws' horses and yelled for Potter to hit the ground. Bullets were flying, but the only casualty among the passengers was a grazed shoulder on Henry Murphy and the cut on Potter's face. When the shooting was over, there were four bodies on the ground, one of them Billy Crabtree's. Two surviving outlaws were already out of rifle range as they ran for their lives. One of them was the one called Jesse, his black hat lying on the ground with a bullet hole through the crown.

With the horses once again under control, the passengers, though noticeably shaken still, began to recover their wits from the chaotic minutes just passed. Ethel Potter tore a strip from her petticoat to fashion a bandage around Frank's head, while Henry Murphy hastened to pull up his trousers. Adam reached down to pick up his .44, and was cleaning the dirt from it when he felt Bonnie at his elbow. "Mister," she said, "you don't say much of anything most of the time. But when your fuse gets lit, damned if you ain't a regular tornado."

Adam dropped his pistol in its holster. "Maybe you could take a look at Mr. Murphy's shoulder," he suggested. "It doesn't look like much." His mind was already on the four horses that had galloped away with empty saddles, especially since he was in need of one to replace

Brownie. Two of them had stopped about one hundred yards away at the mouth of the ravine. One of them, a bay, had already caught his eye. He was always partial to bays. "I expect we'd better collect the guns and cartridges off these bodies," he commented to Potter. "No use lettin' them lie out here to rust." He walked over to two of the bodies and reached down to pull the mask from one of them, only to be startled a moment later. *Rob Hawkins*, he thought, one of the men who had camped with him. Glancing at the other body close by, he found it easy to guess who it was. Short and stocky, it had to be Rob's friend, and he thought for a minute before remembering the name—*Jim Highsmith. I reckon they were looking to do a different kind of mining.* He found it especially ironic when he thought back on how they had cautioned him to beware of road agents. He could almost see Mose Stebbins nodding his head and saying, "I told you you'd better be careful who you turn your back on."

With his dignity somewhat restored, Murphy spoke up. He begrudgingly offered an apology. "I guess I owe you thanks for protecting my gold shipment, and I reckon I was wrong in suspecting you of being part of the robberies on this road."

"I don't reckon you owe me any thanks," Adam replied. "I wasn't protectin' your shipment. I don't give a damn about your gold. I was more interested in savin' the lot of us from ending up like these fellows." He pulled the weapons and gun belts from the bodies.

"I understand how you could feel that way," Murphy said. "Maybe I deserve it, but there is no animosity on my part." He turned to send a scathing gaze in Bonnie's direction, even as she was attending the slight wound on his shoulder. "Perhaps our lives would not have been threatened had it not been for that careless action of yours. Thanks to you, we could have all been killed."

Bonnie met his scornful stare with one equally defiant. "You and your damn gold can go to hell," she spat. "No man's gonna lay hands on me like that and stick a gun in my face without paying for it." For emphasis, she pinched the scrape on his shoulder, causing him to yelp.

"I expect Bonnie's the one that saved your precious gold for you," Adam said. "If she hadn't shot that fellow, they mighta took your gold and left us all alive— or maybe not. One way or the other, they'd have taken the gold."

"We can stand around here jawin' until them other two decide to come back for another try," Mutt interrupted. "Or we can get the hell on the road again and make the three miles on into Bannack." They needed no further encouragement to climb back in the coach.

"I'm needin' a horse," Adam told Mutt.

Mutt understood. As Adam walked toward the end of the draw, Mutt drove the horses slowly up behind him. "I'd appreciate it if you'd ride along with us to Bannack. I kinda like havin' you along."

"Be glad to," Adam replied, "if you'll give me time to catch me a horse. I might have to chase one all over the territory if they spook easy."

About a minute was all it took, for the bay gelding that Billy Crabtree had ridden stood patiently waiting while Adam approached, and made no move to resist when he took hold of the bridle and stroked the horse's face. After letting the horse smell his shirt for a few seconds to become familiar with his scent, Adam climbed into the saddle and walked the gelding slowly over to pick up the reins of the second horse, a sorrel. Both horses seemed content to go with him. The only problem, a minor one, was the necessity to lengthen the stirrups to fit his long legs. But that could wait until he got to Bannack.

It was close to ten o'clock when the coach pulled up to a stop in front of the Meade House, and the weary passengers climbed down, thankful to have arrived safely in Bannack. They were met by the night clerk of the hotel, who stood ready to welcome them and help with luggage. "Runnin' a little late, ain't you, Mutt?"

"Made a little stop I hadn't planned on," Mutt replied, then went on to explain.

"My Lordy me!" the clerk exclaimed. "You're lucky nobody got killed. I don't know which one of the sheriff's deputies is on duty tonight. I reckon you'll wanna go tell him what happened."

"There ain't no hurry about it," Mutt scoffed. "He ain't likely to do anythin' about it. I'll let the station boss go see the sheriff in the mornin'."

Understanding Mutt's indifference toward reporting the attempted holdup to the law, Adam shrugged and dismounted from the bay gelding. He looped the reins of both his newly acquired horses to the hitching rail, in case they hadn't accepted the fact that they now belonged to him. He got his saddle and saddlebags from the coach, then paused for a moment to look around him. While the little town on Grasshopper Creek was already declining from its heyday of a year or so before, it still managed a lively business in the saloons, with all four roaring away full blast. In addition to the saloons, there were three hotels, two stables, plus quite a few stores, all of them built of logs. It looked like the kind of town that would attract Jake.

Looking furtively over his shoulder, lest he might suddenly be attacked, Henry Murphy handed the key to the padlock to Mutt and waited impatiently for him to unlock it. "Why, I declare," Mutt exclaimed upon opening the compartment, "it's empty. There ain't nothin' in here."

"What!" Murphy sputtered, failing to notice the devilish grin on Mutt's face. He grabbed the door of the coach for support when his knees threatened to fail him.

"I'm just japin' ya," Mutt said with a hearty chuckle for his joke. He took the pouches from the box and handed them down.

Humiliated to the point of anger, Murphy took possession of his gold, but not without threatening the grizzled stage driver with the loss of his job. "Your superiors will certainly hear of your outrageous behavior on this trip. You'll be looking for another job by tomorrow."

"Yes, sir," Mutt replied. "Glad you enjoyed your trip. Thanks for travelin' with A. J. Oliver and Company." He looked at Adam and grinned, thoroughly pleased by Murphy's reaction.

Adam stepped out of Murphy's way as the disgruntled passenger hurried into the hotel to put his treasure in the hotel safe. When Mutt climbed down, Adam remarked, "I don't believe Murphy has much of a sense of humor. He might cost you your job."

Mutt chucked again. "Hell, the company has enough trouble findin' drivers dumb enough to take the run between here and Virginia City. I ain't worried about it. Besides, I couldn't resist it. Did you see him grab hold of the door?" He threw his head back and indulged himself with another hearty laugh. "I thought he was gonna pee his britches." He gave Adam a hand with his saddle and when it was securely settled on top of the saddle that was already on the sorrel, he said, "I 'preciate you ridin' along with us, and I sure as hell wanna thank you for savin' all our butts back there in that ravine."

"I wanna add my thanks to that," Frank Potter said, walking up behind Adam. "You know, we were dead for sure when that woman jerked that outlaw's bandanna down. So me and my missus are beholden to you." He stuck out his hand and Adam shook it. "I just wish you were goin' on to Salt Lake City with us." He flashed a wide smile then and said, "I ain't ever seen greased lightning before, but I reckon I can say I've seen it now."

Hardly knowing how to respond to the accolades, Adam hesitated in his response. He really wasn't comfortable in the role of hero. Finally he managed an answer. "Well, I'm glad everythin' worked in our favor. We were just lucky, I reckon. It could have turned out a whole lot worse."

Mutt watched Adam's embarrassment with a great deal of interest. Some men would rush to the nearest saloon to crow about running off a gang of road agents. When the Potters left to follow their luggage inside the hotel, Mutt asked Adam what he was going to do now that he had reached Bannack. "Well," Adam replied, "I reckon I'll have to see about these horses first. Then I'll have to start lookin' for my brother."

"There's two stables in town, one of 'em next door to

the stage office," Mutt suggested. "Why don't you put your horses up there? Then I'd be proud to buy you a drink. Whaddaya say?"

"I could use a drink," Adam replied, hesitating, "but I need to see if I can find out what happened to my brother."

"This day's about done," Mutt said. "By the time you get your horses took care of, and I check my coach in at the office, it'll be too late to get started. So you might as well have a drink or two and start on it in the mornin'."

Adam thought it over for a moment before replying, "You know, Mutt, I believe you talked me into it."

"Maybe you'd like to buy me one, too." They turned to see Bonnie Wells standing behind them. "Hell, I could use one after that ride."

Mutt only hesitated a moment before answering, "Maybe I would at that. I ain't ever met a woman with more starch in her. Whaddaya say, Blaine?"

"Suits me," Adam replied. "I reckon the lady deserves somethin' for takin' care of one of those outlaws. What was his name?"

"Billy Crabtree," Bonnie said. "I thought he mighta been riding with that bunch of cutthroats. Billy always had money to spend, but damned if I know that he ever worked anywhere to get it."

It occurred to Adam at that point that he had not asked Bonnie if she knew his brother. Jake was as likely as any man to seek out the services of a prostitute. "You ever run across my brother, Jake Blaine?" he asked.

"Is that your brother?" Bonnie responded. "Sure, I know Jake. I never done any business with him, but I saw him a few times when I was working here before.

He was sweet on a young girl from Kansas that used to work in the Miner's Friend."

Her reply captured Adam's attention immediately. "The Miner's Friend," he repeated. "Where is that?" When she pointed toward the upper end of the street, Adam asked, "Do you know where to find Jake?"

"Well, no," she replied. "I've been up in Virginia City for the past six months. Even when I was living here, I didn't know where he stayed. I don't think he had any permanent camp, just drifted around like a lot of them."

Thinking that he at least had a start in his efforts to track his brother down, Adam thanked her and offered to buy her drink himself. "Give Mutt and me time to take care of the horses and we'll meet you at the Miner's Friend. That okay with you, Mutt?"

"One's as good as another," Mutt said, "long as they've got whiskey." They parted then, Adam and Mutt to the stable, and Bonnie to the saloon.

"Mister, seems to me you either got too many saddles or not enough horses," Wilber Jenkins drawled when Adam led his horses into the stable.

"That's a fact," Adam said, relieved to find someone still at the stable at that hour. "To tell you the truth, I'm lookin' to trade these two extra saddles and pick up a packsaddle and some supplies. I left most of mine by a badger hole between here and Virginia City."

"Talk to Mr. Thompson when he comes in in the mornin'," Wilber said. "He might be interested in tradin' with you."

"I'll do that," Adam said. "This one stays with me." He threw his saddle in a corner of the stall, and left the other two near the door where they could be easily seen. "I've got a couple of rifles and two handguns here that I'd also like to trade." When his horses were taken care of, he went to meet Mutt and Bonnie.

Idaho Territory until a short time before then, Bannack was now part of Montana. Gold was discovered along Grasshopper Creek in '62 and the rush was on for the next couple of years. The town had even been the capital of Montana briefly in '64, before it was moved to Virginia City when the gold began to peter out and folks moved on to new strikes in Alder Gulch. As Adam walked up the street, he could read the unmistakable signs of a dying town in the dark storefronts he passed, many of them empty. The throbbing pulse of the saloons was the only indication that life was still vigorous in the failing town, and he walked past two of them before reaching the door of the Miner's Friend, where he found Mutt just coming from the stage office.

"I give 'em my report 'bout the holdup," Mutt volunteered as he stepped up on the narrow boardwalk. "Broadus Sims is the station manager here for A. J. Oliver. He said to tell you thanks for protectin' the stage. He wanted to come with me and buy you a drink, but I told him it would probably not be a good idea to make a fuss over you. Too many men around here are in with that sorry bunch of road agents. No use causin' you more trouble."

"I'm glad you talked him out of it," Adam said. "I expect he'll report the incident to the sheriff, or is that your job?"

"Neither," Mutt replied. "It wouldn't do no good to tell the sheriff about it. Hell, he's Plummer's man, same as the outlaws he's supposed to be catchin'. I expect he'll be sore as hell when he finds out the stage got through with all the money on board." He went on to remind him, "There ain't no real law and order in this town or Virginia City. Henry Plummer was the sheriff here before he got hisself appointed deputy marshal over in Virginia City. The sheriff here now is Albert Ainsworth, just one of his men, and there's a lot of honest folk hereabouts that's pretty sure Plummer's behind every robbery and murder that happens on these mountain trails between the towns. Course there ain't no way to prove it, and every time somebody questions it, they likely show up dead or missin'."

"My God, man!" Adam exclaimed, even though it was not the first time he had heard it. Once again, he found he had to ask, "Why don't the people elect their own sheriff, somebody who will do something to stop the murders?"

"The outlaws outnumber the honest folk," Mutt explained. "You might as well paint a target on the back of anybody you name sheriff, 'cause he won't last out the day." He paused to look right and left of him before continuing. With his voice almost in a whisper, he said, "A bunch of the miners and store owners has got together to put a stop to the lawlessness—vigilantes, like I told you. They've already strung up six of the ones that have been identified. I expect they'd be interested in talkin' to you." He paused to see Adam's reaction.

"Me?" Adam responded. "What for?"

"After the way you handled that rifle when they tried to rob us, there ain't no doubt in my mind that they could sure use a man like you."

"Well, I ain't interested," Adam quickly replied in

no uncertain terms. "I've got no part in the trouble the miners are havin' in these gulches. Like I told you, I'm just lookin' for my brother. Soon as I find him, I'm gone. I wish the honest folks here the best of luck, but it ain't none of my concern."

Although somewhat disappointed, Mutt said, "I reckon I can understand how you feel, and I can't say as I blame you." He shrugged off the discussion. "Let's go in and have a drink. Bonnie's probably already hitched up another couple fellers to buy her whiskey."

Inside, they found Bonnie waiting for them at the bar. She was alone, but it was not for lack of trying. There were a few younger women in the saloon, and each one commanded the attentions of a group of admirers. It was still a bit early in the evening for Bonnie. Her usual hunting season was in the wee hours of the morning when the volume of whiskey already downed by the patrons had effectively erased the lines of age in her face. Turning to greet them, she said, "I was beginning to think you had forgot about me." Then she turned to aim a remark at the bartender. "See, asshole, I told you I had friends coming."

"Well, pour us a drink, bartender," Mutt ordered grandly.

The bartender set two more glasses on the bar and poured. "She's already had two. Said you'd pay for 'em," he said.

Mutt cocked a wary eye in Bonnie's direction, but pulled out his poke. Adam put up his hand to stop him. "I'll take care of the lady's first two," he volunteered. After settling with the bartender, he turned to Bonnie and asked, "Do you see the girl you told me about, the one you said Jake was sweet on?"

"Yes, I do," Bonnie promptly replied. "Lacey Brewer. That's her sitting at the second table with those four men."

Adam turned to follow the direction of Bonnie's gesture. The girl he saw was young, as Bonnie had said. He could not call her a pretty girl, but she did present a neat appearance, and he could not help comparing her to Bonnie. He could understand the attraction that Jake felt. "Did you talk to her?" he asked. "Ask her about Jake?"

"Hell no," Bonnie replied, "and I don't recommend you asking her, either, until you can catch her away from that crew she's partying with."

"Why is that?" Adam asked.

Before answering, Bonnie shot a knowing glance in Mutt's direction. "Because that bunch is some of the sheriff's friends, and they might resent the intrusion." Mutt nodded his silent agreement.

Adam was rapidly getting the impression that Mutt had not exaggerated when he implied that the outlaws had overrun the town. "Why do the honest folks stay here?" he asked Mutt. "If the placer minin' has dried up, like you say, why don't they just move on?"

"It ain't that simple," Mutt said. "These folks is kinda trapped here. They can't get out with what gold they found because the damn outlaws are watchin' every road outta here. The only time they ain't watchin' every road is when the winter sets in hard, and then the snows close up the mountain passes and you still can't get out." He glanced over his shoulder then to make sure no one could overhear. "It's changin', though, and pretty damn quick. Like I said, the honest citizens has had enough."

"Vigilantes?" Adam asked again. Mutt nodded in

reply. "Well, I'm awful sorry the folks hereabout are in such a fix, but I've got to find my brother. So I'm gonna go talk to that young lady. What was her name?" Bonnie told him again. "Lacey Brewer," he repeated.

Mutt caught his arm as he turned toward the tables. "Maybe you oughtn't ask her right now. Bonnie's right; it might be better to wait till you can catch her alone."

Adam looked at Mutt, then back at the table again. "Hell, who knows when that might be? She'll probably go off somewhere with one of 'em, or all of 'em, and I don't intend to wait around that long."

"Just when I was beginning to like you," Bonnie commented drily as Adam walked away.

"Don't start writin' his eulogy just yet," Mutt said. "This might be interestin' to watch."

None of the four men at the table noticed the tall, broad-shouldered man as he approached until he caught Lacey Brewer's eye. When she continued to gaze in Adam's direction, one of the men turned to see what had distracted her attention. "Who the hell is that?" he uttered, causing his companions to follow his gaze. Nothing more was said at the moment, while all four looked the stranger over thoroughly. The one who had spoken looked accusingly at Lacey and repeated, "Who the hell is that?" For it appeared he was coming to their table.

"What are you asking me for?" Lacey replied. "I've never seen him before." She paused a moment to appraise the approaching stranger. Then, with a mischievous smile, she said, "I believe I'd remember him if I *had* seen him before."

Her remark served to stir up a fit of jealousy that was already well developed in the man sitting close beside her. Adam could feel the intensity of the man's gaze as he stopped beside the table and asked, "Are you Lacey Brewer?" She nodded, her eyes wide with curiosity. "Can I speak to you for a moment?"

"What about?" her companion demanded before she had a chance to respond.

"Well, that would be between the lady and me," Adam answered calmly as he made a quick judgment of the man's potential for causing him trouble. He possessed an unusually youthful face, and he wore a thin black mustache, an obvious attempt to appear more mature.

"Is that a fact?" the man replied. "Well, the answer is hell no, she can't talk to you. She's talkin' to me." He glanced smugly around him at his friends to get their smiles of approval. "Now, you can drag your ass back over to the bar with that old whore and that broke-down stage driver." His last remark drew a snicker from one of his friends.

Hoping to avoid an unpleasant encounter, but anxious to learn anything the girl might be able to tell him about Jake, Adam paused for a moment before pursuing the matter. He decided he wasn't willing to waste time waiting for her belligerent friend's permission. "Look, mister," he said in as calm a voice as he could fashion, "I don't want to interrupt your little party with Miss Brewer. I just want to ask her a couple of questions. Then you can have her right back." He shifted his focus to the girl then. "Is that all right with you?"

Still puzzled by the tall stranger's interest in her, and curious to know what he wanted to ask her, Lacey shrugged and said, "I guess."

"The hell you do," the man said, and grabbed her

arm to hold her in her chair. Glaring at Adam, he warned, "Now, I've had a bellyful of you. I ain't gonna tell you again." His free hand dropped to his side to rest on the pistol he wore.

"Mister," Adam said, "I told you I'm not lookin' for any trouble. I just wanna ask the lady a couple of questions. It's not worth gettin' riled up about. I'll just take a minute, and you can go right on with your party."

One of the others at the table, an amused spectator to that point, decided to wade in on the fun. "Hell, Lon, he's just lookin' to get his ass whipped. Why don't we take care of that for him?"

With his patience wearing thin, Adam still tried to maintain a calm and noncombative manner. "I told you I wasn't lookin' to cause any trouble," he said, but he knew he had better survey the situation and hope they had already had enough to drink to slow their reactions.

"You ain't, huh?" Lon responded. "It don't look that way to me. Why ain't you lookin' for trouble?"

"Well, for one thing," Adam replied, "there's four of you. I don't care much for the odds."

"You shoulda thought about that before you opened your mouth," Lon smugly informed him. "They seem about right to me."

Adam shifted his attention back to Lacey. It looked as if speaking to her privately was going to be out of the question, so he asked her, "I heard you know Jake Blaine. Do you know where I can find him?"

"Why, you son of a bitch . . . ," Lon exclaimed, infuriated that Adam chose to ignore his threats. He made a move to get up from his chair, dropping his hand to his revolver in the process.

"Don't do that," Adam warned, stopping him before

he was halfway up, the muzzle of his Henry rifle already pointed at Lon's chest. "This ain't worth anybody gettin' killed over, but if that's what you've got your mind set on, I'll accommodate you." The calm, unhurried tone of the big man conveyed a message that it was no idle boast.

Lon sank back in his chair, his face now a twisted mask of anger. "Mister, you must be loco. You don't know who you're dealin' with."

Adam quickly checked Lon's three friends while keeping his rifle on Lon. They were slow in reacting, still taken by surprise with the unexpected confrontation. One of them, a wild-eyed man with a face as sharp as an axe blade, appeared to be making up his mind, so Adam shifted his gaze briefly to warn him. "I know what you're thinkin'," he said. "He can't get all of us before we get him. Well, maybe you'd better think on it real hard. Because I guarantee you I can cut you down, and chamber another cartridge before your friend here has a chance to get that .44 out of the holster. So I'll get you and him for sure, and maybe you." He nodded toward the fat shaggy-haired man sitting next to him. "It ain't so easy drawing a pistol while you're sittin' down in an armchair, is it?" There followed a few moments of uncertain hesitation on the part of the four seated at the table. The solemn, confident manner of the man standing over them with a cocked rifle was convincing enough to cause the four to reconsider any foolish moves. "Like I said before," Adam continued, "I apologize for interruptin' your party. I'll only take a couple of minutes of Miss Brewer's time and nobody gets hurt." With a nod of his head, he motioned for Lacey to get up. "We'll just walk over here to the bar where I can keep an eye on your friends while you tell me what you know about Jake Blaine."

Satisfied that the confrontation had been settled without bloodshed, Adam turned to follow Lacey to the bar. It was not to be that easy, however, for Lon was still steaming over having to back down in the face of the leveled Henry. Thinking Adam had dismissed the incident, he reached for his pistol. Adam's next move was so swift that Lon didn't know what had happened when he recovered consciousness a few minutes afterward with a two-inch gash on the side of his head and a broken nose, left by Adam's rifle barrel. He also missed hearing Adam's comment to him as he fixed the other three with a warning gaze. "Now, there wasn't any need for that. You're a hardheaded bastard, aren't you?"

"There's all different ways to commit suicide, I reckon," an astonished bartender commented to Mutt as the three at the bar watched Adam and Lacey walk to the end of the bar, "but your friend has found one surefire method. Them four he just buffaloed ain't all he's gotta worry about. There'll be a dozen men lookin' to take a shot at him now."

Mutt shook his head thoughtfully, as much amazed by Adam's bold approach as anyone else in the saloon. Like the bartender, he knew the whole town was run by outlaws, with the sheriff right in the thick of it. "I ain't knowed him but half a day," Mutt said, "but damned if he ain't the most determined man I ever saw."

"Determined to get hisself shot," the bartender remarked. "I wouldn't stand too close to him if I was you."

"It tickles me," Bonnie declared. "Ol' Lon Bridges ain't used to somebody knocking some sense in his head like that. That mean bastard. He was one reason I left Bannack in the first place—till I found out it ain't no better in Virginia City."

At the end of the bar, Adam rested his rifle on top with the muzzle pointed at the table he had just left, watching Lon and his friends while he questioned Lacey. "I'm lookin' for my brother, Jake," he said. "Bonnie, over there, said you knew him pretty well. I was hopin' you could tell me where to go to look for him."

"You're Jake's brother?" Lacey asked. Adam answered with a nod. "I don't know where he is," she said. "I ain't seen him in about three weeks. He said he was coming back for me. He was gonna take me with him."

"Take you with him?" Adam had to ask. Jake was as fond of the ladies as anyone, but his style was to love 'em and leave 'em. Could he have fallen for this frail young flower of the dance halls and saloons? "Take you with him where?" he asked.

"Home," she replied innocently, her eyes like those of a puppy that's been left behind by its master.

Well, that's sure as hell some news that ought to tickle the old man, Adam thought, picturing his father when Jake introduced her. Looking even closer at the girl's face, he could not help questioning her morals. "And you're here workin' the saloons while you wait for him?"

"I have to eat and pay for my room," she replied simply.

"Yeah, but . . . ," he started, but did not finish the comment. "Oh, what the hell?" he blurted. "Can you tell me where Jake was campin'—where he was stayin'?"

"I don't know for sure," she answered. "I've never been to his camp. All I know is that he had a place somewhere on the other side of the hills to the east of town, with a fellow named Finn. He was going to come back to get me. I waited for a week, but my money ran out, so I had to go back to work." She studied his face for a few moments, waiting to see if he was going to offer any help, but he remained undecided. "Well, I'd better get back to the table before I lose the chance to pick up some grocery money," she concluded.

Adam was lost in indecision. He was not of a mind to waste money on a barroom whore, but he was reluctant to toss the young girl back to the likes of the four at the table. Jake must have seen something beneath the powder and paint that he found worthwhile. Adam didn't have much time to make up his mind because two of the men helped Lon up on his feet, and started walking him toward the door. The one remaining, the wild-eyed one with the thin face, paused for a few moments to fix his threatening gaze upon Adam before following his friends. No one of them made any attempt to call for Lacey to come with them. "I was coming back," she called to them, distraught to see her rent money walk out the door. Her plea was answered with a sneer from the wild-eyed outlaw.

Carefully watching the four men leave, his rifle muzzle following their path to the door, Adam reluctantly returned his attention to the distressed young woman, her face a worried frown as she saw her chance for a payday disappear. Fearing himself as big a fool as his younger brother, he reached in his pocket for the little pouch his father had given him. "Here," he said to Lacey as he put one of his remaining double eagles in her hand. "This'll hold you for a few days—make up for the business you just lost."

Misunderstanding his gesture, she frowned and

asked, "You want it now?" She glanced at the stairs that led up to the rooms over the saloon.

"No, hell no," he exclaimed. "That ain't what I gave you the money for. I gave you the money so you wouldn't have to do that for a few days."

"Oh," she replied, not fully understanding, but grateful nonetheless.

Having moved down the bar in order to overhear the conversation between Adam and Lacey, Bonnie interrupted. "I'll take a day off, too, if you wanna pay me," she said.

"I can't afford but one fancy lady," Adam replied. "Now, I've wasted enough time in this place. I've got to get an early start in the mornin', so I'd best see about gettin' some sleep."

"I know your brother," the bartender volunteered, surprising Adam, because up to that point he had not shown any indication of wanting to help. "I didn't know his name, but I know the young feller that came in to see Lacey. Him and another feller name of Finn that sometimes came in with him said they had a claim southeast of town on a little stream runnin' down to Grasshopper Creek. Lacey's right about that."

"That's a helluva lot of ground to cover, lookin' for one cabin on a hill that's crowded with 'em," Mutt commented.

"If you ride up from town about even with Harvey's Dry Goods," the bartender offered, "you'll be lined up with a notch in the ridge. I'm pretty sure your brother said his camp was on the south side of that notch—if that'll help you a little."

"Much obliged," Adam said. He turned to Mutt then. "I reckon I'll be goin'."

"What about us?" Bonnie asked, nodding toward Lacey.

"I reckon that's up to you," Adam said. "I don't remember takin' you to raise. Do whatever you were gonna do before I got on the stage."

"I thought I might bunk with you tonight," Bonnie said.

"I'm bunkin' with my horse," Adam replied with a shrug. "If you wanna sleep in the stable, you'll have to talk to the stable owner." He turned to leave.

"I reckon I'll get a room," Bonnie said with an exaggerated pout.

"You can stay with me tonight," Lacey said to Bonnie.

"Adam, I don't know if it's healthy for you to walk out that front door," Mutt said. "You might wanna go out the back."

"I reckon," Adam said. The thought had already occurred to him. In fact, he counted an ambush a sure thing. "Might be a good idea for you folks to stay here until after I'm good and gone."

The bartender shook his head slowly as he watched Adam move through the crowded saloon toward the back door. "Yonder goes a walkin' dead man," he said to Mutt.

Well aware that he had very likely set himself up for a hell of a lot of trouble, Adam slid the bolt on the back door of the saloon and stood just inside while he let his eyes adjust to the darkened alley behind the building. When he was satisfied that there was no one in sight as far as he could see through the partially opened door, he took a cautious step out on the four-by-four back stoop and searched the alley in the other direction. It appeared that, if the men at the table had ambush in mind, they were counting on him using the front door. If that was the case, he decided, he had best get moving before it occurred to them to cover the back.

There was what appeared to be a store of some kind next to the saloon, so he made his way quickly around to the other side of it. Then, holding close to the side of the building, he moved silently along the side toward the front. He had not taken three steps before he stopped stone cold in his tracks. A movement in the shadows at the front corner of the building caused him to drop to one knee and raise his rifle, preparing to fire. He hesitated, however, when he realized that the figure crouched beside the porch was concentrating his gaze toward the front door of the saloon, and was unaware of Adam's presence behind him.

Still intent upon avoiding bloodshed if possible, he very carefully backed away, keeping a wary eye on the figure in the shadows. It would have been easy to continue walking behind the buildings until he came to the stable where his horses were, but he was concerned now that Mutt might be targeted when he left the saloon, simply because he had come in with him. So he circled around the next building in line and made his way to the street again. The only lights were those from the two large windows in the saloon and they provided two square patches of light in the middle of the dusty street. He could barely make out the figure he had almost surprised at the edge of the porch. That accounted for one of them. Where, he wondered, were the other three? He stepped back in the deeper shadows beside the building when two men on horses came up the street, on their way to the saloon. As soon as they passed, he walked briskly across to the other side of the street, confident anyone staking out the saloon door would hardly notice him. Once across, he started inching his way back toward the saloon, seeking out every dark recess that could hide a potential assassin. There were many between the vacant stores that lined that side of the street. He paused at the corner of the barbershop to study the alley between that building and a harness shop beyond. After a moment, a match flared in the darkness when someone lit a smoke of some kind—Adam's guess was a cigar or cigarette, because of the short duration of the flame; it usually took longer to light a pipe. In a moment or two he saw a red glow freshen, then break apart to form two tiny red glows, telling him that there were two of them in the alley next to the barbershop. *That's three of them,* he thought, and shifted his gaze back across the street toward the hotel on the opposite side of the saloon, where he speculated the fourth party might be hiding.

At this point, he wasn't sure of the best way to handle the situation, but he couldn't take a chance on having Mutt walk into an ambush. *Damn it,* he thought, *why in hell didn't I tell him to walk out the back door with me? No good to dwell on it now.* He decided he could at least make enough noise to expose the ambush. The events of the next moment left him with no time to consider his actions, forcing him to rely on his natural reflexes. For at that instant, Mutt appeared in the doorway and stepped out on the stoop. Adam had no choice. The bushwhacker at the corner of the hardware store got to his feet, stepped away from the building, and aimed his pistol at Mutt, who was unaware he was about to be shot. Adam had no time to think about it.

He felt the Henry rifle buck twice as he threw two shots in rapid succession to knock the would-be assassin against the front wall of the store. His shots ignited a brief hailstorm of rifle and pistol shots that sent Mutt diving for the ground beside the stoop. Without hesitating, Adam swung his rifle around to pump three more shots into the dark alley where he had seen the muzzle flashes. There was no time to try to measure his results because the fourth gunman stepped out from the corner of the bakery to draw a bead on Mutt, huddled up against the saloon stoop. The Henry barked once more, dropping the man in his tracks.

Not sure where the rifle fire had come from, Lon Bridges decided it was too hot to remain, sufficiently jarred by the sight of his two companions gunned down. He promptly turned and ran down the alley to the back of the building where they had left their horses. Left to face the devastating rifle fire by himself, Junior Brown fled after Lon. Adam made it to the rear of the building in time to see their retreat. He resisted the urge to throw a few more shots in their direction, opting instead to see if Mutt was all right.

Now that everything was quiet again, a few curious souls ventured out of the saloon to witness the latest shootings in a town no longer surprised by the random mayhem. Mutt climbed slowly to his feet, not sure if he had been hit or not. He cautiously examined his left shoulder where his shirt was wet and sticky with what he feared was blood, although he could feel no real pain. "Mutt!" Adam called out as he crossed the street. "Are you all right?"

"I don't know," Mutt answered as he stepped out

into the patch of light from the saloon windows. "I reckon. I don't feel no wound." He pulled the wet shirt away from his shoulder and looked hard at it. In a moment, his face screwed up in disgust and he swore, "Damn!" Adam tried not to, but he couldn't help laughing when it became apparent what Mutt's wound was. When the shooting started, he had dived for cover in the very spot where the last drunk had vomited the contents of his stomach off the side of the stoop.

Elbowing her way through the crowd of spectators, Bonnie came up to face Mutt. She shook her head in exasperation, as a mother would a precocious child. "Damned if you ain't a pretty sight," she said. "I expect you're gonna have to take your yearly bath if you ain't already. You don't smell too good." She turned her attention toward Adam then, and her expression changed to one of serious concern. "You're bound and determined to set yourself up for every two-bit gunman in the town, aren't you?"

"I just wanna find my brother," he replied. He heard the bartender, who was standing in the doorway of the Miner's Friend, tell someone to fetch the deputy sheriff, so he decided not to linger any longer at the scene.

"Wouldn't be a bad idea for you to make yourself scarce," Mutt advised. "They're gonna be lookin' for you." Adam only nodded in reply as he walked away, heading for the stables where he had left his horses. Wilber Jenkins had told him that he slept in the tack room, so Adam hoped he wouldn't have to break in as he had done in Virginia City. "And, Adam," Mutt called after him, "thanks for savin' my ass."

"Man's got a habit of saving other folks' asses,"

Bonnie commented thoughtfully. "I hope to hell he can save his own."

As it turned out, Adam thought he might have to resort to another break-in, for he found Wilber to be a sound sleeper, so much so that he had evidently slept through the gunfire. It was necessary to almost beat the back door of the stable down before he was able to rouse the sluggish sleeper, who had apparently indulged in a generous bedtime toddy. *If anybody comes looking here for me tonight,* he thought, *at least they're going to make a hell of a lot of noise before they get in.*

Chapter 5

The night passed without incident, and Adam was awake and ready to ride shortly after sunup. He was obliged to wait, however, for Art Thompson, the owner of the stables, to arrive in order to talk about trading his extra saddles and weapons. The sun was well up over the eastern ridge when Thompson arrived. He was met at the front door by Wilber, who told him Adam was waiting for him.

"Howdy," Thompson said upon meeting the tall stranger. "Wilber says you might have some saddles you wanna get rid of."

Adam nodded toward the two saddles he had left at the door of the stall. "I'm needin' a good packsaddle for my other horse," he said. "I'm thinkin' they're worth that one I saw in the tack room and a lot more besides. It you're in a tradin' mood, and ready to get the best of the swap, I'll throw in those two handguns plus the rifles, for the packsaddle, last night's charge for my horses, forty pounds of grain, and fifty dollars' gold."

It was too good a deal for Thompson to question how Adam came to possess the saddles, but his masculine side required him to counter the offer. "Thirty dollars," he said.

"Forty," Adam replied.

"Done," Thompson exclaimed, satisfied that he had skinned the stranger properly, even though suspecting that Adam was not willing to drive a hard bargain because of the questionable means by which he might have acquired them. He looked at Wilber and grinned.

Wilber returned the grin and said, "Well, I reckon I'll go on over and have my breakfast now."

"Why don't you wait around for a minute or two until I'm all packed up and ready to ride?" Adam suggested. "I might need a hand." He wasn't sure where Wilber went to eat breakfast, or whom he might talk to, but he felt he would be a little more comfortable if he was on his way before Wilber had the chance to tell anyone he was still in town. Wilber shrugged indifferently, and waited. When Adam was ready, he walked the bay out to the front door of the stable and paused to look the street over before nudging the horse to a leisurely lope toward the dry goods store the bartender had mentioned. Once he was even with the store, he turned to scan the ridge east of the town. Spotting the notch he had been told about, he headed the bay directly toward it and started up the slope. He had halfway expected someone to take a shot at him, but everything seemed peaceful as he left the town behind him.

More than half of the claims were deserted, but there remained a good many tents and crude structures of all kinds with rough-looking bearded men who stopped to stare at him as he approached. He was reminded of the hillside littered with badger holes that cost Brownie his life. He repeated his inquiry at each camp, but none admitted to knowing Jake Blaine. It seemed unlikely to him that no one had heard of Jake, and he began to wonder if the information as to the whereabouts of Jake's camp was correct. Maybe the bartender was mistaken. He was about to conclude as much when he recalled Jake's partner, a man named Finn.

"Finn?" the grim-looking miner replied. Holding a double-barreled shotgun at his side, he had put aside the pick he had been working with and stood watching Adam approach his camp. "Yeah, I know Michael Finn," he said after just having denied knowing Jake Blaine. "He's a good man. Whaddaya lookin' for him for?"

Considering all Adam had heard about outlaws preying upon the miners along the gulch, he was not surprised by the man's suspicious nature. "I'm told he and my brother were partners. It's my brother I'm lookin' for, but nobody seems to know him."

"So that's who you're lookin' for," the miner said, "Finn's partner." He leaned his shotgun against a knee-high boulder. "Hell, I knowed him. I just didn't know him by name. Ever'body knows Finn, though. He's been here since the first, but he ain't had a partner but about a year. You say he's your brother?"

"That's right," Adam replied. "I was hopin' you mighta seen him recently. We got word that he was on his way home, but he never showed up."

The miner took a moment to scratch under his chin whiskers while he studied Adam's face, apparently trying to decide if Adam was telling him the truth. It was a fact that Finn had come to Bannack right after the first strike, and he was still here. The logical thinking was if Finn hadn't pulled up stakes and moved on to Alder Gulch, then he must still be digging rich ore out of the earth. He had suffered run-ins with outlaws several times, hoping to find a hidden treasure. This formidable stranger might just be one more. After a lengthy pause, he decided Adam was really looking for his brother. "I can tell you how to find Finn's camp," he said. "If anybody knows where your brother is, I expect it would be Finn."

He was a little man, but in stature only, with large forearms and strong shoulders, obvious evidence of many years of hard work. His face was partially hidden behind a dense growth of whiskers liberally streaked with gray, but his eyes were clear and youthful as they measured the stranger on the bay horse when he entered the mouth of the deep ravine.

Not spotting the man until he suddenly stepped out from behind a boulder, rifle in hand, caused Adam to pull up abruptly, and ask, "Are you Finn?"

"I'm Finn" was the simple reply, offering nothing more while he waited for Adam to state his business.

"My name's Adam Blaine," Adam said. If the little Irishman recognized the last name, he gave no indication, waiting for Adam to continue. "I was told my brother, Jake, was your partner, and I'm tryin' to find him. He sent word that he was on his way home, but he never showed up. So I came lookin' for him. I'm hopin' you can help me."

There was just a hint of softening in the gaze fixed so firmly on Adam as Finn made up his mind. Finally he spoke. "So you're Shorty's brother—I always called him Shorty." He nodded his head as if to confirm the statement, while continuing to evaluate the stranger. "Bless me if you ain't a bit taller than your brother."

"A bit, maybe," Adam confirmed.

"Your father must be a large man as well—John, I believe Shorty said his name was."

"Nathan," Adam corrected, already impatient with the seemingly small talk. Then, judging by the expression on Finn's face, he guessed that the little man was seeking to verify his legitimacy.

"Right you are," Finn said. "My mistake." He continued to study Adam's face for a few moments more before deciding to trust his instincts. "I'm sorry for my lack of hospitality," he went on, speaking with the thick brogue of his native Ireland. "But I've had a few of Sheriff Ainsworth's bullyboys snoopin' around lately, and I have to keep an eye out for the back-shootin' bastards. I expect they would have put a bullet in my back long ago, but they think I've got a cache of gold dust hidden somewhere around here. And their sneakin' around ain't found nothin' yet."

"Well, I'm not interested in your gold," Adam said. "I'm just concerned about Jake."

"I believe you," Finn replied. "And now that you're tellin me he's missin', I'm concerned as well." He paused to recall the exact day Jake had left his camp. "It's been two," he started to say before changing his mind, "no, three weeks when he left here on his way to town—I think to see some little saloon girl he knew."

"He never got there," Adam said. "I found the girl and she said he never showed up."

Finn didn't respond at once. He could well imagine
why Jake didn't make it to Bannack. There were hundreds of gullies and rock piles between his camp and
town. Jake's body was no doubt lying in one of them.
Finally he shook his head back and forth sadly. "I
warned the boy to be careful, that Ainsworth's men
were still watchin' the camp, waitin' to see if I'm gonna
pack up and try to sneak out. He'd already had a run-in
with some of 'em over the girl that came close to gunfire. If I hadn't been there to talk some sense into his
head, he wouldn't have walked away from that. There
were too many of 'em. There are always too many of
'em. He wouldn't have had a chance. They ain't the kind
of men to forget somethin' like that, and if somethin'
bad has happened to your brother, I'd be willin' to bet
they had a hand in it. I know that they threatened to kill
Jake." Finn paused again, watching Adam's reaction to
what he had just said. There was no change in the calm
facial expression, but the big man's eyes seemed to be
looking right through him with a steel-blue intensity,
causing Finn to sense the deep presence of a violent
capability. The younger brother had demonstrated a
rough and ready demeanor, willing to stand up to any
challenge. But this solemn man standing before him
now was the more lethal of the two, cold and calculat-
ing, with blood that ran as cold as Jake's had hot.

"Which trail did Jake take to town?" Adam asked.

Finn turned to point. "At the mouth of the gully,
then to the north, the way I always go to town. It's a
ride of about four miles. I ain't been there since Shorty
left. I don't go no more than I absolutely have to. Sometimes, if some of Ainsworth's boys see me in town, I'll

come back to find my camp all torn up, lookin' for somethin' they ain't never gonna find."

Finn's statement caused Adam to recall something Mutt had said, that the folks who had struck it rich were prisoners in the valley, afraid to try to take their gold out. The thought that was searing his brain, however, was the matter of Jake's fate. He had to find out for certain what had happened to his brother, and he feared that it was too much to hope for that Jake was all right. Hidden by his stoic expression, a fire of rage was spreading through his veins as he thought of the free-spirited fun-loving younger man, and his fear of what might have happened to him. Life on the Triple-B, herding cattle, had never appealed to Jake. He was too much like a colt, yearning to stretch his legs. *Maybe I'll find the young colt, and all my worry will be for nothing*, he thought. He turned to step back up in the saddle. "I'm much obliged to you, Mr. Finn," he said as he wheeled the bay. "I'm goin' to look for my brother."

Concerned for what Adam was going to find, Finn felt a deep compassion for the somber older brother. "You're welcome to come on back here to camp for the night. It's getting along in the afternoon and there won't be much daylight left." When Adam paused to consider the invitation, Finn went on. "Be less trouble if you leave your packhorse here while you're lookin'," he said.

Adam paused to think it over. "'Preciate it," he said after a moment. "I'll take you up on that." He dismounted again and took the packs off the roan, then hobbled it and left it to graze. "I'll be back about dark if I don't find somethin' any sooner."

Adam had ridden about half of the four miles to the

town, checking every gully and ravine he came upon, when the trail he followed took a sharp turn to avoid a deep ravine whose sides were thick with scrubby pines. Judging it too steep to risk riding down into the bottom, he dismounted and made his way down the slope on foot. It was here that he found the body, a little more than halfway to the bottom. It had caught on a sapling pine and was lodged there, swollen and decomposing. The shock of finding his brother in this way was enough to cause Adam to sit down hard on the slope in an effort to control his emotions. The advanced stage of decomposition made it difficult to identify the corpse as Jake's. Had it not been for the shock of sandy hair, he might have held out hope that it was not his brother. When he had left Finn's camp, he had tried to steel himself for what he might probably find, but no amount of discipline could prepare him for this crushing grief over seeing what they had done to Jake. Feeling a sudden weakness in his knees, he sat down beside the body, which had been stripped of everything except shirt and trousers—they even took his boots. Thinking what he was going to tell his father, he remained there for some time, remembering Jake on the last day he had seen him—so much alive and eager to start out for the gold fields. After a while, his grief began to turn to anger, and he knew he could not return to the Triple-B until those who had murdered his brother had paid with their lives. With his way clear before him now, he got to his feet and climbed back up to the top of the ravine.

Finn was waiting for him when he returned. It was sooner than he expected, so the little Irishman presumed he had bad news to report. "You found him?"

"I found him," Adam replied, his impassive emotions

now under control again. "I wanna borrow a pick and shovel to bury him."

"I'll go with you," Finn said.

It was the hardest thing Adam had ever had to do. Bent in a permanent position around the tree trunk, the body had not been discovered by buzzards yet, but when he and Finn pulled it away from the tree, they discovered a whole colony of worms that were well into their macabre occupancy. The sight caused Adam to gasp involuntarily, sickened by the desecration of his brother's body. Although able to maintain a grim face, he was barely able to control the fire of vengeance raging in his very soul. Finn realized there was nothing he could say that would console the big man, so he worked away in silence as the two of them dug Jake's grave near the top of the ridge. When it was done, and Jake was in the ground, Finn watched as Adam collected some rocks to fashion a crude marker before attempting to offer his condolences.

"I'm sorry," Finn said. "That ain't easy on you to find him like that." When Adam made no reply, he asked, "What are you gonna do now? I expect you'll be goin' back to tell his father."

There was still no immediate reply from Adam, so deep was he in a mental whirlpool of sorrow and rage. Finn thought he had not heard his question and started to repeat it when Adam spoke. "Do you know any names?" he asked, obviously deep in thought. He looked up sharply at Finn. "Them that threatened Jake?"

"No, sorry," Finn replied.

Adam recalled the man whose nose he had broken in the saloon had been called Lon by his friends.

"Was one a baby-faced little bastard named Lon Bridges?" Finn shook his head no.

"Adam," Finn was quick to comment, "you might not be thinkin' straight at a time like this. It's not just two or three men you're dealin' with; it's closer to a hundred. They're all connected. They know everything that's goin' on between here and Virginia City. There's no sense in puttin' yourself in danger. It won't bring your brother back, and is likely to present your father with two dead sons. If you had a little altercation with Lon Bridges, they're most likely already lookin' for you. Go home, boy."

"If they're lookin' for me, then I reckon I'll make it easier for 'em," Adam said as he stepped up in the saddle. "But I don't wanna bring any trouble your way, so I'll pick up my packhorse and find me a place to camp."

"Hell, it's close to dark now," Finn said. "You might as well stay with me tonight. I ain't noticed any of Ainsworth's boys close to my place for a day or two, anyway. Give you a chance to get something to eat and rest your horses, maybe think a little bit more about what you're gonna do."

"I'm obliged," Adam said. "I ain't particularly hungry, but I could sure use a cup of coffee."

Lon Bridges held a small mirror up before his face and stared at the reddish blue bruises around his swollen nose. "That son of a bitch!" he exclaimed when he gingerly touched the bridge of his nose with his fingers. "He's a dead man if I ever see him again."

"Big feller, totin' a Henry rifle?" Jesse Doyle asked. "I'm bettin' he's the same son of a bitch ridin' shotgun on the stage—killed Hawkins and Highsmith and that tall feller they brought with 'em. And Sykes is lyin' in the cabin with a hole in his leg. The son of a bitch shot a hole in my new hat." He scowled at the memory. "Damn it, I just bought that hat."

"Plummer's gonna be mad as hell when he finds out you boys didn't get that four thousand dollars," Lon said. "He ain't gonna be too happy about losing four men while you was at it. He's the same jasper that killed Ned and Curly last night after he broke my nose. That's six men he's caused to go under since he came to town, countin' Billy Crabtree, I reckon you could say, even if it was really that bitch that did poor Billy in."

"You reckon he might be a marshal they sent in here to try to clean up the town?" Doyle wondered aloud, then answered his own question. "Nah, Plummer's a deputy marshal. They'da told him if they was sendin' in another marshal."

"I'm thinkin' he's a hired gun the damn miners brought in," Lon said, "and the sooner we shoot him down and hang his body up for ever'body to see, the sooner the proper citizens of Bannack are gonna see who runs this town." He placed his fingertips tenderly on his bruised face again, and commented, "And I'd purely enjoy doin' the job." He was about to say more when one of the men outside the cabin called out that a rider was approaching.

Lon and Jesse walked out to stand on the small stoop to see who had found his way through the narrow mountain pass to their hideout in the valley. "Oh, hell," Jesse muttered when he recognized the figure sitting tall in the saddle. "It's that new gunslinger, Briscoe, Plummer hired, come to collect Plummer's share of that four thousand."

"He's gonna be hotter'n a hornet with a toothache," Lon said, at once thankful that he had not been in on the botched stagecoach holdup.

"I can't help that," Jesse replied. "He wasn't there when that whole job blew up in our faces. We wasn't ready for no hired gun ridin' shotgun." He spoke with a show of bravado, but every member of Plummer's gang held a healthy respect for Briscoe. Plummer's special agent, Briscoe acted as a lieutenant for the crooked deputy marshal to the outlaws that worked for him. Plummer had a reputation for adeptness in handling a gun, but most of his men agreed that Briscoe was better. There had been some resentment at first because Briscoe did not ride routinely with the gangs that did the actual work of robbery and, in many cases, murder. They soon learned, however, that he wasn't hired to be a road agent, and several men who had thought to hold out on Plummer were unfortunate to find out his real purpose. No one knew much about Briscoe's background. There was some speculation that he had at one time been a lawman down Kansas way. Some said Plummer sent for him after Briscoe had participated in the massacre at Lawrence, Kansas, when riding with Quantrill's Raiders. Those old enough to have any knowledge of that time knew there was an assassin named Briscoe who rode with Quantrill. But he was an older man, and had seemingly disappeared right after the Lawrence raid. Some thought him dead, but his body had never been found. "This feller's too young to be that Briscoe," Lon said.

"Maybe this one's old Briscoe's ghost," Jesse joked.

"Maybe so," Lon replied. "He's sure as hell a loner— don't hang around with anybody—just stays to hisself till Plummer sends for him." All anyone knew for sure about Briscoe was that he was as lethal as a rattlesnake.

"How do, Briscoe?" Lon called out when the tall rider sitting rigidly in the saddle approached close enough to hear his greeting.

Briscoe nodded in reply, saying nothing until he rode up to the door and dismounted. Glancing about him, his gaze darting from the faces of the two men leaning on their saddles in front of the cabin, and back to focus on Jesse Doyle, he spoke. "Plummer says he'll split the gold with you, and you can keep anything you took from the passengers."

"Well, now . . ." Jesse hesitated, reluctant to admit the failure of their mission. "Them things don't always come off like we plan." Seeing the immediate frown on Briscoe's face, he hurried to explain. "We ambushed the stage just like we was supposed to, but we didn't get no gold. It was a trap. That's what it was. They was hopin' we'd hold 'em up." He continued to embellish as he related the incident. "Them miners hired themselves a gun hand from somewhere, and we was took by surprise—even had a whore with a pistol. She kilt Billy Crabtree, and that hired gun shot Rob Hawkins and Jim Highsmith, and that feller they brought with 'em, before we knew what was what. Me and Sykes was lucky to get away. Hell, that feller shot the hat off my head and Sykes took a bullet in the leg."

"That ain't all." Lon stepped in. "He started up a row with me and the boys in the saloon last night." He pointed to his face. "Caught me when I wasn't lookin'. There wasn't nothin' I could do about it with a Henry rifle lookin' me in the face. Then he snuck around the buildin' and bushwhacked us. He got Ned Waits and

Curly. Me and Junior was lucky to get away." Briscoe made no remark, but leveled his critical gaze at Lon. "There ain't no doubt but what them miners sent for the son of a bitch," Lon went on. Then, hoping to escape Briscoe's wrath, he boasted, "But you ain't gonna have to worry about him much longer, 'cause I'm fixin' to settle with him for bustin' my nose."

There was no show of anger in Briscoe's face as he listened patiently without interrupting either report, but then there was never any emotion in the stone-cold face of Plummer's man. When he spoke, it was without passion. "You two are about the sorriest pieces of shit I've ever seen. I've got to go back and tell Plummer his men in Bannack got their asses whipped by one man with a rifle." That, he decided, was the sum total of the explanations he had just heard. "Maybe your bunch ain't the men to handle these jobs if you can't take care of one man you claim is a hired gun."

"There ain't no doubt about it," Jesse protested. "What else could he be? The way he handled that rifle, it damn sure looked like he knew what he was doin'.'"

Not particularly impressed, Briscoe remarked, "Sounds like he mighta been bulletproof, too. Plummer probably figured you boys could handle a situation like that if it came along. Maybe he was wrong."

"Now, hold on a minute, Briscoe," Jesse quickly responded, not wishing to risk Plummer's displeasure and possibly losing out on notices of future gold shipments from Virginia City. "Plummer ain't had no cause to complain about our work before. Hell, give us a chance to kill this bastard before he decides to cut us off. Anybody can get caught by surprise once in a while. We'll get him. Won't we, Lon?" He turned to Lon for confirmation.

"That's a fact, Briscoe," Lon replied. "He's as good as dead, and them miners will know better'n to try somethin' like that again."

Briscoe studied the faces of both men for a long moment while he considered their boasts. The report he took back to Plummer would no doubt decide their fate as far as members of this gang of road agents was concerned—and as in most cases of this nature, could mean their extermination. If they eliminated this gunman quickly, and without loss of any more of Plummer's men, Plummer might forgive them this one botched robbery. "All right," he finally decided, "I'll give Plummer your side of it, and he'll be waitin' to hear that you took care of this gunman, whoever the hell he is, so business can get back to normal."

"'Preciate it, Briscoe," Jesse said, obviously relieved. He looked at Lon and smiled, then glanced at the other two, who were listening to the conversation with more than a little interest, since it affected their immediate future. "We was just gettin' ready to cook up some grub. You can unsaddle your horse and join us—start back in the mornin'."

"I'll be startin' back right now," Briscoe announced unemotionally. "It's a day and a half's ride to Virginia City, and I don't need to waste any time."

It was a typical response from the mysterious gunman. Briscoe never showed any signs of mixing with the other outlaws on a social basis. He was a loner, and it seemed to Jesse and some of the others that Briscoe thought himself too good to mingle with the rowdy bunch. "Ain't you even gonna stay long enough to let your horse rest up a little?" Lon asked.

"No," Briscoe replied. "He ain't that tired. I'll rest

him after while when I'm ready to eat." He turned and
stepped up in the saddle again, taking a moment to fix
Jesse with his cold gaze. "You make damn sure you
take care of that hired gun," he said before abruptly
heading back out of the valley.

"Tell Plummer he can count on it," Jesse called out
after him. Then, mumbling to himself when Briscoe
made no indication of acknowledging his promise, "I
oughta shoot your ass, you son of a bitch." The thing
that stopped him was the suspicion that Briscoe had
eyes in the back of his head.

Holding the blue roan to an easy lope until he cleared
the mountain pass, the grim rider turned the horse's
nose to the north. Contrary to what he had told them at
the cabin, he was in no particular hurry to get back to
Virginia City. He just preferred solitude over camping
with the likes of Lon Bridges and the others. Common
thieves, they didn't have two cents' worth of brains
in the four of them. Good only for holdups and murders, they hadn't even been capable of that on this last
job. He wouldn't be surprised if Plummer got rid of all
of them.

As he kept an eye out for a suitable place to camp, his
thoughts turned to the matter of the purported hired
gun the miners brought in. It could be true. Although
many of the citizens of Virginia City suspected Plummer of being the mastermind behind the robberies
between that town and Bannack, none dared to state it
publicly. Plummer's public persona was as a fighter of
crime, even to the extent that he was a member of the
Virginia City vigilantes. But recently some of the merchants and miners of the Bannack community had
made a separate move to rid the territory of outlaws,

forming a vigilance committee of their own. They had Plummer worried to the point where he had tried to get a list of members of the vigilante posse that had hanged six road agents last month, but the masked men could not be identified, even to the deputy marshal. An additional cause for worry, Plummer's sheriff in Bannack, Albert Ainsworth, had no notion as to who or how many the vigilantes were. And if they had in fact hired a gunman to come in and start cleaning house, then Briscoe figured he was going to be given the job of stopping him. *We'll see how those two idiots back there do with the job*, he thought, indifferent to the assignment.

Chapter 6

Lacey Brewer left her room over the Miner's Friend and made her way slowly down the stairs. Stopping halfway down, she paused to look over the crowded barroom until her gaze lit upon Bonnie Wells, sitting at a table with two rough-looking miners. Bonnie had decided to rent a room upstairs, next to Lacey's, and it appeared that she was working hard to pay for it. As Lacey stood watching, however, the two miners got to their feet and departed, leaving Bonnie to sit alone. Lacey couldn't help feeling empathy for the weary prostitute and it caused her to worry about her own future, for she was surely destined to end up as Bonnie had, too old and too worn to attract any but the most desperate of customers, and then only after they were properly intoxicated. Those troubling thoughts caused her to think of Jake and wonder what had happened to him. He had been her one hope for changing the path she was walking, and now he had failed her, just as her husband had failed her.

Her mother had warned her that she was making a mistake to marry at the tender age of fourteen, and tried to convince her that although Thad Brewer was young and handsome, he was far too immature to take on the responsibilities of a married man. It wasn't long into the marriage before her mother's predictions became reality with Thad's determination to finish sewing his wild oats. Their daily life soon deteriorated to constant arguing whenever Thad was home, which in turn caused him to spend less time there, and eventually led him to drink. What money he earned working on his uncle's Kansas ranch disappeared in the saloons and bawdy houses almost as soon as he got it. Finally his uncle had enough of his absences and unreliability and told him not to come back.

Promising Lacey that he was going to change his ways and become a dependable husband and provider, he set out for Salt Lake City with his wife and their meager belongings. Taking a room in a cheap hotel, Thad began a search for gainful employment. They had been in Salt Lake for less than a week when Lacey awoke one morning to find Thad gone, leaving her with the bill for their room and no means with which to pay it. Threatened by the hotel manager to be put out on the street if the bill was not paid immediately, Lacey was faced with the first desperate decision of her life. The manager, an unscrupulous father of two children, suggested a means for payment of her debt. After a couple of days of relentless pressure from him, she finally succumbed to the degrading and shameful act that was to be the first step in what she reluctantly accepted as her profession.

Realizing that she had allowed her thoughts to drag

her back through the sorrows that made up her life, she tried to force the painful memories back into the recesses of her mind where she endeavored to store them. She told herself she was a fool to think Jake Blaine was any more than another drifter looking for a good time.

Bringing her thoughts back to focus on the jaded woman sitting alone at the table, she expressed a bored sigh and descended the stairs to join her. Bonnie looked up when Lacey pulled a chair out. She gave her young friend a tired smile and asked, "You finally decide to give up the righteous life and jump back into the muck with the rest of us?"

"I don't know," Lacey replied as she plopped down in the chair, oblivious of the malevolent leering of a half-drunken miner at the next table. "I've still got most of the twenty dollars Jake's brother gave me."

"Yeah, well, that ain't gonna last very long," Bonnie said. She looked around at the evening crowd in the Miner's Choice and commented, "It's a little early yet to be picking up any business." She glanced back at Lacey and raised her eyebrows enviously. "You don't seem to be having any trouble sparking interest, though."

Forgetting her own situation for a moment, Lacey felt a wave of sympathy for her older friend. "It's just look-ers," she consoled, "probably think I remind them of their sister—or their daughter. You're right, it's still too early in the evening. They want to party for a while first."

Bonnie favored her with a knowing smile. "Oh, I know what the score is. Believe it or not, I was as young as you once, but you won't catch me crying about that now. I get by. Long about one or two o'clock, I'll drag some dirty ol' drunk upstairs for a ride. If he's drunk enough not to know the difference, I'll skin him of any extra money he's got left in his pockets and shove him out the door. He won't know how much money he had, anyway."

Bonnie's dreary description of her anticipated evening caused a numbing feeling in Lacey's body, for she knew Bonnie had just described her future if nothing happened to get her off the path she felt forced to walk. At this point, it would have to be some form of miracle—and miracles, as she had thought Jake to be, were few and far between.

As if reading her thoughts, Bonnie sought to advise the young girl. "Honey, it's best if you don't put too much stock in what some young stud tells you about how much he respects you and wants to make things better for you. Some of 'em really mean it at the time, when their temperature and everything else is up. But after they're sober and get back to the mine, or their claim, or to the ranch, it don't seem like such a good idea in the light of day."

"Oh, you don't have to tell me that," Lacey responded. "I don't believe a word half of 'em say." She said it strictly for Bonnie's benefit, for in fact, she had believed Jake when he said he was coming back for her. And she was convinced that his failure to return was only because he had met with some tragedy. As for his brother, Adam, she wasn't sure what to think about him. He had given her money, but was that only to make up for what Jake had promised, and now would that be the end of his concern for her?

"Uh-oh," Bonnie said, interrupting her thoughts. She nodded toward the front door and warned, "Here come some of your other boyfriends."

Lacey turned to see Lon Bridges and Junior Brown in the doorway. They stood for a few moments, scanning the barroom, until Lon spotted the two women sitting at the table. Lacey immediately regretted her decision to join Bonnie, but it was too late to avoid Lon now, so she decided to pretend it was the wrong time of the month to accommodate any urges he might have. She found out, however, that he had other things on his mind this evening.

"Where the hell is that bastard that broke my nose?" Lon demanded when he approached the table.

"I don't know," Lacey replied.

"Don't lie to me," Lon threatened. "I'll beat the hell outta you."

Bonnie stepped in to defend the young girl then. "She doesn't know where he is. He left here after he fixed your yellow ass and he ain't been back. Leave her alone."

"Who asked you anythin'?" Lon snapped. "You can mind your own business, or I'll teach you to keep your nose outta mine." He fixed her with a threatening glare for a moment before adding, "I ain't Billy Crabtree. You try somethin' like that with me and I'll break your neck for you." Turning his attention back to Lacey, he demanded again, "Where's that big son of a bitch?"

"Right behind you."

The entire saloon went dead quiet. Lon's heart seemed to come to a sudden stop, gripped by a numbing fear that destroyed the boastful air he had walked in with. The deep emotionless voice that had issued the statement carried an unspoken threat of death. After what seemed an eternity, he turned to face the man whom he thought he was stalking, realizing at that instant that he was the prey, and not the hunter. The Henry rifle that he had met before was looking at him again, and the look in the eye of the man who held it was as cold and hard as the steel of the barrel. "You're makin' a big mistake, mister," he managed to stammer.

"I found Jake's body in that ravine," Adam stated softly.

"I don't know nothin' about no body," Lon blurted, looking nervously at Junior Brown for his support, but Junior was hesitant to make any sudden moves with Adam's rifle already cocked and leveled at Lon. Realizing that he had no choice, Lon made the fatal move. "Get him, Junior!" he yelled, and reached for his pistol.

The report of the Henry rifle ripped the thick, smoke-filled saloon and Lon winced in pain as the .44 slug tore through his gut, causing him to drop his pistol to the floor. In one quick motion, Adam cocked the rifle and swung it around to cover Junior while Lon staggered backward and doubled over, clutching his stomach while sliding down the wall to a sitting position. Still trying to make up his mind, Junior hesitated when Adam's somber gaze locked on his. He immediately held his hands out in front of him, palms out, his eyes pleading until Adam gestured toward the door with his head, and the frightened man quickly took the opportunity to escape. Satisfied that Lon was in no condition to strike back, Adam turned to face the empty doorway where Junior had just fled, his rifle leveled to fire. As he anticipated, after a few short moments, Junior suddenly reappeared, his revolver out ready to fire. Adam dropped him as he was pulling the trigger, sending a wild shot that smashed the lamp hanging in the middle of the room. A brief look confirmed that his shot had been a kill shot in the man's chest, for Junior lay still, sprawled in the doorway. Adam turned back to Lon, who remained propped against the wall, his face twisted in pain as his torn insides bled out. "The two of you ain't worth a hair on my brother's head," Adam lamented as he watched Lon's final moments draining away. "A damn waste of cartridges."

Cocking the Henry again, Adam looked around him at the speechless spectators to the brutal execution, ready to react to any threat. When no one showed any notion to raise a hand against him, he turned his attention toward the two women still seated at the table, frozen in their chairs. "Are you still whorin'?" he asked Lacey.

"Not since you gave me that money," she answered fearfully.

"Well, that ain't gonna last you very long," he said, echoing Bonnie's earlier comment. "Take whatever you can find on him," he directed, nodding toward Lon's body. "Maybe there's a little to keep you up for a while, and I'll try to get back to see if I can help you. Right now I've gotta get outta here. I expect the sheriff's already on his way." He started to leave, then hesitated, realizing he had not explained the reason for his actions. "I don't know if you heard me say it, but in case you didn't, I found Jake's body in a deep ravine between here and the south hills. That's the reason he didn't keep his word to you."

There was no attempt to hide the sorrow in her face when hearing the final evidence of what she feared had actually happened. She made no reply, but it was obvious that the young girl was devastated. Deep in her mind, she acknowledged the fact that she was not truly in love with Jake, but she was certain that she could have learned to love him in time. Her distress was primarily triggered by knowing that she was doomed to life as a prostitute with Jake gone.

"Where's your horse?" Bonnie exclaimed to Adam when Lacey showed no sign of reacting. "I'll bring it around back!"

"He's already there," Adam replied. "That's the way I came in."

"Well, you'd better get gone before Ainsworth and his outlaws show up," she advised excitedly, "or you're gonna be sitting on the same train to hell with Lon and Junior." He wasted no further time, striding quickly toward the rear of the saloon. A wide path was cleared for him by the spectators, and Bonnie watched him until he disappeared through the door. Shaking her head in wonder, she commented to anyone listening, "That man is determined to bring all hell down upon himself."

Outside, Adam took a cautious moment to scan the darkened alley before he untied his horse and climbed in the saddle, in case the sheriff's response might have been quicker than he anticipated. The noise from inside the saloon told him that the patrons had recovered their voices sufficiently to resume their evening pleasure, now with the added excitement of a couple of killings. Nudging the bay sharply with his heels, he galloped up the alley toward the south end of the town, since the sheriff's office was at the north end. With no sign of pursuit when he reached the end of the alley, he swung his horse to the east and disappeared into the night. Once he had climbed the ridge, he slowed the horse until he reached the common trail, making an effort not to leave sign of his flight. He had a horse and his supplies back in the gully where Finn made his camp, and he wanted to make sure he didn't lead a posse to call on the little Irishman.

Back inside the saloon, Lacey and Bonnie stood amid the other spectators as everyone crowded around to get a look at the bodies. Among the curious, a tall, thin man with thinning gray hair edged his way up beside Bonnie and peered down at the late Lon Bridges. "Hello, Clyde," Bonnie said. "Haven't seen you in a while."

"Somebody said you went to Virginia City," Clyde Allen replied.

"I decided to come back. You been busy down at the claims office?"

"Not so much anymore," he answered. "Who was that fellow that did this? He seemed to know you and Lacey. Is he the same fellow that shot those road agents that jumped Mutt Jeffries a day or two ago?"

"Same man," Bonnie replied.

"I figured as much," Clyde said. "He's a regular grizzly bear, ain't he?"

"He just doesn't stand for anybody treading on his toes," Bonnie said. "He ain't a man you wanna make mad at you."

"No, I can see that," Clyde replied, his mind on other things. As one of the members of a secret organization of vigilantes, he was more than a little interested in a man who had rid the town of eight known outlaws in two days' time. In the three months since the formation of the vigilance committee, it had taken them that long to hunt down and hang six blatant outlaws. "I don't suppose you know where I could find him," he said. "I'd like to talk to him."

"I have no idea," Bonnie replied. Turning to Lacey, she asked, "Did he tell you where he was going?"

Lacey slowly shook her head. "No, just that he'd try to come back to see me if he could."

Clyde nodded and said, "Well, if he does, tell him I'd like to talk to him."

Michael Finn looked up quickly from his campfire, not sure if he had heard something out there in the dark. As a precaution, he moved away from the fire and retreated into the shadows. He had seen no sign of the one or two riders who showed up from time to time to check on him, but that didn't mean they were not still keeping a steady watch on his movements. One thing he was sure of was, if they finally decided to move on him, he was going to make it extremely costly for them. There it was again! He was sure this time that it was the sound made by a horse's hooves on the rocky trail leading down from the side of the ravine. A moment later, Adam's packhorse whinnied to confirm Finn's suspicions. Reaching for the rifle he always kept handy, he prepared to welcome visitors. In a few seconds, he heard a now familiar voice.

"Hello, Finn, it's me, Adam Blaine! I'm comin' in."

"Come on in, Adam," Finn called back, and relaxed his grip on his rifle. He walked back out to the fire and waited for Adam to ride in before asking, "Did you find anything in town?"

Adam stepped down and took the coffee cup extended toward him. "No, I didn't—spent most of the day lookin' around. I ran into Lon Bridges in that saloon where I had a run-in with him before." He paused to take a sip of the boiling hot coffee.

"Well, since you've come riding back to my camp, I guess I can figure that it didn't go so well for Lon."

"No," Adam replied in his usual stoic manner, "I guess you could say that."

"So I reckon we can say Lon Bridges' days of waylaying innocent folk on the trails around Bannack are over."

"I reckon," Adam said.

"My God, man," Finn finally exclaimed in frustration, "are you gonna tell me what happened? Or should I wait to get the story in the newspaper?"

Still drained of emotion, Adam shrugged and replied, "I shot Lon and the fellow he had with him. That's all there is to tell. What else do you wanna know?"

"Sweet Jesus, but you're an emotional man," Finn responded facetiously. "Tell me what happened when you found him. Was it a blazin' shoot-out between you and the two of them? What about that joke of a sheriff? Is he chasin' you now?"

"I wouldn't be surprised," Adam replied, still puzzled over why Finn needed a detailed accounting of the execution. "There ain't nothin' more to tell. Lon drew on me and I had to shoot him. He didn't give me no other choice. Now I expect I'd best get my gear and move on before I bring Ainsworth and his boys down on you."

"Well, if there wasn't anybody chasin' you here, why would they come to my camp to look for you?" Finn replied. "Did anyone see which way you headed when you left town?"

"No, I'm pretty sure they didn't," Adam said. "I was careful about that."

"Then they've got no reason to think they'd find you here, so you might as well spend the night with me,

and figure out what you're gonna do come mornin'."
When Adam paused to consider the suggestion, Finn
asked, "What *are* you plannin' to do—go back home?"

"I reckon," Adam replied. "I don't know . . ." He
hesitated, not sure himself. He had a feeling that there
was unfinished business here. The deaths of Lon Bridges
and Junior Brown had not resulted in the feeling that
the ledger was balanced concerning Jake's death, and
that troubled Adam. He was left with no more than the
feeling he might expect after killing a coyote slinking
around his cattle. He thought about the events of the
past couple of days, events that had caused him to be
responsible for the deaths of seven men, eight counting
the one Bonnie shot. It was not something that sat well
with his conscience, yet when reviewing the incidents
as they had occurred, he could not see that they could
have been avoided. Only the two this evening were
premeditated. He told himself that Jake had been
avenged, and there was no cause for more bloodshed.
But then there was the matter of Lacey Brewer. What,
he wondered, was his obligation to the young
prostitute—if any? He wished that he could know
Jake's mind on the subject of Lacey, if he really had
intended to take her back to the Triple-B. It was not at
all like the Jake Blaine he knew. Could he have hon-
estly fallen for the pitiable young girl? And did Adam
now have the responsibility to live up to his departed
brother's promise to a prostitute? "Damn it to hell!" he
suddenly blurted without thinking, startling Finn,
who was waiting for him to answer the question he
had posed some brief seconds past.

"What's the matter?" Finn asked. "Is anything wrong?"

"Everythin's wrong," Adam answered in obvious

frustration. "I'll never know who killed Jake." Then, looking to the little Irishman for help in making his decision, he posed a question. "Was Jake serious about that girl in Bannack? Did he ever talk about her?"

"Yes, he did," Finn replied. "He talked about her a lot. I think he saw a lot more in the girl than a common whore. He wanted to take her out of that evil town and give her a chance to live a respectable life. I don't know if he was thinkin' on marrying the girl or not. He never said. I think he was more determined to save her from the trap she was in." He shook his head slowly in sad memory of the young man's comments about Lacey. Looking back at Adam then, he said, "I never met her but once when I went with Jake to the Miner's Friend, so I'm afraid I can't say if she was pullin' the wool over his eyes or not."

Finn's comments were not of much help to settle the quandary in Adam's mind. *Damn it*, he thought, *she ain't my responsibility. She ain't the first girl Jake made promises to that he had no intentions of keeping. It ain't up to me to do a damn thing for her.* But it was no use. He knew he would not fail to keep his brother's promise. He had not been there to help him before he was killed, so he should carry out his wishes as best he could. After all, he was his brother. *What the hell am I going to do with her? What's she going to do on the Triple-B? Pa and Mose will think I've lost my mind.* "Well," he finally decided, "I reckon I'm gonna take the young lady home if that's what Jake wanted."

"I see," Finn uttered softly, his mind churning with speculation of a different nature as he studied Adam carefully, seeking to see into the big man's very soul. He had been thinking of his dilemma for months before Adam arrived, and had almost approached Jake with the problem, but decided against it. He knelt by the fire, staring into the flames for a few moments more before speaking of it. Finally deciding that Adam was a man to be trusted, he stood up to face him. "I've been in this hole since the fall of '62," he started. "I found pay dirt, a helluva lot of it, and I kept findin' it long after it played out in the claims around me. People moved out and others moved in, but the vein I struck never quit yielding high-grade ore. Well, I kept it quiet and every night I hauled the day's yield down to the bottom of this ravine and buried it under the bank of the stream."

Astonished by the little man's frank disclosure of his fortune, Adam interrupted Finn's confession. "Whoa, you ought not be tellin' people where you've got gold buried."

Finn smiled knowingly. "I ain't tellin' nobody but you. Maybe I'm wrong, but I think I can trust you." He continued. "Anyway, the vein finally ran out early last summer, but I already had more gold than I can ever spend the rest of my life. Ainsworth's men have been watchin' me almost every day, so I kept at it, so they wouldn't start to think I had all I needed. When your brother joined me, I think that kept Ainsworth at a distance. Jake would go into town to see that little girl, and I don't think Ainsworth's men even recognized him as my partner. If they did, they mighta killed him sooner. We found a little bit of pure stuff after that, enough to make Jake think he was strikin' it rich. But he didn't know that there was a king's fortune buried under the bank."

He paused to pour more coffee in his cup and topped

off Adam's, while he thought about the likable young man who had been his partner for about a year. Jake never seemed to have the capacity to stick with the hard work of mining for any length of time before having to take a little vacation. Every once in a while, he would take off for as long as a week—to spend time with his little saloon girl, Finn supposed. Then he'd show up again, ready to go to work. If Adam knew his brother well, he probably guessed as much.

"Well, what I'm gettin' around to is this," Finn finally continued. "I wanna go with you." Adam recoiled in surprise, but remained silent, for it was obvious Finn had more to say. "I've got what I came for," Finn went on. "But like a lot of miners in the gulch, I'm trapped here in this hole, and it don't look like there's gonna ever be any improvement in law and order. I ain't a prayin' man, Adam, but I believe God is tryin' to tell me that He sent you here for a number of reasons. And one of 'em is to give me a chance to get outta here with my fortune while I've still got a few years left to enjoy it."

Adam was speechless for some moments, taken aback by Finn's request. He was hard put to consider himself an instrument of God. "Are you sure you wanna hitch up with me? Hell, half the outlaws in the territory are already gonna be lookin' for me. You wanna risk all you worked for on the chance that I'll get away from here without gettin' my ass shot off?"

"Yes, I do," Finn replied, nodding his head in determination. "I can't stay here forever waiting for someone to come in and get rid of the lawless bunch that runs the town. The army ain't likely to send in a troop of soldiers to escort me out of this valley. So I figure you're my only chance to finally get out. From what

I've heard since you arrived in town, I can't see how I could find a better man to team up with, and you could use another gun. Whaddaya say?"

Still astonished by the proposal, Adam hesitated, thinking of the added risk of trying to smuggle a string of pack mules out with him and Lacey. "Damn, Finn, I don't know. You'd be takin' a helluva chance of losing everythin', includin' your life."

"I would expect to pay you," Finn said. "I wouldn't ask you to do it for nothin'." He paused to study Adam's obvious uncertainty about the prospects of success. "Adam," he continued, "I know the risks. But I can't wait here and die with the gold hidden in a stream, and that'll happen just as sure as we're sittin' here talkin' about it. Ainsworth will soon get tired of waitin' for me to pack up, and send his bullyboys in to take care of me. I'd sooner get shot tryin' to get out to somewhere where the fruits of my labor could be enjoyed."

Adam shook his head in amazement. "Two men and a prostitute against I don't know how many bushwhackers," he said. "It ain't a bright idea, but it'll sure as hell be interestin'. If you're certain that's what you wanna do, then I reckon we'll give it a try, but I don't expect you to pay me for it."

"I insist," Finn stated with a happy grin. "If we get outta here with any gold, it would be my pleasure to pay you."

"How long will it take you to get ready?" Adam asked.

"I'm ready now," Finn said. "I've been ready for months."

Adam looked around him then and had to remark, "How the hell are you thinkin' about carryin' all this gold? I don't see but one horse. Exactly how much gold do you have to carry?"

"I've got ten bags with about fifty pounds in each one, and I've got three mules to carry them."

Surprised again, Adam asked, "Where the hell are they?"

"Down at the bottom of this gulch where the gold is hidden," Finn replied. "I bought 'em from a man who gave up and went back east a few months ago. I keep 'em down at the stream where they'll be out of sight of Ainsworth's spies ridin' along the ridge." He gave Adam a wide grin. "Give me time to dig up my sacks and I'll be ready to go."

"We'll start on it first thing in the mornin'," Adam said. "Lord help us," he added.

Chapter 7

It was still early evening when Lacey heard the knock on her door. She paused before answering it to decide if she should or not. *I told Fred I wasn't entertaining any gentlemen for a spell,* she thought. Fred, the bartender, had merely laughed when she had told him, and had said that she'd have to start entertaining them pretty soon because her rent was about due. *He probably told some friend of his that I was in my room,* she thought. The problem facing her was that Fred was right. She really had no alternative if she was to survive. She had even asked for a job in the hotel kitchen, but had only succeeded in bringing Grace Marshall's wrath down upon her for trying to take the waitress's job. There was no other respectable employment for her.

The knocking on her door continued, and whoever it was seemed to know that she was there. So when it was apparent that her visitor was not going to go away, Lacey finally gave in and went over close beside the door. "I'm sick," she lied. "I can't party tonight."

"Open the door," a low voice replied softly. "I ain't here to party."

"Who is it?"

"Adam Blaine. Open up, I wanna talk to you."

Lacey felt a surge of emotion run through her breast, for she had given up on ever seeing Jake's somber brother again. "Just a minute, Adam!" she exclaimed excitedly, and hurriedly unlocked the door.

Adam stepped quickly inside after a glance up and down the deserted hallway, and locked the door again. "What's the matter?" he asked. "How sick are you?"

"I'm not sick," she answered, and explained that she thought he was someone the bartender had sent up to her room. "And I haven't been doing any of that since you told me not to," she was quick to reassure him. Like a puppy begging for a treat, she gazed earnestly into his eyes, hoping to hear something that would mean her salvation.

"Tell me how serious this thing between you and Jake was," he said. "You said he was comin' to take you home. Was he talkin' about your home or his? Were you two thinkin' about gettin' married?"

Looking into his eyes, she was struck with a feeling that he would know if she lied to him, so stern and somber was his gaze. She had always told the truth before, except in cases where she felt forced to lie to protect herself. This, she thought, might be one of those times, but his eyes seemed to be burning right into her brain. After a moment's hesitation, she confessed, "Jake was such a sweet young man. He came to see me when he could, and it troubled him to see me in this place, so he decided to take me away from here. I don't think we were in love. At least he never said he loved me." She paused and shook her head sadly. "How could he fall in love with a prostitute? I think he just felt sorry for me, so he said he was going to take me to his home north of the Yellowstone—said I could start a new life there." She shrugged and sighed, feeling that she had not presented much of a case for herself. "That's about it. He never said anything about marriage."

Adam did not respond at once while he considered what she had told him. He had halfway expected a tale of a classic love affair, but instead, she had been openly honest about the relationship. She wasn't making it any easier for him to decide if he was, in fact, under any obligation to her. *Life is tough*, he thought. *You make your own choices and pay the price for any wrong decisions— if she wasn't so damn young and innocent looking.* No matter how much he tried to rationalize, he couldn't bring himself to condemn her to the life of a prostitute. When he finally spoke again, it was to state, "If you still wanna go with me, get your things together, 'cause I'm fixin' to leave this place right now. I gotta warn you, though, it's gonna be a rough trip, and we might run into trouble. There's a lot of folks lookin' for me. You know who they are, so you know there's a good chance we won't make it." He waited for her reaction then.

The excited look in her eyes should have been a sufficient answer, even before she replied. "I'll do anything to get away from here," she said without hesitation. "You're a good man for doing this—"

"Don't go thankin' me yet," he interrupted. "I might get you killed before we make it, so get into somethin' you can ride in." He turned his back then while she put on some clothes suitable for travel, a gesture that struck her as rare. "You can ride my packhorse," he said. While she gathered her things, he told her that they would be traveling with Michael Finn and a string of mules. "Somethin' else liable to bring trouble down on us," he thought aloud.

"I'd rather be shot than stay here," she informed him. "You can turn around now. I'm ready."

He unlocked the door and opened it to find Bonnie Wells standing there waiting, hands on hips. "What the hell's going on?" she demanded. "I heard your big feet tryin' to tiptoe up the hall." Seeing Lacey behind him, carrying a satchel, she at once realized what was taking place. "Well, I'll be damned," she exhaled. "You came back for her. I never thought you would." She grabbed his sleeve and warned, "Ainsworth's boys are looking all over the gulch for you."

"I figured," Adam replied. "That's why we're kinda in a hurry. So pardon us if we don't stop and visit."

"Whoa!" she said, refusing to release his shirt. "I'm going with you. This place is drying up faster than spit on a hot skillet."

"What?" Adam blurted in surprise. This was not something he was prepared for. Taking one woman with him was insane enough; two would be impossible. "You just got here. You don't even know where I'm goin'."

"I don't care where you're going. I'm going with you. I'll worry about where I end up after I get there." She turned to Lacey then and said, "Help me get my things, honey."

Adam stood in the darkened hallway, feeling totally helpless while the two women ran quickly to Bonnie's room to gather up her belongings. "I ain't got a horse for you," was all the argument he could think of at the moment.

"That's not a problem," Bonnie called back cheerfully over her shoulder as they disappeared into the room next to Lacey's. Long accustomed to a sense of survival, Bonnie knew she was many years beyond an age where she could hope for someone to step forward to rescue her. And she had no intention of remaining in Bannack to witness the obvious death of the mining town. Consequently she was ready to take the first opportunity to escape, and she didn't care if she was invited along or not. Experiencing a rather dark optimism, she was optimistic nonetheless and, like a cat, believed she would land on her feet.

The temptation to leave without them was hard to resist. Adam felt that he had been buffaloed by the hardbitten whore, and for a man who was accustomed to being in control, it was a frustrating experience. *Damn me for a softheaded fool,* he scolded himself, and for a brief moment, he was about to curse Jake, too, for without his younger brother's compassion for a sorrowful prostitute, he wouldn't have found himself in such a fix. Knowing that Finn was probably getting antsy waiting for him at the top of the ridge above town, he took a few steps down the hall to the top of the stairwell where he could see half of the saloon downstairs. What he could see told him that it was a typical night in the barroom, and no one seemed to be interested in what was going on upstairs. "Damn," he muttered, still disgruntled over the way things had evolved. Walking back to Bonnie's door, he met the women coming from the room. They both appeared excited as if they were going on a hayride. "You're gonna have to ride on one of Finn's mules," he said to Bonnie.

"Finn?" she responded. "Who the hell asked him along?"

"I expect he'll ask me the same question when he sees you," Adam replied as he led the way down the hall to the back stairs, where he paused. "Might be a good idea for you to go down and make sure there's nobody standin' around the back door," he told Bonnie.

"See, you're using me already," she said, and started down the steps. At the bottom, she looked back and waved them on. After they had filed out the back door, the two women stood in the dark alley while Adam went behind the outhouse to get his horse, unaware that Fred, the bartender, had caught a glimpse of them as they left. Not overly curious, but enough to see who it was, he shrugged and returned to the bar.

"I hadn't planned on ridin' three on one horse," Adam said as he led the bay back to them.

"It's not a problem," Bonnie said once again. "I've got my own horse." Astonished, Adam asked where it was. "I've got a little arrangement with Wilber Jenkins at the stables," she explained. "Wilber ain't got much money to spend on partying, so I made him a special deal. We swap rides. I like to take a little ride once in a while, so he lets me take one of the horses when Mr. Thompson ain't around. Then every time I do that, I give him a free ride." She shrugged nonchalantly. "It's just a little side arrangement—doesn't happen very often, and not once since I've been back this time. He oughta be ready for a ride." When her explanation was met with doubting expressions from both Adam and Lacey, she insisted, "Wilber will still be willing to do it."

"It's nine o'clock at night," Adam bluntly pointed out. "He'll know somethin's goin' on."

"Don't worry about it," Bonnie said, "I'll take care of it." She started out toward the stables, then stopped after taking a dozen steps and looked back at them. "Don't get any ideas about taking off without me, 'cause if you ain't here when I get back, I'll scream so loud I'll wake up the whole town." That said, she proceeded to the stables, leaving Adam to wonder if the hard-seasoned prostitute would actually do what she threatened. With an impatient sigh, he turned and helped Lacey up behind the saddle, and they waited.

Just as she had said, Bonnie appeared at the head of the alley a little more than a quarter of an hour later, riding a little chestnut mare. Adam could not decide if he was glad to see she had been successful or hoped that she wouldn't show up. His immediate concern, however, was what Wilber Jenkins knew about their plans. A word from him and the sheriff's deputies would immediately be upon them.

"I told you not to worry about it," Bonnie said. "I told Wilber that I needed to take a little late-night ride to clear the smoke and sweat of the saloon outta my head—told him it was a female thing." She laughed as she pictured him when she rode out the door. "He's probably asleep, drunk as he was already. I told him I'd give him a free ride when I got back."

An Irishman, three mules loaded with gold dust, and two whores, one of them a horse thief, was the thought that flashed through Adam's mind as he guided the bay up the slope behind the alley.

Like Adam, Michael Finn was openly dismayed when he learned of the addition to their escape party. He had not been in favor of taking Lacey with them on a journey that might prove to be dangerous enough without having a woman to take care of. But he knew he had no say in that decision. He was the one who had asked to tag along. But Bonnie Wells? He wondered what Adam could have been thinking to agree to take her along.

The undisguised look of alarm on Finn's face adequately conveyed his reaction to her presence. Bonnie was quick to address his concern before Adam had a chance to. "What are you looking like a bear with his foot in a trap for?" she demanded of the short, bull-like Irishman. "I'll carry my weight on this trip, and I can shoot a gun as good as most men."

"I don't doubt it," Finn said, relaxing his expression of apprehension, almost smiling in response to the brazen prostitute. "You just might get the chance to prove it before this little party is over." He glanced over to exchange knowing looks with Adam.

"Let's get movin'," Adam said. "We need to be way the hell away from here come sunup."

Since taking the regular road to Virginia City was out of the question, and an open invitation to bushwhackers, Adam and Finn had decided on a longer and decidedly more rugged route, planning to bypass Virginia City entirely. So Adam led the party directly north toward Badger Pass and the mountains. Proceeding at a cautious pace to avoid the risk of crippling any of the horses or mules in the darkness, they were unable to make very good time until, when about two miles north of Bannack, a three-quarter moon climbed over the crown of the mountains to the east of them. With a little better light to see by, they were able to pick up the pace to a fast walk. Dawn found them approximately ten miles from Bannack, just south of Badger Pass, safe enough to stop to rest the animals and eat breakfast.

Both women were quick to do their part, and soon had coffee boiling and bacon frying over the fire that Adam built. While Lacey tended the meat, Bonnie took the liberty to inventory the supplies Adam and Finn had packed. "Well, I'm glad to see you brought some flour and a little baking soda, but it looks like you didn't plan to eat anything but bacon and coffee." She glanced at Adam for comment, but he merely shrugged in reply. "Some dried beans mighta been nice," she went on.

"We weren't planning a picnic," Finn responded abruptly, "or I'da brought some champagne for the ladies."

"Hell, you didn't even bring any whiskey," Bonnie commented as she rummaged through the packs of food.

"You just don't know where to look," Finn snorted. "Now, just you keep out of the rest of my packs."

Bonnie took the coffee Lacey handed her and sat down to drink it while she waited for more of the bacon to finish cooking. While she drank it, she studied the packs that the mules carried. After a few moments of silent speculation, she asked, "Is every one of those sacks filled with gold dust?"

"Whether they are or not," Finn replied, "is no concern of yours."

She counted ten bags. "Ten sacks," she exclaimed, and took a loud sip of her coffee for emphasis. "You must be the richest man in the world. How much is it in dollars?" When he ignored her question, she commented, "No wonder we're sneaking around in the mountains. I thought it was just because Ainsworth was after Adam. Does he know you've got this much gold?"

"I reckon he suspects it," Finn answered. "And when

he realizes I've packed up and moved out, he'll have his men lookin' all over these hills for me. You just forget about what's in the sacks. Those sacks are filled with my blood and sweat and over two years of hard labor. You'll be needin' to worry about gettin' shot."

Preferring not to participate in the discussion, Adam got up to check on the condition of his horses. Satisfied that they were both healthy and rested, he helped Finn check his mules. All the animals seemed fit to travel. "I know we haven't had any sleep, but I think it would be best to put a little more distance between us and Bannack. It's probably a day's ride to the Beaverhead River, so I think we should keep at it till we strike it. Whaddaya think, Finn?"

"Suits me fine," Finn quickly agreed. "The farther we can get, the better."

Adam looked to Bonnie then. "Think you ladies can hold up till we get there?"

"Don't worry about us," Bonnie replied, speaking for them both. "It's sure as hell not the first time I've been up all night."

"Well, I reckon we'll get started, then," Adam said. With breakfast over and the horses and mules packed, they changed their direction of march to an eastern bearing, planning to strike the Beaverhead River at the end of the day if everything went smoothly. A great deal depended upon the difficulty they might encounter trying to keep a constant course through a country of hills mostly barren of trees between there and the river. At least the weather was favorable, with chilly nights and mornings, and pleasant days, giving them one less thing to worry about.

In the saddle again, Bonnie brought her stolen mare

up close beside Finn and leaned over to whisper in his ear, "Ten sacks—you know, I never realized what an attractive devil you are, old man."

"You go to hell," Finn retorted, gave his horse a kick, and moved away from her. She threw her head back and laughed.

Unable to match the boisterous bravado demonstrated by her older *sister in the service*, Lacey endeavored to stay as close to Adam as possible, still fearful of what each new dawn might bring. She knew that, in the event of danger, it would be Adam's strength that would decide her fate. The desperation of her situation lay upon her like a leaden shroud. It was not the possibility of death that frightened her, for she had decided that death was preferable to the prospect of spending her remaining years in the desecration of her young body. If they were fortunate to escape those who would do them harm, she would still have no notion as to what might lie ahead for her. At what point would Adam tell her that she was out of harm's way, and was therefore on her own? What would she do? She only knew one occupation. The thought caused her to shudder. Sometimes she wondered if she could go back home to her parents in Kansas. But it had been so long since she had contact with them, and she was reluctant to return an abandoned wife, afraid they might be able to read the shame she had brought upon herself. As usual, thoughts of this nature brought only despair, so she moved even closer behind Adam, seeking solace in his strength.

Gathering darkness found them still in the hills, following a stream that they figured emptied into the Beaverhead, although there was no sign of the river yet. Adam stopped and waited for Finn to pull up beside him. "Looks like we've got a little piece to go before we strike the river valley," he said. "Maybe we oughta just make camp right here while we've still got enough light to see what we're doin'." He paused to twist right and left in the saddle to take a longer look at the spot. The streambed was fairly wide there, with high ridges on both sides. "Won't be much danger of anybody seein' our smoke between these ridges."

"Looks all right to me," Finn said.

Pulling up in an effort to hear the discussion, Bonnie offered her opinion. "Good a place as any," she agreed, and dismounted without waiting for a final decision from the men. "My ass is about to take root in this saddle," she said, already regretting the fact that she had not stolen a saddle that was a little more comfortable for her behind. "Come on, Lacey. You can help me get a fire started, and we'll get some supper going." She cast an accusing glance in Finn's direction and added, "Such as it is with what supplies we've got."

Finn turned to Adam and remarked sarcastically, "The woman's the very definition of the word *lady*." Adam couldn't help grinning. He had to admit that he had never met anyone like her. "I guess we're campin' here," Finn said, and dismounted. He and Adam unsaddled the horses and relieved the mules of their packs, gladly leaving the cooking to the women.

After the animals were taken care of and left to graze, Adam took his rifle and climbed up to the top of the ridge to the south of their camp. Making his way through a scattering of pines that skirted the lower third of the hill, he found the upper part almost barren of trees. Near the top, he found a spot that allowed a long look over the way they had come, even though the rapidly growing darkness limited his vision. Still, he stood there for a while, wondering how clean a getaway they had accomplished, him and his little party of misfits. The thought caused him to shake his head in disbelief, and brought images of his father when they showed up at the Triple-B—if they showed up. Then a picture of Jake formed in his mind—wild and carefree; his younger brother's need for excitement and adventure had led him to his ill-fated rendezvous. *We've all got a path to travel,* he thought, *some more rocky than others. No use crying about it.* Holding his rifle by the barrel, he propped it on his shoulder and started back down to the camp.

About a half day behind the fugitives, a posse of six men was also in the process of making camp. Deputy Sheriff Ed Bellou had been assigned by Sheriff Ainsworth to lead the posse. There was no doubt in Ainsworth's mind that the mysterious stranger who had suddenly shown up in Bannack was a gunman hired by the vigilantes. The night before, the bartender at the saloon had happened to walk to the back door in time to see the two prostitutes follow the gunman, who had already seriously reduced the number of outlaws that preyed on the Bannack trails. Ainsworth had severely chastised him for not coming to tell him immediately, even to the point of threatening to hang him as an accomplice. It was Ainsworth's feeling that the man was probably heading back to Virginia City to continue his stalking of Henry Plummer's agents. He could think of no plausible explanation for taking the two prostitutes with him, but it was fairly easy to speculate on the presence of Michael Finn. Evidently, Ainsworth thought, part of the deal was to escort Finn out of the territory, for which he would be paid for his services with gold from Finn's claim.

The mission of the posse was twofold, then: to eliminate the miners' hired gunman and to confiscate Michael Finn's gold. There was one other item: the theft of a horse from Art Thompson's stable. It was of no real importance to the men of the posse, other than to lend an air of legitimacy to the job. Finn's attempt to smuggle his gold out from under the noses of Plummer's army of outlaws was not even known until that morning. Ainsworth had already given orders to find Adam Blaine, convinced that he had been hired by the vigilantes. One of three men who had been keeping an eye on Finn's activities, a grubby little man named Blackie, rode in to town early that morning to report Finn's departure. Blackie informed Ainsworth that there had been no fire or sign of life of any kind in the Irishman's camp that night, so he had ridden down in the ravine to find the camp deserted. With something at stake of greater value than Adam Blaine's life, Ainsworth hurriedly assembled a posse. He assigned Blackie to the posse, along with two more of the many outlaws in the gulch with only one name. One, a bony, bald-headed man called Skinner, was reputed to be an expert tracker. The other was a short, potbellied man named Cox. To round out the six, Jesse Doyle and his partner, Sykes, were added, especially since Jesse had talked rather loudly of his intention to settle with the rifleman himself. As soon as the posse left, Ainsworth went to the telegraph office to send a wire to Henry Plummer in Virginia City, informing him of the possibility of a huge gold shipment being smuggled out of Bannack. He assumed the fugitives would take the common road to Virginia City.

"There ain't no doubt about it," Skinner said after tracking the party of prostitutes and the gunman to a high ridge above the town where they hooked up with Finn. "That ol' bastard is leadin' three mules, and there's three other horses with him." It was a fact that the others could have figured out without Skinner's unique tracking ability, for there had been little effort to hide the tracks in the dark.

It also took little thought to confirm that the hired gun was in cahoots with Finn, because he had been spotted leaving Finn's camp the day before. As for the other two riders, there was little doubt of their identity, since the two prostitutes were still missing. "I figured they had to turn back east," Jesse said when they came to the point where the fugitives had changed directions, "'cause they sure as hell weren't gonna keep headin' north into the mountains."

"They're headin' for the Beaverhead," Ed Bellou said. "We shoulda figured that. We coulda cut 'em off and been waitin' for 'em at the river."

"Why do you figure he took them two whores with him?" Blackie asked.

"Hell, who knows?" Bellou replied. "Maybe he's got needs he can't do without." His comment caused a wave of chuckles among the group of men.

"He must have powerful needs if one whore ain't enough," Skinner remarked.

"We'll catch 'em," Jesse said, finding no humor in their task. "They can't be makin' very good time with them mules and two women along."

Had they known how accurate Jesse's remark had

been, they might have been tempted to push on in the
dark, for their prey was only a half day's ride ahead. As
it was, however, they decided it not worth the risk of
losing them in the event they might have changed
directions again, possibly intent upon heading toward
Butte instead of Virginia City. So they went into camp
where they were, with intentions of getting started
again at first light. To a man, all silent speculation was
centered upon the three mules and how much they
might be carrying—and how much each individual's
share might amount to, especially if they were to
decide not to cut Plummer in on a share. It was easy to
figure that Plummer was not entitled to a share, since
he had had no hand in tipping them off, as he did in
the stage and freight shipments. Then there was Ainsworth to be concerned with, making another split in
addition to six ways already. Jesse realized that he was
not the only one speculating on Finn's gold when Sykes
poured a cup of coffee and sat down beside him.

"Reckon how much gold that old fart has on them
mules?" Not waiting for an answer, he went on, speaking softly lest he be overheard. "I wish to hell Ainsworth
hadn't sent them extra fellers with us. We coulda done
without them three jaspers, split that gold three ways
and skedaddled down to Texas."

"Hell," Jesse retorted, "we coulda done it with just
the two of us. All we need is to get one clear shot at that
damn big gunman. Settle his hash and the rest of 'em
ain't gonna cause no trouble a'tall."

"That sure is a fact," Sykes replied. "Somethin' to
think about. I reckon we'll see what's what tomorrow."
There was no more discussion between them, but the

thoughts never strayed far from their minds. They were not alone in their mutinous thinking.

"Them two are sure doin' some serious talkin' over there," Skinner commented as he and his two friends sat apart from Jesse and Sykes. Like them, the three had been watching the trails around Bannack and Virginia City, preying on innocent travelers, all under the direction of Henry Plummer. Plummer's army of outlaws was so extensive, however, that not many of the smaller gangs had any real contact with the others. Consequently, there was a feeling of competition between them, certainly no sense of loyalty, and even a sense of suspicion. After all, they were all callous cutthroats and bushwhackers.

"They might be of a mind to helpin' theirselves to that load of gold dust on them mules," Cox suggested. It was an easy thought to speculate upon, since it was on his mind as well.

"It's bound to be a helluva lot of gold ol' Finn is packin' outta here," Blackie said. "He'd been diggin' in that ravine he was camped in for a long time before we started keepin' an eye on him."

"Yep," Skinner said. "I bet there's enough gold on them mules to set three smart fellers up for life. Sure makes you think about it, don't it?"

"I can't see why those two jaspers are ridin' with us on this job, anyway," Blackie commented. "Hell, we were the ones settin' on that claim all the time, waitin' for Finn to make his move. They didn't have nothin' to do with it. Matter of fact, Bellou said they were the ones that messed up that stage job a few days ago. They got no right to share in this job." He snorted in disgust for emphasis. "In the first place, we don't need this many of us to take care of two men, and one of them a gray-headed old miner." He paused to throw the dregs of coffee from his cup. "That's got to be an awful lot of gold dust they're carryin'."

"Won't be near as much after Plummer, Ainsworth, and Bellou get their cut of it," Cox pointed out.

"I know what you're thinkin'," Skinner said. "But if we was to do somethin' like that, Plummer would be after us before the sun went down."

"To hell with Plummer," Blackie growled. "If we was to take that gold and cut out for Mexico or somewhere, he ain't likely to catch us before we're long gone from this territory. And he ain't likely to go that far to look for us once we're out of here."

Ed Bellou walked over and sat down near them, effectively ending the conversation, but the seed was planted, and the soil was fertile in the minds of the three, just as it was in the minds of Jesse and Sykes. "We oughta catch up with 'em before late afternoon tomorrow," Bellou speculated.

"I expect so," Skinner replied. "Ainsworth sent a lot of us just to take care of two fellers and two whores. He musta thought we'd run into trouble."

Bellou shrugged indifferently before answering, "Well, there's that one feller who's mighty handy with a rifle, and Ainsworth figures there's enough of us to surround 'em and kill the whole bunch without takin' too many chances ourselves." This was, in fact, the reasoning behind sending six men to do a job three should have been able to do, but Bellou was there to make sure the gold was returned to the sheriff's office in Bannack.

He was young, handy with a gun, and loyal to his uncle, Albert Ainsworth. He was also smart enough to notice that his posse was split into two separate factions, with Jesse and Sykes on one side of the fire, and Cox, Blackie, and Skinner on the other.

Chapter 8

Adam paused for a moment to look down at the two women sleeping close to the dying fire. A chilly mass of air had descended upon the hills during the night, bringing the temperatures down to a more normal level for this late in the summer. *They must have gotten cold*, he thought, for sometime before dawn they had moved close together for warmth. He looked over toward the stream to see if the horses were all right before rekindling the fire. Finn stirred and rolled out of his blanket, aroused by the sounds of Adam feeding more wood to the fire. "Chilly," he commented, then stumbled off downstream to answer nature's call. Adam answered with a grunt and continued to tend the fire. Once it was blazing to his satisfaction, he went to the stream to fill the coffeepot.

By the time he returned with the coffee water, Bonnie was up and sitting by the fire, her blanket wrapped around her shoulders. "Good morning," she offered painfully. Not satisfied with his pace of progress, she reached for the pot. "Here, give me that. I'm dying for a cup of coffee, and you look like you're gonna take all day to make it." He willingly relinquished it. When she had the coffee working on the edge of the fire, she reached over and gave Lacey's toes a little shake. "Rise and shine, honey. Let's make a little breakfast." Before she started it, however, she took a walk downstream to answer the same call Finn had just heard. Passing him on his way back, she commented, "Wouldn't hurt you to walk a little farther from camp, old man, at least till you get past some of those bushes."

"Huh," he snorted. "It ain't like you ain't ever seen one before."

"Never seen one that small before," she retorted, and continued past the clump of bushes she had referred to.

While Bonnie and Finn were both out of earshot, Lacey moved up beside Adam at the fire. "I want to thank you for coming back for me," she said. "I don't know if I really did before, so I want you to know I appreciate it."

"You did already," Adam replied. Then, noticing the concerned look in the young girl's eyes, he softened his tone and said, "Don't worry, Lacey. I'll do the best I can to get you outta here to someplace where you'll be better off." The look of gratitude told him she had needed the reassurance. She even smiled, and it occurred to him that it was the first time he had seen her smile. He began to see why Jake had made promises he couldn't keep.

In the saddle again, the party continued their journey along the creek bank. To Adam's way of thinking, it was poor country to try to hide in, with hills all around them, barren of trees. It seemed that every gulch and valley they rode through was a perfect spot for an ambush, so he kept his eyes moving all the time. All it would take was for someone to guess where they were heading and cut them off instead of tracking them. There weren't that many choices regarding trails to take in this wild part of the territory. As an extra precaution, he left the others and climbed a hill every two miles or so, to take a look ahead and behind. He could hope that no one in Bannack was aware of their flight yet, but he knew he couldn't count on it.

They had ridden for over an hour when the sun finally rose high enough to warm the chilly air that lay low in the narrow valleys they followed, as the stream made its way to the river. Soon they emerged from the hilly country and entered the broad river valley of the Beaverhead. Shallow and peaceful at this time of year, the river offered cover along its banks with thick stands of willows and some cottonwoods, with berry bushes hovering over the edge. A dozen yards or so away from the water, however, the valley appeared treeless and barren of anything beyond short grass, framed by the same sparsely treed hills they had been riding through all morning. Relieved at least to find no waiting party of bushwhackers, they turned north and followed the winding river.

"Maybe they still ain't found out we've gone," Finn said when there appeared to be no one in the broad river valley but them.

"Maybe," Adam replied.

"How far you figurin' on followin' the Beaverhead before cuttin' back east again to strike the Madison?"

Adam shrugged. "Well, I can't say I know this part of the country all that well, but I believe the Ruby River joins this one somewhere just south of that range of mountains between the Jefferson and Madison. I just wanna make sure we're far enough north of Virginia City before we head east, so when we get to the Ruby, at least we'll know we're a good ways above Virginia City." Their conference was interrupted then by Bonnie.

"How long are you two planning on riding before we stop to eat?" she asked. "This little mare I borrowed is showing signs of needing a rest."

Adam looked up at the sun to guess the time of day. It was high overhead, a little past noon, he figured. Bonnie's mare had shown signs of a lack of stamina, which had already troubled him in the event a flat-out race for survival was necessary. The other horses and the mules still had shown no indication of fatigue. He pulled his horse up beside Bonnie's and looked the mare over. "I expect you're right," he said, "but I think another hour won't hurt her." He wheeled his horse and started out again. It was nothing but pure luck that saved him, for the .44 slug that split the air between them would have impacted with the center of his chest moments before.

"Go!" Adam yelled, and kicked the bay gelding hard with his heels. His shout was really unnecessary, because as soon as the report of the rifle sang out, all members of the party responded by taking flight. The riverbank, thick with brush and willows, offered the only cover close by, so Adam headed for it with the others close behind. The bank was about five feet high at that point, enough to provide cover from that side of the river, but not enough to protect the animals. With no time to look for a better spot, and two more shots to hurry them, he directed them to move the horses and mules downstream to a point where the willows were thickest, hoping this would take them out of the line of fire. "I'll stay here and hope they think we're all here," he told Finn. "On my packhorse, there's a couple of pistols and an army carbine. Give the women each a weapon and hope to hell they don't have to use 'em."

"You'll need me and my rifle," Finn protested.

"Let's see what we're up against," Adam said. "I don't wanna take a chance on losing our horses."

"All right," Finn said, and moved quickly down the bank. He was reluctant to leave his fortune guarded only by two women, anyway.

"Damn the luck!" Bellou cursed. It had been a long shot, but one that the deputy was sure he could have made if his target had not picked that instant to wheel his horse away. His gut feeling had caused him to scout on ahead of the others while they stopped to water their horses. Something had told him that the man he stalked had to be just ahead. Horse droppings they had seen, still warm and fresh, had told him so as well. Now he was intent upon pinning the four of them down on the riverbank while he waited for the rest of his posse to catch up. He reasoned that, if he could keep them occupied till then, then he could send half of his men across to the other side of the river and catch Finn and his hired gun in a cross fire. So he reloaded his rifle and continued to pick away at the riverbank.

Approaching at a gallop, the remainder of the posse pulled up to Bellou, and scrambled from their saddles when Adam rose long enough to send a series of .44 slugs in their direction. "Where are they?" Jesse shouted excitedly. When Bellou pointed to the spot on the bank where the rifle fire had come from, Jesse complained, "Why the hell didn't you wait for us to move up closer to 'em?"

"Wasn't no use to," Bellou replied. "I had a shot at that big son of a bitch. I coulda pretty much ended the whole thing right there, but he moved right when I squeezed the trigger." Sykes was about to complain as well, but Bellou cut him off. "What's done is done," he said. "We've got 'em pinned down, anyway. They can't go anywhere without stickin' their noses out." He motioned to Cox. "You and Skinner and Blackie go on back upstream a ways and find you a place to get across. They ain't got no protection from the other side of the river. The rest of us will give you a head start, and then we'll move in a little closer. We oughta have 'em in a trap."

Cox glanced briefly at his two friends and exchanged a nod of agreement with each of them. "Sounds like a good idea," he said, and motioned for them to follow him.

"And, Cox," Bellou called after them, "I ain't lookin' to take no prisoners back, so kill 'em all."

"Women, too?" Blackie asked.

"Women, too," the deputy replied. "Ain't nothin' but a couple of whores." He turned to Jesse then. "You and Sykes start pepperin' that bank. We'll wait a spell, then work our way over behind that rise." He pointed to a hummock about fifty yards from the river and directly in front of the spot where he had last seen Adam's muzzle flash.

"I don't trust them three," Jesse stated.

"I don't trust any of you," was Bellou's response. "But I reckon as long as you all do like I tell you, we'll finish this business up in short order, and take that gold dust back to Bannack."

* * *

Back in the willow thicket, Finn and the women huddled beneath the bank, listening to the exchange of rifle fire upstream. "You need to go help Adam," Bonnie urged. "I don't want anything to happen to him."

"I can't leave you women to guard the livestock," Finn said, equally worried about the odds Adam was left to face.

"The hell you can't," Bonnie at once retorted. "I can handle this carbine as good as you." She looked at Lacey, huddled next to her, nervously holding one of Adam's pistols. "You know how to shoot that thing?" she asked. With little enthusiasm, Lacey nodded. "There you go," Bonnie said to Finn. "We'll handle things here. You go on." Finn hesitated, unable to make up his mind. "We ain't going anywhere with your gold," Bonnie reassured him. "And if you get killed, you won't care whether we did or not. So go help Adam."

Finn paused a moment longer, then decided she was probably right. "Don't let anythin' happen to my mules," he said in parting.

"Bonnie said they could handle it," Finn said before Adam could question him. "Where are they?"

"Behind that rise yonder, about a hundred yards. I'm pretty sure there's six of 'em, and they ain't gonna stay there long before they try to move in closer." They were forced to duck then as a couple of shots kicked up sand a few yards away. Adam looked up again in time to see three of them scurry away from the rise on foot and make for the riverbank. "I was wonderin' when they were gonna do that," he said. "I was thinkin' that, if it was me, I'd split up and come around on the other side of the river." He thought it over for only a few moments more before deciding what had to be done. "We're gonna be in a world of trouble if that bunch sets up behind us on the other side. You get on back to the women and move on downstream. I'm gonna cross over and see if I can stop those three comin' down the other side of the river. If I'm lucky enough to get in a couple of shots before they spot me, maybe I can keep 'em from catchin' up to you."

"Damn!" That was all Finn could respond with, and Adam could clearly see that the Irishman was undecided if he should stay or go.

"Go ahead, Finn," Adam instructed firmly. "I'll stop those three from gettin' behind you. You just worry about keepin' the other three in front of you." Finn only hesitated a moment more before hustling off downstream again. The thought ran through Adam's mind, as the squat little man ran along the bank, that it was almost unnecessary for Finn to bend over. Nothing was visible but the crown of his hat bobbing along. Once he was out of sight, Adam brought his mind back to the situation confronting him. He wished then that he had had more time to pick a place to defend themselves from. This section of the river offered very little for cover. "Well, we'll do the best we can," he muttered to himself, and stepped into the water.

So intent was he on the task ahead of him that he barely noticed the cold that gripped his legs as he pushed out into the middle of the river, holding his rifle and cartridge belt high over his head. Much to his relief, the water only rose to just beneath his armpits before becoming shallow again, as he hurried across as quickly as he could manage. Picking a place where the willows

formed a wedge that protruded out onto a small sand-
bar, he dropped to his knees to keep from presenting a
silhouette to the three who might already be approaching. A few shots from the other side of the river caused
him to look in time to see the three who had stayed
making a break for the cover of a low hummock some
fifty yards from the spot he had just vacated. He considered throwing a few shots back in their direction, but
was reluctant to give away his position and spoil his
surprise for the three working their way down on his
side of the river.

After hurriedly tying the horses on some brush behind
the rise, Jesse and Sykes followed Ainsworth's deputy
toward the hummock. As he ran, hunched over in an
effort to expose as little as he could, Jesse's eyes were
fixated on Bellou's broad back before him. Thinking of
the conversation he and Sykes had engaged in the
night just past, he made a sudden decision to yield to
the temptation to eliminate one claim on Finn's gold.
With his pistol already in hand, it was easy to simply
raise it a little and pull the trigger.

"What the hell?" Sykes jumped when the deputy
collapsed with a neat bullet hole in the center of his
shoulder blades. Confused by the unexpected sound
of the shot before him, he dropped to the ground and
looked behind him, thinking the shot must have come
from somewhere in that direction. As he looked at Jesse
then, it registered with him what had occurred, and he
was quick to raise his own .44 in defense in case he was
next on Jesse's list. He was met with a wicked smile on
Jesse's face.

"That's one less split on all that gold, partner," Jesse

explained. "When we finish off this bunch hidin' in the river, and get our hands on that gold, maybe we'll cut a few more shares. Whaddaya say?"

Relieved to see that he was still considered Jesse's partner, Sykes answered with a grin, "I never liked that son of a bitch, anyway. When we're done, there'll be more'n enough dust for the two of us. Right?"

"Oh, hell yeah," Jesse replied, quick to reassure him. "Me and you are partners. We'll be ridin' high when we hit some of them Texas towns, or maybe go to California if that suits you better." Resolved to their task then, they stripped Bellou's body of anything of value, then crawled up to the edge of the hummock and began to lay down a fresh barrage upon the clump of willows, unaware that it had been abandoned. "We'll take care of business, then come back and round up the horses."

Meanwhile, on the far bank, Adam knelt and waited. It was not long before he caught sight of the three men slipping stealthily through the trees. While the willows afforded cover from sight, he knew their slender trunks wouldn't offer much real protection in the event of a hailstorm of .44 slugs. So he took careful aim on the man in the lead when he had approached to a distance of perhaps fifty yards. As soon as he squeezed the trigger, he immediately sprang to his feet and retreated before even taking time to confirm the kill, a kill that he was sure of nonetheless. As he had anticipated, the willow thicket he vacated was riddled with .44 slugs from the remaining two outlaws, shredding leaves and sending shards of bark flying.

When there was no return fire from the willows, Cox and Blackie knelt down beside Skinner, who was obviously mortally wounded by the rifle shot dead center in his chest. "Help me," Skinner begged pitifully as he tried to keep from choking upon the blood filling his lungs.

Cox and Blackie exchanged quick glances, then peered anxiously at the willow thicket from whence the fatal shot had come. "One of 'em crossed over to this side," Cox said, stating the obvious.

"He ain't fired again," Blackie said. "You reckon we hit him?"

"I don't know," Cox replied, "but we damn sure better find out." A new burst of shots from the other side of the river served to tell them that Bellou and the others had moved in closer to the river. "We'd better get movin' before the rest of 'em decide to cross over, too." He started to rise to a crouch, but Skinner grabbed his sleeve.

"Don't leave me here, fellers," he begged. "I need help gettin' back to my horse."

Blackie gave him a cursory glance and said, "You're done for, Skinner. We got to look out for ourselves."

Cox pulled his sleeve out of the dying man's grasp. "Ain't much we can do for you. Might as well settle back and wait for it."

"Oh, Lordy, don't leave me," Skinner cried out feebly as his two partners hurried off through the brush, intent upon capturing the gold dust, and leaving the doomed man to deal with his pain.

Moving cautiously through the willows recently abandoned by Adam, Cox and Blackie advanced to find the rifleman gone. "He's runnin'," Cox whispered. "Come on." He led the way, his eyes set on a large cottonwood leaning over the river. Blackie followed, both men oblivious of the man lying close beside a rotting cottonwood log that jutted halfway out over the bank.

Just keep moving, boys, Adam thought as they moved past him. Then he slowly drew his rifle up to rest on the log. Rising to one knee, he waited for them to reach a spot where he could get a clear shot at both of them. Just short of reaching the big cottonwood, both men stepped into an open patch. Adam squeezed off the first round, his bullet producing a little cloud of dust from Blackie's buckskin vest as it thudded into his back, dropping him like a stone. Adam cocked the rifle as quickly as he could, but Cox's reactions were swifter than he had anticipated, and he whirled and fired before Adam could chamber another round. Though hurried, with no time to take careful aim, Cox's shot grazed Adam's head, knocking him senseless to the ground.

"I got him! I got him!" Cox shouted triumphantly. "That big son of a bitch, I got him!" He ran to the river-bank to confirm it and found Adam lying unconscious on the ground. Hearing his shouts across the river, Jesse and Sykes came out of the trees to see what the shouting was about. Seeing the two outlaws, Cox yelled to them, "He got Blackie and Skinner, but I by God got him!"

"You sure?" Jesse yelled back.

"Damn right, I'm sure," Cox returned, and cocked his pistol, preparing to make certain. His bullet tore harmlessly into the ground beside his foot when the impact of the .44 rifle slug from Jesse's rifle slammed into his chest, dropping him beside Adam's body.

"By God, things couldn'ta worked out much better'n that," Jesse said as he ejected the empty shell. He looked at Sykes with a satisfied grin. "Them three jokers were good for somethin' after all. They got rid of the only one we had to worry about. And what tickles me is he got two of them first. That gold's all mine and yours, partner—no splits with anybody else."

Sykes could appreciate the way things were seemingly falling in place to land Finn's gold in their hands, but he was still cautious to some degree. "We've still got to catch up with that old man and the two women," he warned. "That's still three against two. Maybe we shoulda waited before you shot Cox. We mighta needed him."

"Shit fire, Sykes," Jesse remarked, "an old man and two whores ain't enough to worry about. Let's get after 'em before they take off a-runnin', now that they ain't got their big hired gun to protect 'em."

"Maybe so," Sykes replied, hesitating, "but you'd be just as dead from a bullet fired by a scared female. And I've heard some things about that ol' gal, Bonnie."

"Don't think I ain't thought about that," Jesse insisted. "But look up yonder about a quarter of a mile." He pointed to a stretch of the river that appeared to be free of trees with nothing along the banks but some low shrubs. "If one of us moves on up ahead of 'em, we oughta be able to catch 'em in the open when they cross that clear patch. And if they don't come outta the trees, we can box 'em in between us and plink away at 'em until we pick 'em all off. Which you wanna do, get in behind and do the pushin' or ride on downstream to cut 'em off?"

"I'll ride," Sykes said, and started back up the bank.

"All right," Jesse called after him, "I'll make it so hot for 'em, they'll have to keep movin' toward you." He hesitated for a moment to watch Sykes run back toward the rise where the horses were tied before adding, "Try to get a shot at Finn. Get him and I expect the women will be ready to quit." Sykes acknowledged with a hand thrown up as he ran for his horse.

Some two hundred yards downriver from where Jesse stood, Finn and the two women made their way as best they could while holding close to the bank. It was not an easy task, and slow going, to lead the horses and the string of mules through the willows and shrubs that lined the water, but they were afraid to leave the cover the foliage provided. There had been shots fired behind them—on both sides of the river—some possibly by Adam, but there was no way to tell what was happening. Finn saw no alternative but to keep moving and hope that Adam somehow managed to stop the men pursuing them. It was Bonnie who dissuaded him. About to cross over a stream that cut a deep gully in the bank, she yelled to Finn, "We ain't got much farther to go before we're gonna be crossing a wide stretch of open prairie between here and that next patch of trees. If they catch us out in the open, they'll make short work of us."

Looking up ahead, where she had indicated, he could see that she was right. "It is a bit risky," he said, and pulled up to consider the gully they were in the process of crossing. "We're gonna have to make a stand someplace, I reckon, and this is as good a place as we're likely to find."

The gully was just deep enough and long enough to afford some protection for the horses and mules, so they gathered them at the deepest part at the river's edge. Finn positioned himself at the upstream side of the gully and put Bonnie and Lacey behind him to watch for any attack from that side. He only hoped that Bonnie was as handy with the weapon as she professed to be. Once they were settled and ready to make their stand, there was nothing to do but wait. Adam was back there somewhere on the other side of the river, but there had been no gunshots from that direction for quite some time now. Finn feared that Adam had met with disaster. "Keep a sharp eye out, ladies," he said, "and sing out if you see any of them comin' from your side." He knew the possibility of an attack from below them was very real. The river took a winding snakelike path through the valley. It would be easy enough for some of their pursuers to gallop straight down the valley and cut them off. *I wish I knew where the hell Adam is*, he thought. It might have helped improve his confidence had he known that his adversaries had been reduced from six to two. That might not have been enough, however, if he also knew that Adam was lying wounded by a dead log some two hundred yards behind him on the opposite bank of the river.

Finn shifted his position slightly in an attempt to gain a little better cover from which to fire his rifle. Only a few minutes had elapsed since he had last heard shots in the willows upstream, but it seemed like an eternity. Although he strained to hear any sounds that would signal the approach of the outlaws, there was nothing but the stillness of the riverbank, with an occasional snort from one of the mules. He looked over his shoulder at the two women on the other side of the gully—Bonnie, lying prone on her stomach, her 1864 Joslyn carbine resting across her forearm, ready to fire at the first opportunity—and Lacey, huddled close beside her, holding the Colt .44 as if afraid it might start shooting without her influence. *A fine mess you've found yourself in, Michael Finn*, he thought. There was no time for further lament because of an excited yell from Bonnie.

"There's one of them!" Bonnie exclaimed, and pointed to a single rider galloping some four or five hundred yards wide of them. "He's heading for those cotton-woods up ahead!" She turned to Finn long enough to comment, "See, we'da been in the middle of that open space about now." Taking charge of Lacey then, she said, "You just stay right where you are. You'll be all right. Just point that pistol at anybody you see and pull the trigger. Even if you don't hit anything, it'll give them something to think about."

If the situation had not been so tense, Finn might have been forced to smile. *Maybe we don't need Adam*, he thought wryly, amazed by the woman's obvious spunk to back up her audacious talk. The thought caused him to worry about Adam's fate again, and wonder if one of the shots he had heard might have been the one that put his big friend down. Reminding himself that he had better return his vigilance to the trees behind them, he shifted his position once more, just in time to feel the impact of the .44 slug that struck his right shoulder. Lacey screamed when she heard the sound of the shot and turned to see Finn slide down the steep side of the gully. "I'm hit!" Finn gasped as he slumped against the bank.

"Damn!" Bonnie uttered. "How bad is it?"

"Bad," Finn groaned. "I think it broke my shoulder."

"Damn!" Bonnie muttered again. Like Finn, she

wondered where Adam was, but hesitated for only a moment before taking control again. "All right, just try to hang on for right now. Take that bandanna off and try to stop the bleeding." She took hold of Lacey's arm then and shook the frightened young woman forcefully. "You're gonna stay here and watch that open space. I'm gonna take Finn's place on the other side. And, Lacey, keep your eyes on those trees. If anybody comes out of them, shoot 'em." Though terrified, Lacey nodded bravely and turned her attention back to her side of the gully.

They're done for, Jesse thought as he worked his way closer to the gully where they had taken refuge. He was certain that his shot had found the target. He saw it when it hit Finn and the little Irishman dropped over backward. There was no one to worry about now but the two women, and he was on his way to take care of them, still with a thought to be cautious of Bonnie. *Be a good idea to shoot her right off,* he thought. *Then have a little go-round with the young one before I kill her.* The thought brought a smile to his face as he increased his pace, moving from one point of cover to the next. *Sykes oughta be somewhere beyond that clearing,* he thought.

In fact, Sykes was closer than Jesse thought. Anxious to get his hands on the gold packed on Finn's mules, he decided to leave his horse in the trees, thinking it a good idea to get to that gully before Jesse, or at least soon after. They were partners, but he didn't rule out the possibility that Jesse might hide a couple of those sacks with the notion of coming back for them later. With that in mind, he was making his way as fast as he could on foot through the shoulder-high scrub bushes along the bank, confident that he couldn't be seen. When within fifty yards of the gully, he heard Jesse's arrival at the edge of the gully.

"You women are finished," Jesse called out. "Where's Finn? Is he hurt bad?"

Bonnie glanced at Finn, his face twisted in pain, holding the bloody bandanna over his useless shoulder. She thought about it for a moment before answering Jesse. "He's dead," she called back.

"I thought so," Jesse said. "All right, then, this little party is over. Now, we got no cause to harm you ladies since this is an official sheriff's posse. We'll just take charge of them mules and you ladies can be on your way. So just put your guns down if you're holdin' any."

"We have your word that you ain't gonna hurt us?" Bonnie asked innocently.

"Yes, ma'am," Jesse answered. "You certainly do. We just want the mules." *Then I'll put a hole right between your eyes,* he thought.

"All right," Bonnie called out. "We give up." She put a finger to her lips to warn a terrified Lacey to keep silent as she cocked her rifle.

Feeling helpless to defend himself, Finn made an awkward attempt to retrieve his rifle, which had slid all the way down to the bottom of the gully when he had been hit. Bonnie motioned for him to remain still, but he ignored her signals and tried to ease himself down to his weapon, resulting in a tumble that brought a painful landing several yards from the rifle. At that moment, Jesse appeared at the rim of the gully, his rifle trained on the helpless man.

"Well, now," Jesse commented sarcastically, "he's movin' pretty good for a dead man." As soon as the words left his mouth, he realized his concentration should be on Bonnie. It was too late to avoid the .52-caliber slug that ripped his gut at close to point-blank range. As he bent double in pain, Bonnie reloaded and pumped another round into him, a few inches above the first. Mortally wounded, he tumbled face forward over the edge of the gully, landing a few feet from Finn.

Sykes froze in his tracks, stopped by the sudden report of two quick shots only a few dozen yards ahead of him. Kneeling beside a serviceberry bush, he paused to listen for sounds that might indicate what had happened. The shots he heard didn't sound like Jesse's rifle, more like a carbine, like some of those the cavalry soldiers used. After a few moments, he heard voices—excited women's voices—and it occurred to him that they might have gotten Jesse. There was only one way to know for sure, but he was not eager to meet with the same fate. There was another way to look at it, he realized. If they got Jesse, and it was very likely that they had, the fortune packed on those mules was all his. He faced a huge chance of ending up like his partner, but the risk was worth it. He imagined there was more gold on those mules than a man could ever amass in a lifetime. Resolved to claim what he fancied to be rightfully his, he started moving forward again, inching his way slowly to a point where he might get a look at what he faced.

Pausing every few yards to listen, he eventually made his way to a lone cottonwood that had been blown over by a storm, leaving a large root ball exposed aboveground. This provided excellent cover for him while he listened. In a few minutes, he heard a woman's voice that he guessed might be Bonnie's. She was telling someone to stay where they were while she climbed down to help Finn. In a flash, he got the picture in his mind. Finn was shot! And the old whore was down in the bottom of the gully, leaving no one but Lacey to keep watch. He knew he had to act quickly.

He eased his head up above the top of the root ball. When there were no shots fired his way as a result, he rose a little higher and spotted the young woman lying just beneath the rim of the gully. She held a pistol pointed in his general direction, but at the moment, she was looking back toward the bottom of the gully. *Now!* he told himself, and charged toward the distracted girl. Lacey turned her head back, but not soon enough to prevent Sykes from stomping her hand with his boot. Her scream alerted Bonnie and Finn, but not in time for them to react.

With his boot still pinning Lacey's hand to the ground, and his rifle aimed at Bonnie, he paused to take in the situation. "Go ahead," he goaded Bonnie when she started to grab her carbine. She froze when she realized she had no chance, for she had neglected to reload the single-shot weapon after shooting Jesse. Sykes laughed. "I'll give you folks this much. You sure as hell made us work for it." He glanced at Jesse's body crumpled near the wounded man. "'Preciate all the work you did to dig up all that gold for me." Feeling Lacey's frantic attempts to pull her hand out from under his foot, he reached down and pulled the pistol from her, then shoved her down to join the others. "There, now you're all together. You can all go to hell in one load." Thoroughly enjoying his advantage, he challenged, "Which one of you wants to go first?"

"You go to hell," Bonnie spat, and started to reach for the carbine again. She was stopped by a shot into the dirt beside her hand. It effectively stopped her efforts to resist, and she realized there was nothing she could do to prevent the slaughter of the three of them.

"All right," Sykes said. "I reckon you're volunteerin'." He swung the rifle around slightly to take dead aim at the defiant woman. The shot that rang out came from the other side of the river, leaving Sykes with a startled expression that would remain on his face throughout eternity as the rifle slug smashed the side of his head and tore through his temple. Dead instantly, even as he was suspended in midair, his corpse crashed down the side of the gully to come to rest beside that of Jesse's.

The three stunned survivors, so near death seconds before, were not sure what had happened for a moment or two until Bonnie looked down toward the end of the gully to discover the imposing figure of Adam Blaine, standing on the far bank of the river, his rifle in hand, a wide streak of dried blood running from the side of his head, down his cheek, to the edge of his jaw. She could not remember having seen a more welcome sight in all her life, and she could not help crying out, "Adam!" Her joyous shout caused Lacey to raise her eyes to discover their grim savior, although he was not the one she had been praying to until that moment. Of the three trapped at the bottom of the gully, only Finn was unable to exhibit a look of joy upon his face, as he grimaced from the pain in his shoulder. "Hurry, Adam!" Bonnie implored. "Before the rest of them get here!"

"No need to hurry now," Adam assured her, "that's the last of 'em." His remark brought a shout of joy from

Bonnie and a sigh of relief from Lacey. Even Finn managed a painful smile, although his throbbing shoulder told him that his wound needed serious attention. Adam glanced up and down the river, looking for a favorable spot to come back across. Finding none that looked any shallower than the others, he said, "Looks like I'm goin' swimmin' again," and waded into the water.

"We were afraid we'd lost you," Bonnie said when Adam was across, her face lit up with a happy smile. "How bad is that?" she asked, pointing toward the dried blood on his face.

"Nothin' serious," he said, "just slowed me down for a bit, or I'da been here sooner." His gaze was fixed upon Finn. "How bad is he hurt?"

"Well, it doesn't look too good," Bonnie said. "I haven't had a chance to take a good look at it, but he thinks his shoulder is broken."

Adam frowned, hoping that was not the case, especially since it appeared to be his right shoulder, and there was no guarantee they were free of future attacks. "Well, let's see what we can do for him. Then let's get outta this hole you folks are in." He started at once for the injured little man.

"Damn piece of bad luck," Finn complained as Adam knelt down to examine his wound. "But I sure am glad to see you. You showed up at the right time. That son of a bitch was fixin' to shoot the three of us, and there wasn't nothin' we could do to stop him."

Bonnie and Lacey gathered around Finn to offer their help. "We weren't able to help him with those bastards coming at us from both sides," Bonnie said. "He's lost a lot of blood," she commented as she got a closer look at the hole in Finn's shoulder.

Adam nodded toward Jesse's body a few feet away. "I see you got one of 'em."

"Bonnie shot him," Finn replied, and told Adam how she had tricked the outlaw to drop his guard.

"I'd have gotten the other one if I'd had one of those repeating rifles," she said. Adam smiled and nodded his approval.

Lacey, silent until that moment, spoke up then to confess, "I still haven't fired my revolver. But I would have if he hadn't stepped on my hand."

"You ladies did good," Adam allowed. "Now let's clean Finn's wound as best we can, and then we'll get him on his horse and get outta this hole—find a better place to camp while we decide what to do about gettin' him fixed up."

After the women bound Finn's shoulder, Adam helped him up in the saddle and tied the lead rope for his mules to the saddle. "Can you stay on that horse?" he asked, and Finn allowed that he damn sure would. Then Adam saw to the women, giving Lacey a lift onto her horse. He had to wait for a couple of minutes while Bonnie traded her Joslyn carbine for the seven-shot Spencer that Jesse had carried, as well as the cartridge belt that went with it. The party of fugitives filed up out of the gully. Adam picked out a jagged ridge in the distance and pointed it out to Bonnie. "You keep headin' toward that ridge and I'll catch up with you in a little bit. There are half a dozen horses tied somewhere behind that rise back there and I might as well go back and get 'em." He figured that since they were already trailing a string of mules, they might as well drive some extra horses, too. In any case, he couldn't leave them tied up.

"There's one horse in those trees up ahead," Bonnie said. "We saw him ride by to get around us."

They crossed the Ruby River and continued on for almost a full day when it became apparent that Finn was in no condition to continue. To make matters worse, he began to lose blood again and soon he was unable to remain upright in the saddle. "We're gonna have to find us a place to hole up for a while," Adam told the women, "at least till Finn heals up enough to ride." He looked toward the mountain range to their northwest, whose foothills they would have passed through on their way to reach the Madison. Rugged and thick with juniper, fir, and pine along the lower slopes, with many valleys and canyons formed by their higher treeless peaks, they looked to be the travelers' best choice for a hard-to-find campsite.

Bonnie studied his face as he gazed critically at the mountains. "You're thinking about going back up in those mountains," she stated matter-of-factly.

"I am," he replied.

"Adam, we'll freeze to death up in those mountains if the weather turns cold," she said. "And it's about the time of year when the first cold weather hits."

"I ain't plannin' on spendin' the winter there," he replied, "just till Finn gets a little better. There's plenty of wood for fires, and there's plenty of game for meat. He needs some rest and some fresh meat to build his blood back up. If we're lucky, he'll heal some in a few days and we can get on to hell away from here. If we don't stop somewhere soon, we're gonna drain the life right out of him."

"Can't we just make camp right here by this stream?"

Lacey asked as she gazed at the foreboding peaks. "If we're just going to be here for a few days, this looks like a good spot."

Adam looked at the young girl as if explaining to a child. "I don't wanna cause you to worry, Lacey, but it ain't over with Ainsworth and Plummer. We beat those six that came after us back there on the Beaverhead, but there'll be more to follow them. That's why I pushed Finn so hard to stay in the saddle. I expect they'd like to hunt me down for killin' some of their men, but there's another prize that's too big for them to pass up." He motioned toward the mules. "And I'm afraid they ain't likely to be real forgivin' for any of us, includin' you and Bonnie, especially when they find out the deputy sheriff is lyin' back there dead."

"But you said you didn't kill Bellou," Lacey insisted. "They can't blame you for that."

"There's no way for them to know who shot him. They'll say I did—or got him killed—same thing," Adam said.

"It don't help none at all that he was the sheriff's nephew," Finn groaned.

"Adam's right, Lacey," Bonnie interjected. "They'll be looking for us with everybody they can get on a horse. We've got to find someplace to hide." She looked at Finn, who was bent over on his horse's neck, unable to sit up any longer, oblivious of the conversation. "Ol' Albert Ainsworth would love to get his hands on those sacks, all right." She looked back at Adam and grinned wide. "Let's get up in those hills and get busy making a camp."

Chapter 9

Henry Plummer stood staring at the telegram in his hand, a wire that had taken two days to reach him. "Damn it," he cursed, "a man on horseback could have made it here in that length of time." He glared at Joe French, as if his deputy was somehow responsible for the lateness of the wire's arrival. "All Ainsworth knows is that they left Bannack and headed north. Hell, they could be anywhere. Ainsworth sent six men to track them, and he's pretty sure they might be trying to sneak out with a helluva big shipment of gold, too big to let slip out of our hands." He paused to consider where they could be heading, and decided upon two obvious choices, since they were apparently intent upon avoiding the road between Bannack and Virginia City. "They're either planning to keep riding north to Butte or cut back east and head for Three Forks—doesn't make sense to go anywhere else."

"No, sir," French commented, "unless they're thinkin' to cross some mighty rugged mountains."

Still deep in thought, Plummer was oblivious of French's comment. "Joe," he ordered, "go find Bailey Cruz and tell him I want to see him right now." French turned immediately to follow Plummer's instructions. "Tell him he's gonna need to get his boys together and ready to ride."

"Yes, sir," French replied. Then remembering, he paused before saying, "Ben Caldwell's wife is waitin' out in the office to see you."

Plummer frowned, but said nothing and followed French out of the cells to the office out front. He waited until French had closed the door behind him before greeting the woman. "Good day, Mrs. Caldwell. What can I do for you?"

"Good morning, Sheriff, or is it Marshal now?" Lois Caldwell asked with a bright smile for the town's law enforcement officer. Taller than average, but not towering, Plummer cut a dashing figure among the ladies of Virginia City. With a brutish forehead framed by thick coal black hair, and cold penetrating eyes, he was a handsome man, who seemed to be a pure guardian of the town's merchants. The fact that he was also a quick and accurate man with a gun was more commonly known by the legion of robbers and murderers he secretly led.

Answering her question with a gracious smile of his own, he said, "Either one will do. How may I help you?"

"Ben was going to come talk to you about it, but he's busy parceling a new shipment of flour that just arrived, so I came instead. We were wondering if there was something that could be done to cut down on the wild drinking at the saloon two doors down from our store. Last night we heard gunshots, and when we opened the store this morning, we found part of our front window broken."

Plummer fashioned a frown of deep concern for Mrs. Caldwell's benefit and offered his sympathy. "I'm right disturbed to hear that. I'll certainly look into it right away to find the guilty party. I'll try to get your window paid for. Thanks for stopping by to tell me. Sometimes it seems like my whole job calls for keeping the drunks under control, so citizens like you and Ben don't have to worry about their safety."

"Thank you, Sheriff," Lois said. "We appreciate your help."

"Not at all," Plummer replied. "That's what I'm here for." He walked over to the door and held it open for her, returning her smile as she breezed through. As soon as the door was closed, his thoughts returned to the possibility of a sizable amount of gold dust slipping through his fingers.

About an hour after Lois Caldwell left the sheriff's office, Joe French returned with Bailey Cruz, a stocky, squarely built brute with long black hair reaching his shoulders. "You wanted to see me?" Cruz asked.

Plummer wasted no time in getting to the problem at hand. "Yeah," he replied. "I want you to round up some of your men and find somebody for me." He went on to explain who they would be searching for and which way they had gone. Then he cautioned Cruz that one of the men he would be hunting was the suspected hired gun who had already accounted for more than a half dozen deaths since he hit town. "I'm thinking it might be a good idea to send for Briscoe, since this fellow is supposed to be such a grizzly bear."

His suggestion brought a frown to the otherwise bored face of Bailey Cruz. "Briscoe?" he questioned. "That man spooks me. He's such a damn loner, anyhow, I ain't sure he'll wanna ride with me and my boys. Besides, accordin' to what you're sayin', we're goin' after two men and two women. I don't see why we need no high-priced hired gun to get that job done."

Plummer considered Cruz's remark for a moment before deciding. "Maybe you're right," he said. Briscoe was a mysterious sort of assassin, hard to figure out, and not always easy to find. He could always call him in later if Cruz couldn't stop the fugitives. "All right, what I want you to do is take the road to Three Forks and search all up and down the Madison River in case those people cut across that way."

Cruz looked skeptical. "That's a lot of ground to cover. It ain't gonna be easy to catch somebody cuttin' across when we don't even know where they're comin' from."

"You might not catch them at all," Plummer said. "You're just to make sure in case that posse Ainsworth sent after them doesn't catch up to them."

Cruz shrugged. "You're the boss. Me and the boys'll scout out that whole country. 'Pears to me that it's gonna take a helluva lotta luck to bump into 'em, though."

"There's enough gold with them to make us all pretty happy, so it's in everybody's interest to find them," Plummer said, although he, like Ainsworth, had no idea how much gold Finn had amassed.

"Maybe Lady Luck will be lookin' our way," Cruz said as he headed for the door. "I'll take John Red Blanket with us." He wouldn't presume to tell Plummer his business, but he was still of the opinion that his was a fool's mission. *Riding out in a world of wilderness, hoping you'll bump into four people heading God knows where*, he thought. *Must be one helluva lot of gold those folks are carrying.*

After Cruz had gone, Plummer opened a cabinet behind his desk and weighed out ten dollars' worth of gold dust from a pouch kept there. He handed the dust to Joe French. "Here, take this over to Ben Caldwell's store and give it to them to fix their window. Tell 'em we investigated it and got the money from the drunk that shot it out." It was important to retain the trust of the businesspeople of Alder Gulch, especially in recent times when Plummer had heard rumors of some dissatisfaction with the lack of curtailing outlaw activity on the trails between the claims of the miners.

Bailey Cruz found Tom Seeger in O'Grady's Place, where the gruff professional road agent was in the process of finishing off a breakfast of pork chops and potatoes, washed down with a mug of beer. A cheerless man of constant dyspeptic nature, Seeger dabbled with his food as if reluctant to ingest it. He glanced up to frown at Cruz when he walked in the door.

"We got a job to do," Cruz said as he pulled a chair away from the table and sat down. Seeger's only response was a bored grunt as he continued to gnaw on the bone from his pork chop. "Where's John Red Blanket?" Cruz asked.

"Hell, I don't know," Seeger replied. "I ain't seen him since last night. Ask O'Grady."

O'Grady happened to come in the door from the back room in time to hear Seeger's remark. "Ask me what?" he asked.

"I'm lookin' for John Red Blanket," Cruz said. "You seen him?"

"He's sleepin' off a drunk in my storeroom," O'Grady answered. "And I wish to hell you'd get him outta there, before he wakes up and pukes all over the floor, like he did the last time you fellers were here." O'Grady's Place had become the informal base of operations for Bailey Cruz's gang of cutthroats when they were in town. O'Grady was not particularly happy with the arrangement, but he had let it develop because of the amount of money they spent in his establishment. Now it had progressed to the point where he was afraid to complain about their patronage, even though it had cost him business from the peaceful citizens of Virginia City.

"I'll go drag his sorry ass outta there," Cruz said. "We need him for a little job we've got to do for Plummer."

Before Cruz could embellish, O'Grady turned on his heel and promptly headed for the bar. "Whatever it is, I don't wanna know about it," he said, figuring that the less he knew about their activities, the better. This was especially important in the face of recent vigilante retaliation on some of the road agents that had been identified. It worried him that he knew as much as he did, just from conversations he had overheard in his saloon, and he wondered how long it would be before he might be visited by the vigilantes.

"What are you worried about, O'Grady?" Seeger called after him. "You ain't got no cause to fret unless you start talkin' in your sleep."

"It ain't none of my business what my customers are doin'," O'Grady said as he walked around behind the bar.

"Long as you keep it that way," Cruz said, "you'll be

all right." Back to the business at hand, he instructed Seeger, "We're goin' on a little huntin' trip that oughta tickle you. Plummer wants us to see if we can head off a couple of fellers that run off from Bannack with a full load of gold dust. One of 'em's supposed to be some kinda sharpshootin' hired gun, brought in by the miners up there. There's just the two of 'em, and they got two women with 'em. You know one of 'em, that ol' whore that Plummer run outta town a while back—Bonnie somebody."

"I swear," Seeger grunted. "Bonnie, I remember her. She's the one they said gutted Jack Chatwick, but nobody could prove it."

"That's the one," Cruz said. "Most folks thought the world was better off without Jack, anyway. He rode a fine horse, though—that little blue roan. Joe French didn't waste no time claimin' that horse."

Seeger paused to suck a sizable piece of meat from his front teeth, which he took a moment to examine before popping it back in his mouth. "That hired gun," he asked, "is he the same jasper that had a run-in with Rafe Tolbert and Frank Fancher a few days back—broke ol' Fancher's nose?"

They both paused to recall. "Mighta been. I don't know." Then Cruz got back to business. "Get through suckin' on that bone and ride out to the camp and get Buster and Rawhide. And don't dawdle. We got to get movin'."

"What the hell you need Buster for?" Seeger wanted to know. "He's about as useless as tits on a boar."

"We might need some heavy liftin'," Cruz said, "just in case." The oxlike man was not endowed with a great deal of brains, but he was as strong as a mule, and had no better sense than to do whatever he was told to do. The only person with the patience to deal with him was Rawhide, a lean, saddle-hardened man who was tough as the name he went by. The name, however, came from the rawhide whip he always carried, which he was ready to apply with the slightest provocation. He had somehow adopted the simpleminded brute over the course of a couple of years and Buster followed him around like a puppy—a puppy capable of breaking a man's back if Rawhide gave the word. It was for this reason that some of the men, like Seeger, were not always happy with Buster along on a job. But Cruz liked having the hulking man with the child's brain with him. He had laughingly commented to Joe French that it was like having a grizzly in a harness, as long as Rawhide was there to make him dance. "Meet me back at the stable," Cruz told Seeger, "and we'll get started while there's still plenty of daylight. I'll go get John Red Blanket."

As O'Grady had said, Red Blanket was in the storeroom. Cruz found him sprawled on his belly across a couple of flour sacks, dead to the world. O'Grady's Chinese cook had placed a bucket under the sleeping man's head. "John!" Cruz shouted loud enough to be heard in the barroom out front, but evidently not loud enough to penetrate the deep alcohol-induced slumber of the Crow Indian. "John, damn it! Get up from there!" Cruz yelled at the unresponsive body. He looked around him, searching for something to hasten the procedure, and spying a bucket with a mop standing next to the wall, he picked it up and emptied it over Red Blanket's head, mop and all. It was effective in accomplishing the awakening of the drunken Indian, and the sudden intrusion of light through the half-opened eyelids was enough to signal the same rumblings deep inside his belly as the last time. He made an attempt to get up, but was still on hands and knees atop the flour sacks when the contents of the night before rushed to evacuate his stomach, leaving a putrid waste on the storeroom floor close beside the empty bucket.

"Damn!" Red Blanket exclaimed when at last he could breathe again. "I musta been asleep."

"Yeah, you musta been," Cruz said with more than a hint of disgust. "Come on, let's get outta here. We got a job to do."

"I need a drink of likker," Red Blanket complained as he got himself together and followed Cruz, who was already heading for the door. He stumbled after him, almost bumping into O'Grady's cook, coming for something in the storeroom. They went out into the saloon, ignoring the thunderstorm of irate Chinese profanity behind them.

It was later in the morning when Seeger returned with Rawhide and Buster to find Cruz and a now sober Red Blanket waiting for them with supplies and ammunition on a packhorse. They left town immediately with Plummer's final caution. "I know how much gold that old man has," he lied, "so all of it better damn well be there when you come back with it."

The party Bailey Cruz and his four partners sought was at that moment following a narrow canyon that divided two lofty mountains that stood like giant sentinels on either side of them. There was a wide stream that ran down the middle of the canyon, and Adam continued to follow it until he found a smaller stream that fed into it from a ravine that climbed higher up into the mountain. Thinking this was what he was looking for, he herded the women, the wounded Irishman, the mules, and the extra horses up the ravine, following the smaller stream a distance of about two hundred yards until he came to a waterfall. Beyond it, the slope leveled to form a shelf with a small glen of pine trees surrounded a clearing of grass. "This'll do," he announced, dismounted, and led his horse over to tie it to a pine limb.

"Well, thank goodness," Bonnie said, weary of the saddle. "I thought you were gonna make us climb all the way to the top of the mountain. She slid off the horse and rubbed her sore bottom. "I ain't used to spending this much time on a horse."

"I ain't, either," Lacey echoed, and scrambled off the sorrel.

Adam ignored both complaining women while he looked around his choice for a campsite more closely. *Anybody looking to find us will have to come up this stream the same as we did*, he thought. *And they'll be easy to see until they get to the trees. It's a ways to the edge of the tree line, so they ain't likely to see us from above without coming out in the open. It might not be perfect, but it'll do us just fine for a while.* Satisfied, he went over to help Finn off his horse.

As soon as Finn was settled as comfortable as possible, Adam set about making a more permanent camp. Selecting a stand of younger pines, he picked four for the framework of his shelter and took his hatchet to the few standing in what would be the center. Once they were cleared, he bent the four remaining trees over together and bound their tops together. Using a slicker he had found rolled behind Billy Crabtree's saddle, he covered part of the shelter with it, covering the slicker and the remaining roof with pine boughs. Once he was well along in his structure, Bonnie and Lacey saw what he had in mind, so they joined in to help fashion their temporary home. There was already a good start for a floor provided by a thick layer of pine needles upon which they spread what blankets they had.

Leaving Bonnie and Lacey to finish up and start a fire, Adam left on foot to scout out the mountain above their camp to make sure he knew about anything around them that might give an enemy advantage. He was pleased to find abundant sign of deer, some of it fresh, and he knelt by the stream where they had recently crossed. Studying the hoofprints carefully, as Mose Stebbins had taught him when he was a boy, he estimated that the deer were four in number and had crossed above his campsite no more than one or two hours before, judging by the amount of water that had seeped up in the tracks at the edge of the stream. Possibly they might have been frightened off by the approaching horses. *Fresh meat.* The thought came immediately to mind, but he paused to consider whether or not it would be wise to fire a shot, not sure if anyone might be close enough to hear his rifle. He decided to see if he could track the deer while he thought about it.

After following a trail through the thick belt of pine trees for over a half hour, he discovered a high meadow, just below the tree line. Grazing in the center of the meadow were three does and one young buck. Adam knelt in the trees to watch them while he made up his mind. How much of a risk would it be if he shot one of the deer? He had no notion if there was anyone around to hear the shot or not. *Finn needs some fresh meat*, he told himself. *Hell, we all do. I'm gonna chance it.* He raised his rifle and laid the sights on one of the does. The Henry bucked once and the deer dropped heavily to the ground, shot through the lung. Seeming like the sound of a cannon, the shot reverberated off the steep mountain slope. Adam shook his head and looked around him as if expecting someone to fall upon him at any minute. But all was quiet again, and he told himself that it was highly unlikely anyone had cut their trail this soon after following the stream up from the canyon. He paused a few moments to watch the remaining deer disappear in the trees above the clearing. Then he hurried out to claim his kill.

"It's Adam!" Bonnie sang out when a figure appeared at the edge of the clearing. "Damn, look at that," she said when the tall man walked out of the trees carrying the carcass of a deer across his shoulders. She put her Spencer carbine back where it was next to her blanket and stood up to meet him. "We heard a shot—didn't know what to think, but we hoped it wasn't someone come to call this soon."

"You ever butcher a deer?" Adam asked.

"No," she answered. "But if you can, I can."

"I can show you how," he said, and dumped the deer on the ground. "First we'll have to skin it." He set to work right away, knowing that everyone would be happy to have something other than salt pork for a change. Bonnie did not hesitate to jump right in beside him, with Lacey standing ready to help whenever either of them needed something. In no time at all there were strips of venison on hastily made spits over the fire, and soon the aroma of the roasting meat reached Finn where he lay on his saddle blanket over a mattress of pine straw. Convinced that he was about to enter death's dark corridor a few minutes before, he decided he had enough life left in him to partake of the feast.

"Look at him wolf down that meat," Bonnie remarked to Adam. "Before you came back, he had us about ready to start digging a grave." Addressing Finn directly then, she teased, "Looks like we're gonna have to wait a little longer before we get our hands on that gold."

"Maybe so," Finn replied, "and I'm thinkin' that's reason enough to postpone my departure."

Adam stood by without joining in the playful banter between the two. It was good to see Finn's spirits up. It would help him to heal faster. He feared that Finn might have been correct when he said he thought the shoulder was broken. He needed a doctor and the closest one was in Virginia City, which meant Finn was going to have to hang on for a while longer. So the little Irishman was on his own as far as healing was concerned. Adam intended to see him safely out of this lawless territory, if he possibly could. As he watched the two women tending the fire and seeing to the needs of the patient, he again asked himself how in hell he had come to be in such a fix. His simple mission to find Jake had mushroomed into a traveling circus. He sighed heavily and sat down by the fire to test the venison for himself. Lacey poured a cup of coffee and brought it to him. When he thanked her, she smiled shyly and seated herself beside him. "Finn's going to be all right," she said. "He has a lot to live for."

"I reckon," Adam said. He studied her face for a

moment. "How 'bout you?" he asked. "Are you gonna make it all right?" She was such a contrast in nature to Bonnie, seemingly lost in the danger of their circumstances, and he wondered if she was strong enough to survive another attack if it occurred. *Jake's puppy*, he thought as she gazed up at him with wide innocent eyes.

"I'll make it," she answered. Then after a brief pause, "As long as nothing happens to you."

High above the little camp on the opposite side of the canyon, an interested observer made his way down an old game trail to a position where he could see the camp near the top of the ravine. Though they were far below him, Black Otter could easily count the white people who had entered the mountains to make a hasty shelter. He counted one man and two women, but there appeared to be another—man or woman, he could not tell—who was sick or wounded. They had many horses and three mules that the white man often used to carry heavy burdens. This was not a welcome sight. The white men had not ventured into this part of his mountains before this, and he immediately worried that they would be followed by others, just as had happened west of there in the lower hills. There had been a handful of white men who had come seeking the yellow dirt that they thought so precious, but they had moved on when the yellow dirt was not there.

The day before, when he had been hunting, he had been startled by the sudden report of a rifle on the far side of the mountain. There was only that one shot, but it was enough to cause him concern, so he went in search of the source. The camp had not been easy to find, but he had been fortunate to catch the scent of roasting meat on the wind and followed it to the point where he now knelt, watching the intruders. The question on his mind now was what he should do about the situation. He was inclined to avoid them and hope that they did not intend to stay. Maybe, he thought, he should move his camp deeper into the mountains, but decided that he should keep a watch on them. It would be better to know what they were doing, and if they intended to build a permanent home here. That thought disturbed him. Unlike the others, they did not appear to be searching for the yellow dirt.

Black Otter and his wife were here in these rugged mountains to escape the soldiers who wanted them to live on the reservation at Fort Hall. His people, the Bannocks, had been pushed from their home west of these mountains, in the Idaho country, ravaged by the white man disease, smallpox, and driven by the increasing inroads made by the Siksika into their lands. He had found peace in this rugged fortress of sheer peaks and narrow valleys with plenty of game for his bow, as well as roots and plants to eat in the many streams. It was a good life, but now he wondered if he had discovered a threat to that existence. Gravely concerned, he got up and moved down through the trees to seek a point that would afford him a closer look.

Lying prone at the edge of a small cliff, he found that he could look right into the white man's camp. The one man he had observed from higher up seemed to be the big medicine, for the others appeared to listen respectfully whenever he spoke. Black Otter could see now that the person lying on a blanket near the fire was a man, and judging by the bandaged shoulder, he was wounded. *They are running*, he thought at once, and considered the possibility that others might come seeking to find them. *This is not good*, he told himself. His attention was caught again by the leader of the party. He was a big man and carried himself well, like a warrior and hunter.

There is nothing I can do about this now, he thought as he slowly pulled himself away from the edge of the cliff. *But I will come back to see what they are doing every day.* Getting to his feet, he picked up his bow again and started back up the slope.

Chapter 10

After another night passed in their camp with no real sign of improvement in Finn's wounded shoulder, Adam decided that it might be best to try to get the bullet out. He had hoped to wait until they could reach the doctor in the settlement that John Bozeman had staked out, but Finn continued to run a high fever. "All we can do is try," he told Bonnie, "'cause he ain't gettin' any better, and we can't stay here forever."

"I think you're right," Bonnie said. "I've been thinking the same thing."

"I reckon I'll go tell him," Adam said, and got up from his seat by the fire.

Bonnie caught his sleeve to detain him. "Wait a minute," she said. "It might be best if I tried to probe for that bullet. Your hands are so damn big you might make a bigger mess of it. But you'd better not tell him I'm gonna do it. He might be afraid I'd put him under to get my hands on his gold." She chuckled as if it was said in jest, but she was more than halfway serious.

Adam simply nodded in reply, then went to the shelter where Finn was trying to rest. "Well, Finn," he started, "I reckon it's time we dug into your packs to find that whiskey you said you had."

Misunderstanding Adam's intent, Finn muttered, "You'd best forget about the whiskey. You need to keep your wits about you."

"It ain't for me," Adam said. "It's for you. We're gonna have to get that bullet outta your shoulder before you die of lead poisonin'. And I figure it'll be a sight easier for you if you're drunk as a lord."

His statement brought a long moment of silence from the little Irishman, and his response served to surprise Adam. "I was wonderin' if that was gonna have to be done. The bottle's in my war bag in the second pack, the one that rides close behind my heart." Adam started to go immediately to the packs, but Finn stopped him. "For mercy's sake, though, let one of the women dig for the bullet. You're liable to cut somethin' outta me by mistake."

To the party's amazement, the little man had an unbelievable capacity for whiskey. As soon as he downed one cup of the fiery liquid, he called for another, claiming that he was still as sober as a judge. As the bottle neared empty, Adam began to worry that there was not enough whiskey to do the job. "I might have to knock you in the head to get you ready," he threatened in jest. He was saved the trouble, however, when the level in the bottle got down to enough for maybe one more drink, and Finn simply closed his eyes in midsentence and passed out. "Get at it," Adam told Bonnie, "before he wakes up and wants another drink."

Bonnie worked fast and furious while showing a

surprising dexterity with the skinning knife used for the surgery. Watching in undisguised awe, Lacey stood at hand with a bucket of clean water, which she used to rinse out the cloths that Bonnie continuously soaked with blood. She could not help recalling the stories that had been passed around that some folks suspected Bonnie of sending Jack Chatwick to his reward with a knife in the gut. She shook her head to rid it of such thoughts.

To those watching, it seemed longer, but in actuality Bonnie felt the solid tick of the lead slug with the tip of her blade in less than a quarter of an hour, which seemed an incredible accomplishment in the bloody mess of the wound. A few minutes later, she was able to get a grasp on the bullet and finally pulled it out, holding it up triumphantly for all to see. Adam smiled and gave her a nod of approval and Lacey cheered. "I'd best take a couple of stitches in that wound," Bonnie said, for what was once a bullet hole was now a three-inch gash. "I've got a needle and thread in my bag." Lacey went immediately to fetch the bag.

During the duration of the surgery, Finn responded with little more than a groan here and there, so embalmed with whiskey was he. But when the heated blade of the knife was applied to cauterize the wound, he sat straight up with a howl of pain, only to fall back unconscious. Bonnie deftly drew her needle through the flesh to loosely hold the sides of the slash together, tied the knot, then bit the thread in two. "There," she said with a tired sigh, "all done." She jammed the knife blade in the ground to clean it and said, "Hand me that bottle." When Lacey passed the bottle over to her, she tilted her head back and drained the last few ounces. Throwing the empty bottle into the bushes, she commented, "Maybe we should have thrown him in the creek and washed him before we doctored him. I thought I was gonna pass out, too, when I bit that thread off."

"Do you think he's dead?" Lacey wondered as she gazed down at Finn, who was motionless on the saddle blanket.

"All I did was work on his shoulder," Bonnie answered patiently. "I didn't go near anything vital. Besides, have you ever heard a dead man snore like that?"

Lacey blushed, embarrassed by her naive question. Adam smiled and shook his head. "He's gonna feel like hell when he wakes up. Then I reckon we'll see if he'll do any better with the bullet outta that shoulder."

At the edge of the cliff, high up on the opposite slope of the ravine, Black Otter paused to consider what he had just witnessed. Thinking at first that the man and the two women were going to kill the wounded man, he realized that they were actually intent upon removing a bullet. *They are fortunate to have a medicine woman with them,* he thought. *Now maybe the wounded man will get better and they will go away.* He withdrew slowly from the cliff and started back up through the pines. *Tomorrow I must hunt,* he thought. His surveillance of the white camp would have to wait until later in the afternoon.

Early splinters of light began to filter through the thick pine boughs as Adam descended carefully down through the thick belt of trees that skirted the lower two-thirds of the mountain. He was intent upon adding to their supply of venison, planning to smoke some of it to carry with them when Finn was well enough to ride again. His hunt on this morning was purposely farther away from the camp, in hopes that the sound of his rifle might be lost in the canyons on the other side of their mountain shelter.

Like the stream where he had killed the doe before, there was plenty of deer sign all along the slope he was now working his way down, but so far, there was no sighting of the animals. *They've got to be here somewhere*, he told himself. *There's too much sign for them not to be.* When the game trail he followed took a turn around a thick stand of firs, he decided to cut straight through and catch it again below the firs. He was almost through the maze of trees when he stopped suddenly and dropped to one knee, for there they were, about fifty feet below him where the trail crossed a small mountain meadow. He counted eight deer grazing in the grassy opening in the trees, any one of them an easy shot at that distance.

Since they were unaware of his presence above them, and they showed no signs of preparing to move on, he took his time setting himself for the shot. Bringing his rifle to bear on the target of his choice, he started to squeeze the trigger, but stopped short of firing when a figure about halfway down between him and the deer slowly rose from the middle of a thicket with a bow fully drawn. Frozen with indecision for a moment, Adam held his fire. It was only for a moment, however, for something spooked the deer. An eight-point buck, obviously the leader, threw his head up and snorted. On cue, the entire herd bolted just as the hunter released his arrow, causing him to miss his target. Adam acted without thinking of the consequences his action might bring. Shifting his aim only slightly, he squeezed off a round and knocked the buck to the ground. Still acting on instinct, he quickly cranked another round into the chamber and felled a second deer before the rest disappeared into the trees.

Faced now with what could become an unwanted situation, he knew it was too late for him to question his decision to expose his presence. In truth, he realized that he had fired the first shot to keep the hunter—which he could now see was an Indian—from losing his kill. And the second shot was simply because of an opportunity for them both to get a deer. Right or wrong, it was done. The question now was whether or not a violent confrontation was to follow. He slowly came out of the trees and stood with his rifle cradled across his arms, waiting for the Indian's reaction.

Some twenty-five feet below Adam, Black Otter left the thicket and turned to face the white man. Seconds before, he had been stunned by the sudden burst of rifle fire when his arrow had flown wide of the target. Now he recognized the man as the leader of the little party in the canyon. His initial impulse was to run, for the white man had the rifle that shoots many times. But the man showed no indication of aggression. In fact, he seemed to be waiting to see what Black Otter's intentions were. Well aware that the white man had the advantage, and could easily kill him if he wanted to, Black Otter held up his hand.

Recognizing the Indian's sign of peace, Adam returned it with his hand and began working his way down the slope to meet him. Black Otter waited for him, still unsure if there might be any treachery in the white man's heart. Just in case, he dropped his hand on his skinning knife to make sure it was riding loose in its rawhide scabbard.

Just as cautious, Adam watched the Indian carefully as he approached, noting the question in the red man's face. He was a fine specimen of a man, sleek and smooth muscled, a young man, with no sign of fear in his eyes—only one of caution. "Speak white man talk?" Adam asked.

"Yes," Black Otter replied. He had learned to speak English during the time he had spent at Fort Hall. "Little bit," he added.

"Good," Adam said, relieved, because he spoke very little in any Indian dialect. "I mean you no harm. I come in peace."

Black Otter nodded, and paused to formulate his words. "Shoot gun good. Get two deer."

"One for you, one for me," Adam said, gesturing with his hands. "We'll share, and you pick the one you want."

Black Otter nodded thoughtfully, as if judging Adam's words. "Good," he said, then suddenly notched an arrow and turned away to let it fly. It embedded solidly in a small tree approximately thirty-five yards away. He turned back to Adam then and said, "Deer move."

Adam understood Black Otter's message. He smiled and nodded. "Yes, I saw the deer move right when you released your arrow. Else you'd have got him for sure." Black Otter smiled in return and nodded. And the two stood there smiling and nodding for several seconds before Adam said, "My name's Adam Blaine," and held out his hand.

The Indian tapped his chest lightly and replied, "Black Otter. Friend." Familiar with the white man's way of greeting friends, he grasped Adam's outstretched hand firmly and made two exaggerated movements up and down. Now that the two were standing toe-to-toe, Black Otter looked up at the white man towering over him. "Come down from mountain, still look like up on mountain," he remarked.

Adam didn't understand at first, but then caught the Indian's attempt at humor. "Yeah, I'm kinda tall," he said with a grin.

They went out in the meadow to look at the two fallen deer then, and Adam insisted that Black Otter should have first choice, and assured him that all he wanted was the meat. Black Otter picked the buck. Since the morning chill was still in the air at that high altitude, they decided to gut both carcasses there in the meadow. While they worked, Adam learned that Black Otter did not live in a village, but dwelt alone with his wife in these mountains. He also sensed that the Indian was anxious to know what had brought Adam's little party to his mountains and what his plans were. Adam could not help seeing the relief in Black Otter's eyes when he told him that his party was going to move on as soon as Finn recovered enough to ride. "There are others looking for you?" Black Otter asked.

"Yeah, I'm afraid so," Adam answered. "There are some bad men lookin' for us. They shot my friend, and that's why we found a place to hide for a while."

"They come here?"

"Well, I hope not," Adam replied. "I hope they don't know where we are. I hope we'll be gone before they can find us."

With their loads lightened somewhat, the two men hefted the carcasses up on their shoulders and parted company, each back to his own camp. It was a long walk back to the pine shelter by the stream, made to seem twice the distance with the deer on his shoulders. It would have been a great deal easier if he could have brought his horse, but the slopes he was hunting on were too steep to bother with his horse. In spite of the altitude and the chilly air, he had worked up a healthy sweat when he finally emerged from the pines to confront Bonnie, as before, with her carbine ready to fire. "You know," she informed him, "it couldn't hurt you to sing out before you pop out of the woods like that. One of these times I'm liable to put a bullet in your big ass."

"You reckon?" he answered, unconcerned.

She lowered her weapon and stood watching him as he stepped across the stream. "I see you found us some more meat. I expect you think somebody's gonna have to skin it and butcher it."

"Thanks for volunteering," he said, and dumped the carcass on the ground. He looked over at Finn, propped up against a tree with a blanket around his shoulders. "How you makin' out?" he asked.

"I'm afraid I'm gonna live," he said, then remarked, "We heard two shots. Did you miss with the first one?"

Adam was a little disturbed to find they had heard the shots, since he had hunted so far away in hopes they would not. He related the meeting he had with Black Otter, and the reason for two shots. The women were at once concerned that he had encountered an Indian hunter, but Adam assured them that it was just one Indian and his wife, and they weren't interested in taking any long black scalps—or in Lacey's case, any long sandy-haired ones, either.

After the butchering was done and the women set to work smoking the strips of venison, Adam saddled his horse and rode back down the ravine, the way they had originally come into their camp, still concerned if anyone else had heard the two shots. When he reached the valley floor, where the stream flowed into the wide one that flowed down the length of the valley, he rode across to the other side and climbed the western slope. His purpose was to find a high point where he could get a good view of the foothills they had ridden through on their way to their hideout. Following an old game trail, he soon reached a good spot with unrestricted views of a wide expanse of country both east and west. Satisfied that he was unlikely to find better, he dismounted, took a freshly roasted strip of deer meat, and sat down on a boulder to eat it. He remained there for a good part of the afternoon, with nothing moving in any direction except a herd of antelope that moved slowly toward the towering mountains, stopping to graze occasionally before disappearing from his sight. There could not be a more peaceful world, he thought, and decided he could gamble on one or two more days before striking out for the Madison and home. If his little party of fugitives was still being pursued, he figured that their pursuers would have shown up before now.

The sun set early deep in the mountains, so it was already heading toward evening by the time he again approached the camp. This time he sang out to humor Bonnie, but it was not enough to allow him to escape her scolding. "Where the hell have you been all afternoon?" she demanded when he rode up and dismounted. "If

Ainsworth's murderers had shown up, wouldn't we have been in a fix?"

"Oh, I reckon it wouldn'ta been nothin' you couldn't have handled," he replied, unable to resist baiting her.

"I've got my hands full here," she complained, "taking care of Finn and being a mama to Lacey. Now, since this morning, I find out I've got to worry about that Indian up there watching us."

"You were gone a long time," Lacey said. "I was beginning to worry."

Good Lord in heaven, he thought. *When the hell did I come to be the daddy for these people?* As was his custom, however, he merely smiled and went to check on Finn.

"You making out okay?" Adam asked.

"Yes," Finn replied. "I'm gettin' stronger. If I could have a couple more days, I think I'd be ready to ride out of here." He paused, then said, "I'm thinkin' you've been out watchin' our back trail."

"That's right," Adam said, "and I didn't see sign of anyone comin' our way. If we're lucky, nobody knows where the hell we are. But we'll still have to be careful not to run up on anybody that might be waitin' up ahead of us."

"This is a damn fool job Plummer sent us on," Tom Seeger complained, "ridin' all over hell and back, lookin' for a needle in a haystack. Them folks could be anywhere. Just because we can't find no tracks where they crossed the river don't mean they didn't cross it. Ain't nothin' says they had to cross where we looked. Hell, for all we know, that posse outta Bannack mighta already found 'em and took that gold back." He scowled at the coffee left in the bottom of his cup, then flung it out in disgust. "Damn coffee tastes like mule piss."

"You're awful damn cheerful tonight," Bailey Cruz said. "Course, I'm gonna have to take your word on the coffee, since I ain't ever drank no mule piss." His comment brought a chuckle from Buster, causing Seeger to turn his scowl in the big oaf's direction. Of the five who had been sent out from Virginia City, Buster was perhaps the only one who was not weary of what appeared to be a pointless search. As Rawhide had put it, Buster was like a duck. He woke up in a new world every morning.

Cruz had decided to head west two days before, leaving the Madison with the slim chance they might still run into the fugitives if they had, in fact, eluded the posse and cut back east. It was a rough country, and he was operating on the theory that the fugitives would take a commonsense trail through the hills, trying to escape as soon as possible. And there were only a few such trails that he knew of. Camped now by the Ruby River, he had decided to call off the search, and his final effort was to send John Red Blanket to scout on ahead as far as the Beaverhead, just so he could report to Plummer that he had exhausted all possibilities.

"How long are we gonna lie around here waitin' for Red Blanket?" Rawhide asked. Like Seeger, he was growing weary of the futile hunt.

"Till he gets back," Cruz replied soberly. "I told him not to go no farther than the Beaverhead."

Rawhide picked up a small stick and tossed it at Buster. "Hell, that Injun might come up on some likker somewhere and won't be back for a week." Buster grinned wide and playfully tossed the stick back at Rawhide.

"I doubt there's any whiskey between here and the Beaverhead," Cruz said, "and there ain't no use belly-achin' about it. He'll get back when he gets back."

"How much gold you reckon that old coot really dug outta the ground?" Seeger asked.

"Don't know," Cruz replied. "A helluva lot, accordin' to Plummer."

"If it's that much, it'd be mighty temptin' to keep headin' east with it, if we was to catch up to them people." Seeger's sour expression was creased by a slight grin at the thought.

"It would at that," Rawhide responded. "Wouldn't it, Cruz?"

"I doubt we'll have that decision to make," Cruz replied, although it was an interesting proposition to consider.

It was late that night when Red Blanket returned to the camp by the Ruby, yelling, "Don't shoot. It's me," as he splashed across. Eager to give his report, he pulled his lathered horse up before the dying campfire and dismounted. "I found 'em!" he exclaimed. "I found 'em!"

"Where?" Cruz responded excitedly as he threw off his blanket. "Did they have the gold with 'em?"

"Not them," Red Blanket said. "I found the posse—back on the Beaverhead! They was all dead, all of 'em—bodies on both sides of the river—musta been a helluva fight."

"Damn," Rawhide swore solemnly, still sitting with his blanket wrapped around him. "That hired gun must be the cougar they say he is."

"Any idea where they went after that?" Cruz asked.

"Yeah," Red Blanket said. "It wasn't hard to follow the trail they left outta there, and they was headin' straight east. I tracked 'em till daylight ran out on me about five miles back yonder way, but they were headin' toward the Ruby. And unless they changed direction, I expect they mighta crossed somewhere not far north of where we're settin' right now."

"That means they've still got all that gold," Rawhide said.

"Want me to saddle the horses?" Buster asked.

"No, dummy," Rawhide responded. "We can't go nowhere in the dark."

"We'll scout the river north of here in the mornin'," Cruz said, "and maybe pick up their trail—oughta be easy enough. Nothin' we can do right now, so we might as well go on back to bed." Looking at Red Blanket, he commented, "Your horse looks like he needs some rest before he'll be ready to go again."

"That's a fact," Red Blanket said. "Any coffee left in that pot?" he asked, nodding toward the pot still sitting in the ashes. "I ain't had none all day."

"If there is, it ain't fit to drink," Cruz replied, "but I reckon you know how to make some if you want it."

Always ready for anything to eat or drink, Buster volunteered, "I'll make you some."

Cruz was awake at first light and had the others up shortly after. Anxious to get in the saddle as soon as possible, he had to wait, however, for breakfast of coffee and bacon at the insistence of the others. Their enthusiasm for the chase was evident, but not on empty stomachs. While Rawhide fried the bacon, the other four saddled the horses and broke camp. Buster, as usual, took over the chore for Rawhide. By the time the sun was in evidence over the hills, they were on their way upriver, Cruz, Red Blanket, and Seeger on one side and Rawhide and Buster on the other.

As Red Blanket had predicted, they came to the place where Adam and his party had crossed the Ruby approximately three miles from the place they had camped. "That sure looks like a helluva lot of tracks for four riders," Cruz remarked, "even countin' the mules."

"I expect they musta picked up the horses that posse was ridin'," Red Blanket said.

Since both halves of the search party came upon the tracks at the same curve in the river on opposite sides of the water, it told them that there had been no effort to disguise their trail by wading up- or downriver. Leaving the water, the tracks continued on a straight course to the east. "Sure looks like they were headin' right for the Madison," Seeger commented. "How come we never found no sign of them crossin' the Madison?"

"I reckon they managed to cross it somewhere we didn't look," Cruz replied, "or maybe they didn't cross it. Plain as this trail is, we oughta find out one way or the other." Late in the afternoon the question was answered, for the tracks told them that the party they followed had stopped by a small stream for a short while, then turned north into the mountains.

"Now, why in hell would they do that?" Rawhide gave voice to the question in all their minds, except possibly Buster's. "There ain't nothin' in that direction but high mountains and narrow canyons."

Cruz thought about it for a few moments before speculating, "This might be the luckiest thing that could happen for us. They mighta been thinkin' there was another posse up ahead, waitin' to catch 'em at the river. Maybe they decided to find 'em a place to hole up for a while till the heat blows over, and if they did, it just might give us a chance to catch up with 'em."

They set out in the direction dictated by the obvious trail, straight for the mountains, and more directly toward a narrow canyon with a stream gushing forth. The trail that had been so easy to follow before became more difficult in the confines of the canyon and the diminishing light. Finally, when the sun slid behind the western peaks, and the canyon was plunged into darkness, as if someone had suddenly blown out a lamp, they were forced to stop for the night.

Morning found them waiting impatiently for the sun to send some rays into the deep canyon while Red Blanket, with help from a torch, inched his way a few yards ahead, trying to find at least a hoofprint or two. Finally, as the light filtered down the steep sides of the mountains on either side of them, Red Blanket could see again. "Come," he beckoned to the others, and tossed his torch into the stream. The searchers started out once again, this time following behind Red Blanket as he sought tracks now more difficult to find. "They're bein' a lot more careful 'bout tryin' to hide their trail," he commented. A short time later, he stopped again when he found several tracks headed in the opposite direction. "Just one horse," he told the others. "Hard to say how old these tracks are, but it was in the last day or two." The searchers continued to advance slowly up the stream until Red Blanket held up his hand to halt them at a juncture where a smaller stream emptied into the one they had been following. "Wait a minute till I make sure," he said, "but I think they mighta headed up this little stream." After a few minutes, when he could find no tracks beyond, he was sure they had turned to follow the smaller stream.

Rawhide stood peering up the steep ravine with its narrow sides lined with pine trees. "Boys," he announced, "this is where we best start watchin' ourselves."

"Rawhide's right," Cruz said. "We'd better leave the horses and take it real slow from here on up. There's too many places for a bushwhacker to sit just waitin'. Go ahead and lead out, Red Blanket."

Red Blanket hesitated. "My job's trackin', and I done that. I found 'em. Somebody else can go up first to draw fire."

"Shit fire," Cruz said. "I thought you Crow Injuns was supposed to be brave."

"Brave, yeah," Red Blanket replied. "Stupid, no."

"Hell," Rawhide scoffed, "Buster ain't scared to go up that ravine, are you, Buster? Go on up there and we'll be right behind you. You can be the leader."

The suggestion pleased the simpleminded man-child. "I'll be the leader, Rawhide. I'll lead us up there to get 'em." He started up the ravine immediately.

"Sure you will," Rawhide said. "I knew we could count on you." He turned to Cruz and remarked, "They're probably long gone by now, anyway."

"Maybe, but there don't seem to be many ways to get up and down this gulch, and there ain't no tracks comin' down but that one set Red Blanket saw. I'm bet-tin' they're still up there somewhere." In a single file, they started climbing after the oversized brute, each man with his eyes peeled and darting from side to side of the foreboding gulch. Unnoticed by any of the five, a solitary figure rose from a laurel thicket, high up the stream, and faded into the leafy background.

Lacey dropped the pan she was filling in the stream when she looked up to see the Indian spring from the edge of the pines. She screamed and fled toward the shelter. Bonnie rushed out of the shelter but halted abruptly when she discovered the Bannock warrior running toward her, his bow in hand, yelling something she could not understand. Like Lacey, she took flight, but unlike the frightened girl, she ran to fetch her carbine. Recognizing his name being called, Adam appeared in time to keep Bonnie from shooting Black Otter. "Stop!" he ordered. "He's callin' me!"

"Adam Bain!" Black Otter repeated, mispronouncing the last name. "White men come! You come quick!"

In need of no explanation beyond that, Adam reacted immediately. Snatching his rifle up, he cocked it and ran to where Black Otter beckoned. "Where?" he asked. Black Otter motioned toward the stream and Adam understood at once. He wasted no time moving to a large boulder beside the stream at the edge of the waterfall, and looked below to the five men the Indian pointed out. They were still more than a hundred and fifty yards below him, making their way cautiously up the steep streambed. There was not much time to think, but fortunately he had given the possibility of this occurrence some thought before, so he did not hesitate to act. There was no quick exit from his camp. The only way out was up and around the mountain. The first and foremost problem was the time it would take to saddle the horses and load the packs on Finn's mules.

In those initial rapidly ticking seconds, he took a

hard look at the five men laboring to lead their horses carefully up the steep slope. There was no doubt in his mind who they were and what their intent was. They couldn't be anyone but more of Plummer's men. He wasn't going to wait to ask them. "Bad men?" Black Otter asked.

"Yeah, bad men. Thank you, my friend, for warning us."

"I help you fight," Black Otter said, holding his bow up before him.

Adam hesitated for a moment, thinking that Black Otter had a wife waiting for him somewhere on the other side of the mountain, but the precarious situation he found himself in made it difficult to turn down any offered help. "Again I thank you," he said. With no time to dally, Adam then called Bonnie to come to him. She was carrying her rifle with the cartridge belt slung over her shoulder, and she hurried to answer his call. "There's at least five men that I can count comin' up the stream. Looks like they're still trailin' us. In just about a minute, I'm gonna start throwin' some shots down this hill, and I think I can buy us some time. I need you and Lacey to saddle the horses and load the pack mules. Can you do that?"

"I've saddled a horse before," she replied confidently, "and I guess Finn can tell me how to load the packs."

"Good," Adam said. "Go to it, then. Just saddle the horses we're ridin'. Leave the extra horses. Ain't no need for me to tell you we've got to get outta here."

"You're right about that," the spunky woman replied, and was off to do his bidding.

Adam turned his attention back to the execution party inching its way up the stream. He rested his rifle in a notch in the boulder, aimed at a spot where the stream took a sharp turn around a cluster of rocks, then waited for the huge man leading to reach it. He glanced over at the Bannock warrior and Black Otter nodded solemnly, notched an arrow, and waited for Adam to start the volley.

When the first shot rang out, Cruz dived for cover behind a log lying close beside the stream. He looked up to see Buster staggering, struggling to stay on his feet. He could see an arrow protruding from the big man's chest, but he figured there was a gunshot wound that he couldn't see. *Indians? Was it possible?* The trail they had followed from the Ruby led right up this stream. Had they run into an Indian camp? And how many were there? Behind him, he heard Rawhide yell for Buster to get down, but the mindless brute continued to stand on unsteady feet as two more shots rang out. Buster took two more steps up the stream before he finally dropped facedown, like a giant cottonwood, falling across the middle of the water. "Damn it!" Cruz yelled out. "What are you waitin' for?" He took aim on the boulder above him and sent a rapid-fire volley to cause Adam and Black Otter to duck behind the rock. Following his lead, Rawhide knelt in the water behind Buster's body, using it for protection, while Seeger and Red Blanket scurried over behind some rocks across from Cruz. Their concentrated fire forced Adam and Black Otter to seek better positions to shoot from.

For a while, all of the firing came from the four outlaws below, but as soon as any one of them made a move to advance farther up the stream, Adam cut loose with a rapid series of shots from his Henry and Black Otter loosed another arrow, effectively keeping the outlaws at bay. In between the short volleys, he took quick looks at the camp behind him. It was not encouraging, for it appeared that the women were having trouble loading the mules. When their efforts seemingly became fruitless, Bonnie broke away and ran to join him behind the boulder. "The horses are saddled," she gasped breathlessly, "but me and Lacey can't lift the damn gold sacks and tie them on the packs. Finn's tryin' to help, but he's more in the way than helping." When Adam looked perplexed, she suggested, "I can't lift the sacks, but I can sure as hell shoot this carbine. You go load the mules, and me and the Indian will keep the bastards pinned down." She flashed Black Otter a confident grin, which he acknowledged with a solemn nod.

Adam felt no need to question the wisdom of her suggestion. He backed away from his position at the edge of the boulder so she could slide in and take his place. "Mind you keep your head down," he cautioned her. "You're gettin' too damn handy to lose." She smiled, pleased with his comment.

Adam quickly backed away from the boulder and ran to the shelter where Lacey, with a one-armed attempt to help from Finn, strained to lift a heavy sack of gold dust up high enough to lace it on the pack frame. Behind him he heard the sharp snap of Bonnie's carbine as she opened up on the threat below. He immediately grabbed the gold sack and hefted it up to be tied down, then going to the next in line until, in a few minutes, the mules were loaded. He then took a quick look in the shelter to make sure nothing they needed had been left behind. "All right," he said, "you're ready to get outta here."

"Where?" Finn asked, staring at the thick belt of pines above the camp. "Which way?"

It hit Adam at that moment that he had not really determined the best escape route, since there had been none obvious. His only plan, in the event escape became imperative, was to flee into the dense forest and look for a way around the mountain as best they could. "Wait," he told Finn.

Hurrying back to the boulder where Bonnie was sending round after round down upon the outlaws huddled below, he grabbed her ankle and yanked it a couple of times before he was able to break her concentration on her target. "Slide on outta there," he said. "You've got to lead Finn and Lacey outta here." He turned to Black Otter then. "You know these mountains. Will you lead my friends away from here, somewhere they'll be safe?"

Black Otter nodded. "I take them to my camp."

"Good. Thank you, my friend," Adam replied. "I'll keep these boys right where they are till you're long gone." Black Otter nodded again and started to back away. "Where is your camp?" Adam remembered then to ask.

Black Otter pointed to the north. "That mountain, go round, next mountain, go round. My camp by big stream near bottom."

"Good," Adam said. "I'll be seein' you." He watched the Bannock warrior for a second before turning back to the four pinned down below him.

Approaching the two women and the wounded man, Black Otter addressed Finn, who was standing holding the reins of his horse, although still on unsteady feet. "Adam say you follow me," Black Otter said. "I take you safe."

Finn agreed without hesitation, eager to escape with his treasure, but Lacey was leery of leaving Adam behind. "What about Adam?" she asked. "We can't go without him."

As had become the usual practice, Bonnie took control of the situation. "Adam knows what he's doing," she said. "He'll hold them till we've got a good start. Then he'll come after us. What he wants us to do now is to get the hell outta here, so let's get moving."

Black Otter stood, watching impatiently as Bonnie directed Lacey and Finn to form the animals in single file. When they were ready to march, he walked up to Bonnie and, without warning, suddenly thrust his hand up between her legs, receiving a sharp angry rap across his forearm, which encouraged him to immediately withdraw the hand. His reaction was no more than a satisfied grunt and a solemn nod. Then, his curiosity satisfied, he turned and signaled with his hand. "Come."

"You crazy damn savage!" Bonnie swore in stunned anger. Then she glared at Finn, who was chuckling in spite of their dangerous situation.

"He just wanted to see for himself if there wasn't really any male organs up there," Finn said between chuckles. "You had him wonderin'."

At a later time, she might appreciate the humor, but for now, with the sound of rifle fire at their doorstep, she was not amused. "Get going," she ordered Finn, then hustled Lacey along behind him, and they filed into the pines behind Black Otter.

"This ain't doin' us no good," Cruz complained loud enough for his three partners to hear. "They can keep us pinned down here all day." The rifles up above clearly held the advantage, and he could only hope they would give out of cartridges before he did. He was no longer worried about Indians. Judging by the scant number of arrows, and the fact that they all seemed to come from the same place, he decided there were not enough to make a difference. It was the Henry and the carbine that held them pinned down.

"We got to draw back from here and find a way to circle round 'em," Rawhide said, crouching low behind Buster's body, a carcass by then displaying a couple more arrows protruding as well as a fair amount of weight in lead slugs within.

"Shit," Seeger commented. "Look around you. You see any way to circle around? This damn gulch is the only way up I see. You'd have to be a damn spider to climb up the sides of it. How we gonna get the horses up?"

"Well, we can't stay here," Cruz said. "That's for damn sure. Whaddayou say, Red Blanket?"

"Seeger's right," Red Blanket answered. "Only thing to do is go back down to the bottom and go around this mountain to see if we can find another way up to that waterfall."

With no better suggestions forthcoming, Cruz said, "All right, let's back outta here, then." He pushed back from the log and slid a short way on his belly until he felt it safe to scramble down farther on his hands and knees. Following his example, Red Blanket and Seeger left the rocks in the same fashion. Only Rawhide elected to rise to a crouch and make a run for it down the stream. His mistake cost him his life as a bullet from Adam's rifle caught him squarely between his shoulder blades. The other three hurried to safety, no one of them inclined to stop to check on Rawhide's condition, and the only comment made was Cruz's pronouncement when he looked back to see Rawhide drop in the middle of the stream. "Damn fool."

Above them, Adam rose high enough to peer over the top of the boulder. The one clear target that Rawhide had offered was the only opportunity he had to thin out his attackers. He was certain by this time that there were no others but the five he had seen before the shooting started. Now the odds were improving, since the number had been reduced to three, and they had withdrawn, giving up the siege for the time being. But Adam knew it meant no more than a temporary lull in their attack. At least, he now had time to make his escape after the others, so he left the boulder and hurried to the shelter where his horse was tied. Taking the bay's reins, he led him into the pines above the camp. The floor of the forest lay thick with pine needles, but the trail was not difficult to follow because of the many hooves of horses and mules that had just preceded him.

Near the base of the mountain where the outlaws had left their horses, the three remaining members of the search party were already squabbling over the horses that had belonged to Rawhide and Buster. "I expect the only fair thing to do is to odd-man-out for 'em," Seeger said. "We can cut the cards and the low card don't get no horse. The high card takes his pick, and the next-highest card gets the other one, that piece of crow bait that Buster rode. I got a deck of cards in my saddlebag."

"I don't trust no deck of cards you own," John Red Blanket said.

"What the hell is wrong with you two?" Cruz demanded. "There's enough gold up there to buy a herd of horses. We need to find a way to get up to that camp, and you two are arguin' over two horses. And Rawhide and Buster's bodies ain't even cold yet."

"Well, Lord have mercy on their souls," Seeger replied sarcastically. "I know you're really gonna miss 'em. They was always goin' everywhere together, so now I reckon they're on the stagecoach to hell about now."

"That damn hired gun is pretty damn handy with that Henry rifle of his," Red Blanket said. "I'm tellin' you, Cruz, you shoulda seen that posse from Bannack. He cleaned 'em all out. There was dead men lyin' all over that riverbank."

"And now he's already took care of two of us," Seeger reminded them needlessly.

"So what are you sayin'," Cruz asked pointedly, "that we should just let 'em go and ride on back to Virginia City—tell Plummer we quit on 'em 'cause they was shootin' at us? Maybe you ain't rememberin' they're totin' a helluva lot of gold dust with 'em, but I aim to claim my share of it. If you two ain't got enough gizzard to go after that son of a bitch with the rifle, then get on your horses and turn tail and run. And you can take them two extra horses with you, but the packhorse stays with me."

"Ain't no need to get your bowels in an uproar," Seeger said. "Nobody wants to quit on you. Ain't that right, Red Blanket? Hell, we want our share of that gold dust, same as you. Just sayin' the bastard can shoot don't mean we ain't goin' after him."

Cruz glared at Red Blanket then, and the Indian shrugged his indifference. "All right, then," Cruz said, "let's find us a way up to that camp." He turned his horse to the south and started out around the base of the mountain. They had gone a couple of hundred yards when he said, "Leave Rawhide and Buster's horses here. We can come back for 'em later."

Chapter II

The fugitives had not gone far before the rugged climb became too much for Finn's weakened body. The gritty Irishman tried to keep up the pace, but it was apparent to Bonnie that he was not going to make it much longer. She finally called for Black Otter to stop, and together they lifted Finn up on his horse. "I can walk," he protested feebly.

"Like hell you can," Bonnie said. "You're just slowing us down, you and those damn mules."

"Maybe so," he said gamely. "But if it comes to a choice to leave one of us behind, I'll wager it won't be the mules."

"Looks like you're thinking straight," she said with a chuckle. "You just worry about hanging on to that saddle. If you fall off, you won't stop rolling till you reach the bottom of the mountain—and we don't have time to go down to get you."

Finn couldn't help grinning at the aging prostitute's bluster. He had seen enough of the tough-talking woman to determine that she was not all talk, and he was well aware that their little party would be a lot worse off without her courage. Her warning to stay in the saddle was not wasted upon him, however, for the barren rocky slope they had encountered above the tree line was a lot safer on foot than perched on a horse. Black Otter led Finn's horse, with his mules on a line behind, followed by Bonnie and Lacey leading the other horses. It was easy to envision the catastrophe that could result from the slip of a hoof and the chaotic scene of a tangle of horses, people, and mules careening down the mountainside. The spectacular views of the surrounding mountains and the valley far below them were consequently wasted on the party desperate to escape with their lives. With no choice but to trust the Bannock warrior, who had mysteriously come to their aid, they trudged across the rugged shoulders of the mountain, their destination unknown. Every quarter hour or so, Lacey looked back behind them, hoping to see Adam appear until Bonnie finally told her to watch her footing and forget about Adam. "He can take care of himself," she assured the young girl, but she was not without concern for the safety of their solemn protector.

When they reached a point where Bonnie felt she couldn't climb any farther, Black Otter pointed toward a notch in the slope below them that appeared to be a gully leading down into the tree line. "Go down now," he said.

"Well, hallelujah," Bonnie replied, "I thought I was gonna have to crawl up on my horse, too." Watching Finn grasping his saddle horn for fear his horse was going to slide during the steep descent, however, she was just as happy to be on foot.

Once they entered the mouth of the gully, their way was not so steep. Still, when watching their guide when he paused to determine the best path to take, they could see it was obvious that he had never led a horse along this trail before. His judgment proved sound, though, and before much longer, they were making their way down through the pines again, this time to a hogback that linked them with the neighboring mountain. Black Otter followed a game trail through a belt of pines so thick that it was dark as night at ground level. Still he pushed on, never slowing his pace until they emerged to find themselves entering a large meadow. Across the meadow, and down again through another belt of trees, they followed until on the opposite side of the second mountain. "Not far now," he told Bonnie as they waited for Lacey to catch up. "There," he said, and pointed to a spot across a narrow valley where a broad stream flowed down from the mountain. Bonnie and Finn strained to see what he was pointing to, but they could see nothing but more forest, although a thin ribbon of gray smoke wafted lazily up from the dark trees.

After descending to the valley floor, they were at last able to ride the horses, and Black Otter led them across to the base of the mountain where the stream turned and meandered in a crooked path down the valley. Only then did the three white strangers see the single tipi tucked back in a stand of fir trees. A woman working on a deer hide near the fire stopped and stood up when she saw the party approaching. Her first thought was to run, but then she saw that it was her husband leading the line of horses and mules. She then walked slowly out to meet them.

"Why do you bring the white people here?" Little

Flower asked, at once alarmed as she peered at the odd trio of strangers. She had heard the shooting on the far side of the mountains and had fervently prayed that Black Otter was nowhere near it.

Answering in his native tongue, he said, "They are the friends of Big Hunter. One of them, the man, is wounded. They were attacked by bad white men. Big Hunter stayed behind to let us get away." Big Hunter was the name Black Otter had given his white friend on the occasion when they first met, and Adam had given him a gift of one of the deer he had shot.

At once distressed, Little Flower could not help thinking of the danger she and Black Otter had faced when they had fled from their native land in Idaho Territory to escape the soldiers who wanted to drive them to the reservation. "Why do you bring these people here?" she repeated. "The bad white people will follow them to our camp, and we will have to run again."

"They are running from the bad people, just as we ran from the soldiers," Black Otter replied. "They mean us no harm, and they do not want to remain here in these mountains. I think Big Hunter is big medicine, and I will help him escape these people who would do him harm."

"She doesn't look too happy to see us," Bonnie remarked. The two women and Finn had been waiting while Black Otter explained the situation to his wife. Since no one of the three knew even a smattering of words in the Bannock tongue, they were not certain but what they might be ordered to move on immediately. "Do you understand any of that talk?" Bonnie asked.

"Not a word," Finn replied, just as the conversation

between husband and wife ended, and they both turned to face the three white people.

"Little Flower," Black Otter said, introducing the Indian woman. "She will give you food. Maybe Big Hunter be here soon."

"Who?" Lacey asked Bonnie.

"I guess that's his name for Adam," Bonnie replied. "Here, help me get Finn off his horse." She was ready to accept any hospitality offered, with or without a smile on Little Flower's face. With help from the two women, Finn dismounted and sat down near the fire to rest. The hazardous ride along the steep mountain slopes had taken a lot out of his tired body. "I'll break out that old coffeepot of yours," Bonnie told him. "I doubt if these folks have any."

It was a rugged trail Adam followed, making him wonder if he had not lost it in several places when it led him across wide areas of solid rock where there were no tracks. Remembering Black Otter's directions to his camp, he wondered why it was necessary to keep climbing up the mountain instead of circling it lower toward the base. The question was answered, however, whenever he emerged from the belts of pines to reveal sheer cliffs that stood over deep canyons. Though difficult to travel, the barren mountaintops presented any number of places to wait in ambush for anyone following him. With that in mind, and hoping to stop his pursuers before they could catch up to Finn and the women, he kept an eye out for the best choice for ambush. When he came across an outcropping of rocks that were broad enough to conceal his horse and give him an unobstructed field of fire, he decided that he would find no better. So he dismounted and led his horse behind the wall of rocks. Drawing his rifle from the saddle sling, he selected a protected spot to await his pursuers, thinking they should not be far behind. The time ticked slowly by with no sign of the three outlaws. Still he remained there for a couple of hours before coming to the opinion that they must not have realized that he had withdrawn from the camp. They had evidently given up on continuing up the stream to his camp, and consequentially, did not follow his and Black Otter's trail out of the camp. Maybe they had stopped to take possession of the six extra horses. It puzzled him, for it seemed unlikely that the three had given up and quit the chase, but it was something to hope for. Finally, he decided they had. Looking up at the midday sun, he continued on his way, thinking that it might not be wise to let the sun go down and catch him still high up on the mountain.

Leaving the expanse of rock, he came upon a broad meadow and sighted a deep gully that appeared to lead down toward the pines again. It looked to be a reasonable way down the mountain, so he decided to take it. Much to his surprise, he discovered a trail of hoofprints leading into the mouth of the gully. *Dumb luck,* he thought. The gulch led him to a hogback leading to the next mountain. By the time he found his way to the valley and Black Otter's camp, the afternoon was wearing away.

Seldom taking her eyes off the open valley they had crossed to get to Black Otter's camp, Lacey sat drinking a cup of the coffee Bonnie had made. They had eaten some of the venison that Little Flower had dried before, and while not yet exhibiting cordiality, at least the Indian woman no longer looked at her with a frown etched in her bronze features. Lacey could not blame her for feeling threatened. She would in her place. She glanced away from the valley for a few moments to look at Bonnie. Her sister in the ancient profession never seemed timid in any circumstance, and was already in the process of taking over the camp. She had dived right in with preparing food for them, making coffee, roasting strips of deer meat that Little Flower had provided. Lacey wondered if Bonnie was as fearless as she purveyed. At that moment, Bonnie looked up to meet her gaze and smiled. Then her eyes suddenly opened wide and she exclaimed, "Adam!" They all turned to discover the solitary rider coming across the valley floor. Black Otter immediately grabbed his bow, but there was no mistaking the bold figure riding the bay gelding.

Lacey dropped her cup, spilling the coffee in the sand, as she jumped to her feet and ran to meet him. Bonnie stood up, but remained by Finn's side. *That little girl is working herself up for a big disappointment*, she thought. As far as she could tell, Adam had shown no particular interest in Lacey beyond the concern he might feel for any vulnerable woman. But Lacey was becoming more and more dependent upon their tall rescuer, and Bonnie feared the girl might be interpreting his concern as deeper feelings for her. After all, Jake had planned to carry her away from the evils of Bannack, and Adam seemed to be taking his brother's place. *I hope I'm wrong about this*, she thought, fearing that a second disappointment might be too much for the insecure girl to bear.

"Well, I see you folks got here all right," Adam said to Lacey when she ran up to walk beside his stirrup.

"I was worried about you, Adam," Lacey said. "You were gone so long."

"That's a fact," Finn called out. "We're all glad you showed up. Thought you mighta got into a little trouble."

Adam stepped down. Patting Lacey gently on the shoulder, he told her, "No need to worry about me. If somethin' happens to me, you've still got Bonnie and Finn to get you outta here." To Finn, he said, "No trouble—I waited awhile back up on the mountain for those three fellows to show up, but they never did. I think they musta gave up."

"That don't hardly figure, does it?" Finn replied, thinking of the amount of gold loaded in the ten bags, of which only he knew the real value. "I ain't sure we're done with them yet."

"Me, either," Adam said, "so let's get you ready to ride and get on out of these mountains." He turned to Black Otter then. The Bannock warrior was standing, waiting to introduce his wife. "Pleased to meet you, ma'am," Adam said in response to her curt nod, at once sensing a slight hostility in her manner. *Uh-oh*, he thought, *we got Black Otter in trouble with his missus.* Thinking there was no way he could blame her for her attitude, he told Black Otter that he intended to leave right away for the Madison Valley. "I don't wanna bring any more trouble to you and your wife," he said.

"I help you fight," Black Otter said.

"You've already helped me, my friend, and I thank you and Little Flower again, but I don't wanna bring those murderers down on your camp."

"Stay one night," Black Otter insisted. "Rest, rest horses, go in the morning."

"All right, we'll leave in the mornin'," Adam finally said, much to his companions' relief. He pulled his saddle off the bay and led the gelding down near the water to graze with the other horses and Finn's mules.

"Damn!" Cruz swore loudly. "There ain't nothin' but one cliff after another on this mountain." They had ridden almost halfway around the mountain, and tried climbing up several different ravines that looked to have promise, only to be turned back by a cliff, or a rock ledge. "You're one helluva Injun scout," he said sarcastically.

"Well, I ain't got no way of knowin' what's at the end of a gulch if I ain't ever been up it before," Red Blanket replied. "It ain't got nothin' to do with scoutin'."

"This ain't gettin' us nowhere," Seeger complained. "We might as well go on back and try it up that stream again. They mighta pulled outta that camp by now— mighta come down that stream as soon as we left."

Seeger's comments caused Cruz to hesitate, thinking that he might be right, and the thought of being snookered by the hired gun and his whores was enough to bring his blood to a boil. He was reaching the point where he was ready to follow Seeger's suggestion and go back to the stream below the waterfall, when they came to the hogback that linked the two mountains.

Red Blanket stared up at the trees that covered the high ridge between the two mountains for a few minutes before declaring, "We can ride up that ridge. That mountain ain't so steep on this side. We might be able to go up it, and go round it, and come out above their camp."

His suggestion sounded as if it entailed a lot of hard

work to take the horses up the mountain, but it seemed a reasonable approach to attack the fugitives' camp from above. And no one had any better solution to their problem, so Cruz said, "What the hell? Let's go. There better be a helluva lot of gold up there," he added, as Red Blanket led out.

As Red Blanket had predicted, the climb up the hogback was steep, but not a hard climb for their horses. "We're gonna have to get off the horses and walk up the back of that mountain," Red Blanket advised when they had reached the top of the ridge. He stepped down from the saddle and started to lead his horse back up the slope, but was stopped abruptly by something he saw in the pine straw. "Hold on!" he exclaimed, and held up his hand to halt Cruz and Seeger behind him.

"What is it?" Seeger asked.

"Wait a minute," Red Blanket replied impatiently while he knelt down to examine the floor of the pine forest. Crawling along on his hands and knees, he suddenly let out a chuckle. When Cruz, equally impatient, asked what he had found, Red Blanket got to his feet to announce his discovery. "This oughta tickle you. Them folks has already left that camp. They're on the run." He pointed over Cruz's shoulder. "They came down off that mountain and crossed over this hogback." He turned to point again. "And went yonder way."

This sparked Cruz's and Seeger's interest immediately. "How do you know it was them?" Seeger asked.

"Who else would it be?" Red Blanket replied. "Ain't no doubt, anyway. The way this straw is tore up, it was more'n one or two horses come through here, and it weren't long ago."

"How long?" Cruz wanted to know.

"Hell, I don't know," Red Blanket responded, "not long. I'm an Injun. I ain't no damn fortune-teller, but we can't be that far behind 'em."

Once again, Cruz's mind was working on the possibility of acquiring a large amount of gold, and now it was out in the open. Plummer had said he knew exactly how much there was, but maybe Plummer was bluffing. The thought of capturing Finn's treasure with just the three of them to know how much was really there was cause to consider all the options available. The immediate priority was to overtake the fugitives and take possession of the gold. After that was accomplished, he could take the time to decide the best way to handle the situation, and whether or not he had further need of Seeger and Red Blanket. "Let's go get 'em, boys," he finally exclaimed. "Lead out, Red Blanket, and mind you don't lead us into no ambush."

The first shot came after they had eaten a supper of more venison with some pan bread that Bonnie had made with some of Finn's flour. The bullet found a victim in the form of Lacey Brewer as the young girl passed before the fire, bringing the coffeepot to fill Adam's cup. She issued no more than a whimper before crumpling to the ground with a .44 slug in her stomach. That shot was followed by a volley of rifle fire that swept the camp, sending the fugitives to the ground to seek cover, and Adam scrambling to drag Lacey out of the firelight. Amid the chaos that ensued, he heard Little Flower scream in fear and Bonnie yell Lacey's name. There was no time to see what Finn and Black Otter were doing. Adam had to assume they were taking cover to repel the attack. He pulled Lacey back in the shadows where he had dumped his saddle, and drew his rifle from the sling. He had to take a moment then to try to see where the shots were coming from and how close they were before he could give Lacey his attention. "Lie quiet," he said softly. "I'll be right back." He rolled over several times and inched his way up to a low mound close to the edge of the stream, and waited for the next volley. It came in less than a few seconds, and he immediately sent an answering series of shots toward the muzzle flashes. A few yards away, he heard the distinct sound of Bonnie's carbine. After another moment, the solid sound of Finn's rifle sang out. "Lacey's hit!" Adam called out. "Anybody else?"

"We're all right," Bonnie yelled. "I don't know about Black Otter and Little Flower. Where's Lacey?"

"She's over by my saddle," Adam answered. "I'm goin' back to her now. Keep your eyes peeled." He crawled back to the wounded girl.

"Adam," Lacey cried when he returned to her side, her voice pitiful and frightened. "It hurts bad, Adam."

"Where are you hit?" he asked. "Oh, Lord," he blurted immediately after, when he saw the dark stain spreading rapidly on her shirt. Then, afraid that he might have frightened her, he quickly tried to reassure her. "You're gonna be all right. I know it hurts, but you'll be all right." Even as he said it, he knew her chances were not good. There was nothing he could do to help her.

There was a lull in the shooting and a few seconds later, Bonnie crawled over to join them. "How bad is it, honey?" she asked Lacey.

"It hurts," Lacey whimpered.

Bonnie looked at Adam and he shook his head, telling her what she had feared. Then, seeing Lacey's bloody shirt, she understood. Lacey was gut-shot and bleeding internally as well as soaking her shirt. She put her carbine down and put her arms around the dying girl, holding her close to comfort her. Speaking quietly to Adam, she said, "You'd better keep your eye on the others."

He nodded, then looked again at Lacey. It was obvious that the young girl was fading fast, and it grieved him to see her suffer so, but he felt helpless to do anything that might make it easier for her. The shooting from the valley floor started anew and he told Bonnie he was going to go back to the bank of the stream where he had a better chance of a lucky shot.

Slipping in and out of consciousness, Lacey was fighting to live and she clutched Adam's wrist as he started to leave. "Don't leave me, Adam," she pleaded feebly. Her words were weak and slurred as the life drained out of her body. "I'd have made you a good wife, Adam."

Startled by her dying statement, he didn't know how to respond, but he did not want to hurt her feelings. "I know you would, Lacey. You'da made any man a fine wife." A faint smile parted her lips, she sighed softly, and she was gone. Stunned for a moment, Adam felt his soul filled with rage for the useless killing of the young innocent girl. She had been an easy target, silhouetted against the firelight, so they killed her. It didn't matter that she was no threat to them. They just took the easy shot.

"Adam, you're hurting me."

In his anger over the unjust murder, he hadn't realized that he had grabbed Bonnie's arm, and the powerful grip of his hand had cut off the circulation. He released her immediately. "I'm sorry. I didn't think what I was doin'."

"I know," she said softly, ignoring the random shots that still snapped across the stream, tearing holes in Little Flower's tipi. "It's not your fault. There wasn't anything you could have done to save her life." Her words were unusually gentle, not at all her normal brashness. "The rest of us need you now. If we don't respond to their attack, they're gonna ride right in here and kill us all. Lacey's gone and it ain't your fault."

He heard what she was saying, but he could not discard the guilt he felt for Lacey's death. He had told her he would take her home with him. Had he not, she would still be in Bannack, unhappy maybe, but alive. He hoped that Jake might be there to take her hand and lead her across that dark river into the next world, whatever that was. As for himself, he had had enough. He was tired of running, chased by godless outlaws who preyed upon the innocent, like Lacey—and Finn—and Black Otter. Not only was he guilty of Lacey's death, but he had brought the murderers down on the innocent Indian couple. At that moment, he decided that he was no longer going to run from these gangs of outlaws. It was time for them to pay for their sins against decent folks.

Once his decision was made, a calmness came over him, and when he looked at Bonnie's terrified eyes, he realized that she was frightened by this intense episode that had seemed to consume him. Once again, his somber demeanor returned as he told her what she should do. "Leave Lacey for now. Crawl back over there with your carbine and help Finn throw some shots at the muzzle flashes when you see 'em."

"What are you gonna do?" Bonnie asked, somewhat relieved to see his usual sober self return.

"I'm gonna rout those bastards outta there," he said. "You and Finn keep your heads down." With that, he rolled over the edge of the bank and disappeared into the darkness.

"Wait!" she cried, but he was already gone. *Oh, shit,* she thought, and scrambled off to tell Finn that they were alone. When she reached him, where he had taken cover behind a sizable tree, she gave him the news that Adam was out there somewhere in the darkness, and the two of them were going to have to defend the camp.

"Three of us," Finn corrected her. "I told Black Otter to take one of those extra rifles off the packhorse. He wasn't doin' much good shootin' all his arrows into a dark sky."

Ignoring the chilling water that embraced his legs, Adam made his way across the swiftly running stream. When he reached the other side, he silently climbed onto the bank and knelt in the fir trees to listen and watch for the muzzle flashes again. His wait was not long, for the three outlaws were not trying to conserve their cartridges. His plan was to flank the attackers, and once he pinpointed their position, he began to work his way across the narrow valley, stopping every dozen yards or so to watch and listen. The muzzle flashes told him that the outlaws were not moving and had probably found good protection to shoot from. There was no moon yet and the valley was too dark to determine their exact position, so the flashes were all he had to go on. Foremost in his mind was to get to them before they decided to move on the camp. He tried to recall a picture of the valley and how the stream cut through the firs, but had to reproach himself for not paying enough attention to that detail when he rode into Black Otter's camp earlier. When he reached a point directly on the flank of the shooters, he started inching his way forward in an attempt to get closer. Even when he was within a reasonable range for his rifle, he still could not make out individual targets. The moonless night and the dense stand of fir trees made it almost impossible to see distinct figures. There was no alternative but to wait for a clear shot, for he wanted to make every shot count. His intent was not merely to chase Lacey's killers away; he had made up his mind to eliminate them from the earth. So he waited.

"How long are we gonna keep this up?" Seeger yelled over to Cruz. "So far, we ain't done nothin' but use up over half the cartridges I've got left."

". . . and shot one whore." Red Blanket finished the statement for him, with a little chuckle. At that distance, they couldn't tell which prostitute had been the victim, but she was clearly identifiable as a woman.

"Hell, it was a good shot," Seeger replied in defense. "I just hope it was that salty old bitch and not the young one. We might wanna save her for a little while." Getting back to his question, he asked, "How 'bout it, Cruz, you figurin' on workin' in closer to see if we can't go ahead and take that camp?"

"I reckon that's what we came here to do, weren't it?" Cruz answered, but he was still hesitant about rushing into the camp with the miners' hired gun waiting for just such a move. "I'd feel a heap better if I knew exactly where that stud horse with the Henry rifle is." It occurred to him then that he had not heard the distinctive sound of the Henry for a while, and it gave him pause to wonder why. "You know, that son of a bitch might be thinkin' about—" That was as far as he got before he heard the solid thump of a .44 slug impacting with flesh and bones, followed almost immediately by the sharp crack of the Henry. He turned to see Red Blanket in the small open space between the outlaws and the trees where their horses were tied. The opening in the trees was no bigger than three paces across, but the Indian had been caught in the middle of it while on his way to get more cartridges from his saddlebags. While Cruz gaped, stunned by the sudden attack, Red Blanket uttered not a sound, but staggered toward a tree, where he slid to the ground and slowly keeled over, dead by all appearances.

"Cruz!" Seeger shouted. "We got to get outta here! They've snuck around us!"

"I know it!" Cruz yelled back. "They got Red Blanket. It's that damn killer," he said, for there was no doubt who the shooter was.

"You see him?"

"No," Cruz answered, "but he's off to the right somewhere. I'm pretty sure that's where the shot came from."

"We got to get outta here," Seeger repeated frantically.

"I know it, damn it," Cruz said, as anxious to move as Seeger, but leery of exposing himself even for a moment, as Red Blanket had, and giving the stalker another open shot. There had been only that one shot from somewhere out in the dark valley, which suggested to Cruz that the killer was waiting for the next person to make a mistake. "We've got to be careful, though. Can you get to the horses without crossin' that space where Red Blanket is?" The rifle fire from the camp across the stream was now all but ignored since the real danger was clearly on their flank.

"I don't know, maybe, but I ain't too anxious to try," Seeger replied. "Did you see where the shot came from?"

"No, damn it, somewhere out to the right, most likely in that stand of trees yonder. I'll lay down enough fire to keep his head down, so you can make a run for the horses. All right?"

Seeger wasn't keen on the idea that he should be the one taking that chance, but he knew there was no future in sitting there waiting for the rifleman to pick him off, so he decided to make a run for it. "All right," he responded. "Start shootin'."

Cruz opened up with his repeating rifle, firing as fast as he could pull the trigger and cock it again. Sending his shots toward the stand of trees he had mentioned, he shifted his aim back and forth across the shadowy clump of trees. It had the effect he had intended, for Seeger sprinted across the gap in the trees without a return shot being fired. Grabbing the reins of the horses, he led them back to Cruz, using their bodies as his cover. "Come on!" he exclaimed to Cruz as soon as he was back in the trees. There was no need to repeat it, for Cruz was running to meet him. As quickly as two frightened men could, they jumped in their saddles and galloped off through the firs, toward the mouth of the canyon. Almost ready to celebrate a clean getaway, Seeger suddenly yelped in pain as a rifle slug caught him behind the shoulder.

Hearing the shot that hit Seeger, Cruz flailed his horse mercilessly as the two would-be assassins charged recklessly through the firs that bordered the creek.

Across the creek they splashed, through a bank of berry bushes, and down the valley floor, demanding all their horses could give. Not until they had ridden the length of the valley and come to the pass that led to the broad river valley beyond did they let up on the laboring horses, and then only because to continue at that pace the horses might founder. It was then that Cruz learned for certain that the shot he had heard when they fled had hit Seeger. "Damn the luck," he remarked when he saw Seeger favoring his left arm and his blood-soaked sleeve. "How bad is it?" He looked behind them, peering in the darkness, expecting to see the gunman giving chase.

"I don't know," Seeger answered. "It ain't that bad, I reckon, just hurts like hell." He was cautious not to let on how bad it really felt, afraid that Cruz might be inclined to leave him to fend for himself.

"That son of a bitch," Cruz muttered, talking primarily to himself. "Every time we run up against him, one of us gets shot." Cruz had never been a timid man in the face of most any kind of confrontation with lawmen or outlaws, but there was something eerie about the mysterious gun hand the miners of Bannack had supposedly brought in to clean out the outlaw gangs. He thought back on the events that had happened, and the number of gang members who had been killed, since this stranger with the wide shoulders and the Henry rifle had come to the territory. It was almost as if the man was not human, and Cruz did not want to admit it to himself, but for the first time in his life, he felt fear. And the inclination to run had never been stronger, even though he would pass it off as simply being cautious.

Seeger winced in pain when he turned in the saddle to study their back trail. "I don't think he came after us," he said. "I think he was on foot."

"Maybe," Cruz allowed, thinking back. "He'da had to be to get that close on us without us or our horses hearin' him."

"We're gonna have to let these horses rest, else we're gonna be on foot, too," Seeger said. His real concern, however, was more for his wounded shoulder, and the feeling that he had to rest for a while and try to see what he could do to take care of it.

"I reckon you're right," Cruz agreed, and immediately looked around him for a likely spot. "Yonder," he said, pointing to a crook in the stream where it entered the pass. "We can see him comin' for a pretty good ways, even in the dark." When Seeger expressed agreement, Cruz said, "Lead out and I'll follow you." He reined his horse back to let Seeger go before him, with another thought in mind. He wanted to take a closer look at his partner and how the wounded shoulder was affecting him. As they walked the tired horses toward the stream, Cruz took note of the way Seeger was favoring his shoulder, with his arm dangling limp at his side. He had no intention of hanging back to take care of a severely wounded man while there was the possibility that a deadly killer was on his trail. Thoughts of the gold dust supposedly in Finn's packs had been lost in the past half hour, replaced with an image of the sinister hunter stalking him. *We don't even know for sure that old bastard has any gold worth going after*, he thought. "What?" he asked, realizing then that Seeger had asked a question.

"I said are we still goin' after that gold? 'Cause if we

are, I'm gonna need to take care of this shoulder." He was still trying to downplay the seriousness of the wound. In reality, he wanted nothing more to do with the man traveling with Michael Finn.

"I'm tired of chasin' after those folks," Cruz complained. "I don't think that old man has any gold, anyway. I think Plummer sent us on a wild-goose chase. Ain't nobody ever seen any of that gold. I believe it's just a setup to draw us in, so that damned gun hand can kill off some more of us."

That was what Seeger wanted to hear. "By God, I think you're right. We've done our part in Plummer's little game. Somebody else can chase all over these mountains lookin' to get a lead bullet in the chest for their trouble. Hell, me and you can rest up a spell and head on back." He pointed to a low ridge before the base of the mountain pass. "We can set us up a camp on that ridge, and see everythin' moving in this valley behind us, long before they get close. Whaddaya say, Cruz? To tell you the truth, this shoulder needs a little attention. It won't stop bleedin'."

Cruz thought about it for a moment. He was not inclined to sit in one spot and wait for death to come calling on him. But they had damn near killed their horses in their panic to escape, so it was in their best interest to let them recover before moving on. What about the man they feared? Why would he come after them? He had been successful in running them off; there was no reason to believe he would do anything beyond starting back out to wherever he was headed in the first place. *Come to think of it*, he thought, *he was the one doing the running all along.* "All right," he said, "we'll stop here for the night and see if your shoulder can't get a little better."

Not sure if he had hit anything with his last shot at the fleeing riders, Adam walked into the stand of firs to confirm the kill he was confident of. He found Red Blanket lying on his side at the base of a tree. The fiery anger that had consumed him when he had knelt beside the dying girl had been replaced by an impassive calm that created a sober, businesslike approach to the task he had set for himself. He reached down and rolled the body over on its back, curious to get a look at the man who had sought to kill him and his party. Feeling no emotion beyond what one would feel for the extermination of a rat, he unbuckled the man's cartridge belt and pulled it off his body. He picked up the weapon he saw on the ground near the tree, a Spencer carbine, then walked to the edge of the trees to peer off into the darkness after the two remaining outlaws. He would go after them, but first he must see to the members of his party to make sure they were all right.

Several minutes had passed since the last shots fired from across the stream, and Finn worried that their adversaries might be creeping up close to their camp. He had heard the one shot from off to the side, and he was pretty sure it was from Adam's Henry rifle, but there was still the chance that the outlaws might even now be approaching in the darkness. Thinking along the same lines, Bonnie moved closer to him and whispered, "Whaddaya think? Do you think they're trying to get behind us?" When Finn confessed that he didn't know, but they should keep a sharp eye for whatever they were trying, she assured him that she was going to shoot at the first movement she saw. Luckily for Adam, they heard him call out moments later.

"Finn, hold your fire. They're gone. I'm comin' in."

Exhaling a great sigh of relief, Finn called back, "Come on in, Adam." In a few minutes, he emerged from the darkness, directly in front of them, crossed the stream, and walked into the camp leading two horses. Still wet from his thighs down to his toes, he went to the fire and sat down to remove his boots.

Black Otter moved to stand over him. "Bad men gone?"

"Yep, they're gone," Adam answered. "One of 'em's dead. One of the other two might be wounded. I don't know for sure, but I don't think they'll be back, at least not tonight. I'm sorry I brought this to your camp. I hope Little Flower is all right."

Black Otter nodded. "I think I move camp. Too easy to find."

"It wouldn'ta been if I hadn't led 'em right to it," Adam said. "I'll be goin' after them at first light. I want to make you a gift of those two horses. One of them, the packhorse, might have some supplies you can use." He hoped that the gift might help pay for the trouble he had brought Black Otter's way. The Bannock warrior eagerly accepted the gifts.

Adam glanced over at the spot near his saddle where Bonnie and Little Flower were bending over Lacey's body, and the painful thought that he had been responsible for her death caused a deep frown of guilt to appear on his brow. He motioned toward the Spencer and cartridge belt lying on the ground beside him. "Take the carbine, too. You need more than a bow if you're gonna stay holed up in these mountains." Again, Black Otter accepted the gifts gratefully. He was beginning to think he had been wise to befriend Big Hunter and his friends, for now he had horses and weapons when, before, he had neither.

"Did I hear you say you're goin' after them?" Finn asked. "I thought that since you've chased them away, maybe we'd be moving on in the mornin'—put some distance between us and them."

"I'll be goin' after them at first light," Adam repeated.

"Maybe they've had enough," Finn said, strongly preferring Adam's presence with him and Bonnie.

"Maybe," Adam allowed somberly, "but there's one way to make sure. Whether they're plannin' to come back or not, they need to settle up for what they did to Lacey." Although he made no further comment, Finn's discontent was obvious, so Adam continued. "You and Bonnie can head outta the mountains in the mornin', or you can wait here with Black Otter and Little Flower till I get back. But I'm goin' after those two. I'm gonna make sure they don't cause us, or anybody else, any more trouble."

Finn could see there was no room for discussion on the issue. "Well, I guess my choices are down to one, since I don't know where the hell I'm goin' without you to lead me, now, do I?" He didn't have to mention the primary reason for riding with Adam, for protection for him and his gold.

"I reckon that is a minor detail," Adam replied, almost smiling. Finn had never expressed what his plans were, if any, beyond making it to the Triple-B. For that matter, neither had Bonnie. "That shoulder could stand another day or so of rest, anyway," Adam said.

"Maybe you're right about that, although I can feel I'm gettin' my strength back. Bonnie and I will take care of Lacey while you're gone."

Moving to join them by the fire, Bonnie was in time to hear Finn's comment. "I guess you're going to chase after those two murderers now."

"I am," Adam answered emphatically, expecting some objection from the crusty prostitute.

"I expected as much," she said, to his surprise. "Don't take too long doing it. Finn and I will take care of things here till you get back." She glanced at Black Otter, who had stood silently, listening to their discussion. "If that's all right with Black Otter and Little Flower."

"You are welcome here," Black Otter said. Then with a smile, he added, "Woman shoot gun good."

It was settled, then. Both Finn and Bonnie were smart enough to know that they were extremely vulnerable if they tried to go on without Adam. Not only was he their primary protection, but he was their guide to his father's ranch in the Gallatin Valley. Neither of the two had made any plans beyond that, but to both it seemed to mean their safety.

Chapter 12

The morning was chilly with a light frost that caused the valley to glisten when the sun found its way down between the towering mountains on either side of him. Earlier Adam had returned to the gap in the firs where he had found Red Blanket's body the night before, so he could track the other two outlaws from that starting point. In the light of day, the Crow Indian's face retained the startled expression of shock the man had experienced at the moment of impact. Hardened by the morning frost on skin and whiskers, the face looked unreal, more like that of a replica of a once living person.

Their trail was not hard to find, leading across the stream and heading straight down the canyon. The swath of broken berry bushes on the opposite bank bore testimony to their panic to escape. Holding the bay to a brisk walk, he kept his eyes trained on the tracks left by the two horses until he felt certain they would not stray from the direction first started toward the far end of the canyon. Then he let the bay settle into a lope for a while until the horse showed signs of needing rest. The routine was repeated over and over as he followed the clear tracks.

"You ain't lookin' any too good," Cruz commented to his wounded partner. Seeger opened his eyes to find the gruff outlaw standing over him. "Weren't sure you wasn't dead."

"Well, I ain't," Seeger replied, cranky from the short fits of sleep he had managed to snatch from the seemingly endless night. He winced with pain when he rolled over on his side. "I ain't feelin' too good," he said. "That damn bullet musta left some poison in there. You reckon you oughta take a look at it?"

"What for?" Cruz replied. "I ain't no doctor. Wouldn't be much use for me to look at it." He studied his partner's face for a long moment before asking, "Can you stay on a horse?"

"Oh, hell yeah," Seeger said. "Ain't nowhere near that bad. I can ride. Don't you worry none about that."

Cruz continued to study the wounded man while he made judgment on whether Seeger believed what he said, or was just reacting out of fear that Cruz might run off and leave him. "You sure as hell don't look like you're ready to ride," he said. "Lemme take a look at that wound." He stooped down and tore Seeger's shirt where the bullet had entered behind his shoulder, exposing the red swollen bullet hole. "Damn," he exhaled, "it's all puffy and tender lookin'." He poked a finger on the skin of the shoulder, swollen tight as a drum. Seeger winced with pain at the touch. Cruz stood up again. "Like I said, I ain't no doctor, but that wound looks pretty damn bad. You can rest here for a couple more hours and then we'll take a look at it."

"And then what?" Seeger demanded. "What if it ain't no better? What if it's worse?"

"We'll just see then," Cruz replied. "You just lie back and rest it up some. I'd make us some coffee if we hadn't run off and left the damn packhorse back yonder."

"I can ride," Seeger insisted. "If we had to go right now, I could ride, so don't go gettin' no notions about running off and leavin' me."

"Why, hell, I wouldn't have no reason to do that," Cruz assured him. "No, sir-ree, I ain't gonna leave you." He had already made up his mind that he would, however, if Seeger didn't show enough improvement to carry on. There was no guarantee that the sinister rifleman would not come after them, so Cruz wasn't willing to stay in the area for long. Besides that, they were without even basic supplies, not even a coffeepot, and he didn't care much for living off what he could hunt. He would make his decision in a couple of hours, he decided. However, the time came sooner than he expected.

At first it was just a small dot in the distance, at the far end of the long canyon. Cruz caught a glimpse of it and started to look away, but something drew his eye back to look at it again. He realized then that it was moving, so he kept his gaze focused upon it to see if it was a deer, or an elk maybe. As it continued to grow, he realized it was coming toward them. "What the hell . . . ?" he murmured, and picked up his rifle.

"What is it?" Seeger wanted to know.

"Can't tell yet," Cruz answered as he stepped up on a rock ledge to try to get a better look. "Might be supper comin' to us, if it keeps comin' this way," he said, although the object was moving at a rate too steady to be a casually grazing animal. He continued to watch until the object began to take form as the distance decreased. "Oh, shit!" he exclaimed when he realized that what he had hoped was an elk was a man on a horse, and there was no doubt in his mind what man it had to be.

"What?" Seeger demanded. "Cruz, whaddaya see?" But Cruz's mind was too busy to answer Seeger's questions. He continued to stare down the narrow valley, hoping that the rider might pass them by, hoping it was not who it had to be.

Impatient for an answer, Seeger struggled to his knees, using his good arm for support, in an effort to get a look at whatever had left Cruz speechless. "It's that son of a bitch that shot Red Blanket," he blurted when he sighted the rider. "He's comin' after us!"

"He's got a ways to go before he comes to that crook where we left the stream and cut up this way to this ridge," Cruz said hopefully. "He'll most likely keep right on goin' out in the river valley."

Seeger was not that optimistic about their chances. "Even if he does see where we turned up to this ridge, we got the high ground. Ain't that right, Cruz? And there's two of us." He was talking faster and faster, his fear showing through no matter how he tried to hide it. "I mean, hell, he ain't but one man. Right, Cruz?"

Cruz didn't answer. His attention was wholly on the rider sitting tall in the saddle, riding steadily along the bank of the stream. "Damn," he finally uttered when, approaching the crook in the stream, the rider reined his horse back and studied the tracks left there. Then he turned and looked toward the ridge. "Damn!" This time it was an involuntary exclamation, for even though the rider was over a quarter of a mile away, it seemed to Cruz that he had looked straight at him. He jerked back from the ledge and knelt once more, continuing to stare, when without hesitation, the rider turned his horse toward the ridge. "Damn," Cruz uttered for the third time, "he's comin' right at us."

In a panic to stop the relentless hunter, Cruz cocked his rifle and aimed a shot at the rider. The range was too much for the accuracy of the Spencer carbine, and the shot kicked up dirt far wide of the target. The grim stalker never flinched, even after a second and third shot, but continued to ride directly toward the ridge. The seeming indifference of the man to his shots served to unnerve Cruz to the point of outright terror. It was as if the man was a ghost rider from the supernatural world, for he showed no fear of Cruz's rifle. He became convinced that to stay there and continue to shoot at the grim avenger would profit him nothing but his own demise.

Locked in a moment of frightened confusion, he had to decide what to do. Flight was the only option his mind could entertain, and he acted quickly to put it into action. "He's comin' our way!" he yelled to Seeger. "We need to move offa this ridge!" He ran to his horse while his confused partner sat stunned and helpless. "I'll saddle the horses," Cruz said. "You just sit tight."

There was little choice for Seeger but to trust Cruz to take care of him. So while Cruz threw the saddle on his horse, Seeger tried to have a closer look at the approaching avenger for himself. Like Cruz, he didn't like the look of it. He looked back at his partner in time to see him step up in the saddle as soon as it was strapped on his horse. With no hesitation, not even a look in Seeger's direction, Cruz kicked his horse hard and charged over the back side of the ridge. "Cruz!" Seeger yelled, realizing that he had been left as a sacrifice, so that Cruz could save his skin. He snatched his pistol from his belt and shot at the yellow coward, but there was no real target as Cruz disappeared over the side of the ridge.

Faced with two choices, a showdown with the man reported to be a professional assassin, or a desperate attempt to escape, Seeger chose the latter. Forced to answer the command to save himself by the fear that raced through his veins, he willed his weakened body to get to his horse. And with a scream of pain, he picked up his saddle and threw it on the animal. Gritting his teeth against the searing agony, he tightened the cinch strap, causing a new trickle of blood to run down his arm to drip on the grass. With one final act of desperation, he lifted himself onto the stirrup and threw a leg over. Once over the side, he turned his horse away from the path Cruz had descended, in hopes that the assassin would choose to follow Cruz.

Keeping a wary eye on the rock ledge near the top of the ridge where the shots had come from, Adam became more cautious as he approached what he estimated to be reasonable range. The three wild shots told him that the shooter must have been firing to scare him away. By the sound, the weapon was a carbine, and surely the man using it knew the range was too far for the accuracy of that weapon. The lower part of the ridge wore a spotted apron of pines, and Adam figured if he could reach their cover, he could dismount and work his way up to the top on foot. He assumed the outlaws were waiting in ambush, to catch him in the open when he left the cover of the trees to climb to the top. For that reason, he was not surprised that there were no more shots when he galloped into the pines. *So far, so good*, he thought as he quickly drew his rifle from the saddle sling and dismounted. Then, to avoid the ambush he felt surely awaited him, he ran along the base of the ridge until coming to a narrow ravine some one hundred yards distant.

With his rifle held ready to fire, he climbed up the ravine, leaving the cover of the trees as he moved cautiously over the rocky upper third of the defile to a large boulder at the top. From there, he could sight along the crest of the ridge, but he could not spot his adversaries. Moving carefully a few yards at a time, he continued to stalk the rock ledge from which the shots had been fired. Still there were no more shots. Finally, after advancing to the ledge itself, he realized that he had been stalking an empty ridge. They were gone.

Angry to have wasted so much time, while the outlaws were putting distance between him and themselves, he began a search of the grassy meadow just below the ledge. From the look of it, the outlaws had camped there overnight. Judging by the tracks, the two horses had been tied to the limbs of a couple of stunted pines. Looking farther, he found tracks where the two had fled down the back side of the ridge, but if he could believe those tracks, they had gone in opposite directions. He puzzled over the fact for a few moments, because it would have made more sense to retain their two-to-one advantage. He went back to the place where the horses had been tied to have another look before he decided which of the two trails he was going to follow. "I'm wasting time," he decided aloud, and was about to start back down to fetch his horse, when he happened to notice a spotting of color on the grass blades at his feet. He paused and knelt to look closer. *Blood,* he thought. *So I did hit one of them last night! And he's still bleeding.* This didn't explain why the two men had obviously split up when they left the ridge, however. One thing seemed evident to him now: they were gambling on the fact that he could not chase both of them.

He faced several problems at this point. He had never seen either man close enough to be able to identify him, so he was dependent upon the tracks they left behind. If he could choose between them, he would follow the trail of the one who was not wounded, since the man with the wound might be easier to find later on. The problem with that, however—there was no way to tell which set of hoof tracks belonged to the wounded man. Undecided, he turned to look out over the back of the ridge in the directions each trail indicated. One would seem headed south, toward the broad river valley, the way they had originally come several days before. The other led straight down the backside of the ridge toward the mountain beyond. He stood there, unable to decide for a moment. Then he reached in his pocket and pulled out the one remaining twenty-dollar gold piece and flipped it up in the air. "Heads, it's the mountain—tails, it's the valley." It was heads. He went to get his horse.

"That son of a bitch," Seeger whined as he strained to stay in the saddle. The thought of the cowardly abandonment by his partner was the only thing keeping him upright in the saddle as his horse followed an old game trail up the mountain. He could feel the back of his shirt getting more and more soaked from the blood that had started to flow again. He needed a doctor, for he feared he might bleed to death before he had a chance to recover, and he desperately needed to recover so he could seek his revenge on Cruz. Knowing he was too weak to try to follow the double-crosser now, he had chosen to try to find a place to hide and heal. Now he began to fear that he was going to fall off his horse, so he knew he had to pick a place to rest soon.

He was suffering so much pain from his shoulder that he forgot that he had not eaten since the day before. Even as weak as he now was, food was not a priority at this moment in his life. *If I could just rest*, he thought, *then maybe the shoulder will begin to heal on its own. I could make it then.* It was the last thought he had before passing out and falling from his saddle. The jolt when he hit the ground was enough to jar him awake, but he knew he could not get himself back on his horse again. There was no other option open for him, so he crawled painfully over against a pine tree and sat waiting for whatever his fate might be. The foremost regret he had was not being able to settle the score with Cruz.

The trail Adam had selected to follow was not a difficult one. The outlaw had not taken pains to hide his flight. When he reached the foot of the mountain, he had taken a game trail that appeared to wind its way through the pines before gradually ascending toward the top. Upon coming to a sharp turn where the trail became quite steep and appeared to double back, he was stopped short by the discovery of a riderless horse standing on the narrow trail. His reaction was immediate as he slid quickly from the saddle, expecting gunshots coming his way. But there was nothing except the greeting nicker of the horse. Kneeling on one knee, he scanned the trees from left to right and back again, seeing no one. When he rose to his feet again, the snap of a .44 slug whistled a few inches from his ear, and he dived for cover beside the trail. It was not until two more shots were fired that he located the shooter. With his back propped against a tree at the turn of the narrow trail, a man sat slumped, his pistol in hand. Adam, astonished that his assailant had taken no pains to protect himself, immediately lifted his rifle and drove a slug into the bushwhacker's chest. The revolver fell from the man's hand.

It was obvious that the outlaw was finished, but Adam approached him with caution, lest he suddenly pick up his pistol and fire again. As before, when ending the life of one of the murderous outlaws who had killed his brother and the girl, Lacey, and sought to kill him, Adam felt no pity for the man now dying before him. He kicked the pistol lying on the ground out of reach, then stood gazing at the figure sprawled against the tree.

Seeger's eyes fluttered, then opened halfway. "I reckon my luck ran out," he uttered, his speech slurred and slow. "Why the hell didn't you go after Cruz instead of me? The son of a bitch deserves to die."

"Like you said, your luck ran out," Adam said somberly, then waited for a few moments when Seeger began to cough up the blood that was congesting his chest. "The other one's name is Cruz?" he asked.

Content to send death's messenger to even the score with the man who had left him to be killed, Seeger nodded, then said, "Bailey Cruz, heavyset feller, long hair down to his shoulders." The talking seemed to exhaust him, and his eyelids began to flutter again.

Adam could see that the man was taking his last breath. "Where can I find him?"

"O'Grady's maybe. Kill the son of a bitch." Those were his last words.

Adam stood over him a few moments longer. Seeger's eyes had suddenly opened wide just before he exhaled his last breath, causing Adam to wonder what the poor wretch saw at the moment of death. Whatever it was must not have been very pleasant, he decided, for it had left his face twisted into a mask of terror. Reminding himself then that he had no time to linger there, he took Seeger's guns and ammunition and put them on the horse still standing patiently in the path. Leading the dead man's horse, he rode back to pick up Cruz's trail, leaving Seeger to await the buzzards.

The trail that had angled down the back of the ridge pointed in the general direction of the river valley, south of the high mountains where Bonnie and Finn waited for his return. Not sure he hadn't lost it after coming upon a wide outcropping of rock, he thought of his brother. Jake could track as well as any Indian he'd ever met. *I need you here now,* he thought when finally he had to give up on looking for tracks on the rocky surface. Going strictly on a guess as to where the outlaw had headed, he was relieved to pick up the tracks again at the bank of a small stream where the man he now knew as Bailey Cruz had paused to let his horse drink. As the afternoon wore on, with the promise of evening to come shortly, Adam spurred the horses on,

knowing Cruz's lead might be too substantial to overcome. Darkness found him at the banks of the Ruby
River, where he was forced to end the chase until
morning.

After watering the horses, he rode downriver a
short distance to find a suitable campsite where he
could build a fire that would not be easily seen. A few
strips of deer jerky were all he could produce for his
supper, since he had not taken the time to pack many
supplies with him. He reprimanded himself severely
for not bringing his coffeepot, the one utensil that he
could never do without. Ignoring the angry growls
coming from his empty stomach, he settled down to
pass the night. Sleep didn't come easily, however. There
were too many things to sort out in his head. His single
demanding objective was to run Bailey Cruz to ground
and balance the ledger in that regard. But he could not
forget the obligation he had taken on for the safe deliv-
erance of Finn and Bonnie out of this territory and
safely to the Gallatin Valley. Torn between the contract
he had made with them and the determination to follow Cruz, he found it difficult to decide which was the
more important. Unable to make the decision, he put it
off until morning.

Morning brought rain. The storm clouds began to
form in the wee hours of the morning, pushing their
way toward the mountains. A little before daylight the
rain began to fall, and by the time he pulled his rain
slicker off his saddle and put it on, he was hit with a
pelting shower that lasted for over an hour. Concerned
for the effect it might have on the trail he must find, he
saddled the horses and hurried back upstream to find
the hoofprints that had led into the river were now

effectively erased by the rain. He was left with the discouraging fact that he knew only that Cruz had entered the river here, and not if he went straight across, or stayed in the water to leave the river upstream or downstream. Recalling his indecision of the night just passed, he said, "Well, I reckon my decision has been made for me." But to be sure, he rode a mile or so along the east bank, then crossed over and came back on the other side before finally turning the bay gelding back the way he had come. He would see Finn and Bonnie safely out of the mountains. Then he would hunt Bailey Cruz down. He knew his name, a vague description of him, and he knew at least one place where he might be found. He was not looking forward to a return visit to Virginia City, but that seemed to be where the trail led. It was extremely hard not to simply head there now, but he could not say how long it would take to track Cruz down once he got there. *Once I take care of Finn and Bonnie*, he thought, *then it won't matter how long it takes*. It was more than ten miles to the ridge where he had encountered Seeger. He still had more than half a day from there to Black Otter's camp, but he decided to try to make it before dark.

"Thank you," Bonnie Wells said politely when Little Flower placed a portion of freshly roasted venison before her. The Indian woman responded with a slight nod, her face devoid of expression. When Little Flower withdrew to seat herself on the opposite side of the fire, Bonnie looked at Finn and commented softly, "I think Mrs. Black Otter wishes we'd get the hell out of her home." There was no doubt that Little Flower felt threatened with the two white people in her camp.

From the first, she had been accommodating, but far less cordial than her husband.

"I don't doubt it," Finn replied. "It helped matters very little when those killers followed us here."

"Black Otter seems friendly enough," Bonnie said. "She could warm up a little bit. It ain't like we wanna be here."

Finn took a loud sip of the coffee Bonnie had made before commenting, "Black Otter counts it as good fortune. He gained horses and guns he didn't have before. All she gained was a couple of extra mouths to feed." He slurped his coffee loudly again and smacked his lips in approval. "We'll be pullin' outta here as soon as Adam gets back."

"He's been gone two days already," Bonnie fretted. "What if he doesn't come back? Then what in hell are we gonna do? I'm not planning on spending the winter in an Indian camp," she said, emphatically.

"He said he'd be back," Finn replied. "He's as good as his word. He'll be back." His statement was far more confident than his inner feelings. Finn had worked hard all his life with nothing to show for it, until the last few years. Hard work had finally paid off, for now he was a wealthy man. But his wealth was packed right there in a lone Indian's camp in ten canvas bags, no good to him or anyone else if he failed to transport it to someplace where it had value. Finally able to sneak his fortune out from under the watchful eyes of Sheriff Albert Ainsworth and his gang of outlaws in Bannack, he now found himself in a quandary. He was afraid to lead his mules out of these mountains without some formidable protection. The two gangs that had attacked them had been defeated, but there were still those many outlaws who constantly watched the roads in and out of Virginia City. So the past three nights, with Adam gone, were especially worrisome for him. The thought of starting out for Three Forks or Butte, leading his string of mules, loaded down with a fortune in gold dust, was one that offered nothing short of suicide. He was sure that Bonnie would stick with him. Where else was she to go? She was as spunky and tough as any woman he had ever met, but she was not enough protection against seasoned road agents. *I wish to hell Adam would show up*, he silently prayed.

"I hope you're right," Bonnie said, "because the nights are getting cold up here." She thought of another point that only served to worry the little Irishman further. "You know, you and I just invited ourselves along on this little journey as extra baggage. He was only going to take Lacey home with him, and that was just because he figured he owed it to his brother. He might decide he doesn't owe us a damn thing." It gave them something to think about. She paused, however, before saying more on the subject when she saw Black Otter get up from the fire, pick up his new Spencer carbine, and move quickly to the edge of the clearing. Fearing trouble, she grabbed her carbine and moved up beside him. "What is it?" she whispered.

"Big Hunter," Black Otter replied. A moment later, Adam hailed the camp. The Indian dropped his weapon to his side and walked out to meet him.

Bonnie remained where she stood, and when Finn walked up to join her, she asked, "Now, how in hell did he know that?"

Finn shrugged. "He's an Injun." He didn't care how the Indian knew; he just released a great sigh of relief.

A few seconds later, Adam appeared at the edge of the stream. Behind him, on a lead line, followed a string of seven saddled horses. "Well, I'll be damned," Finn muttered. "You went back for the horses."

"Figured I might as well," Adam replied, "since it looked like those three outlaws didn't have 'em—oughta be two more somewhere around the foot of that mountain." He turned to Black Otter then. "Can you gimme a hand with 'em? Half of 'em's yours."

The Bannock warrior was all smiles as he looked the horses over thoroughly. "You stay," he said to Adam, "make Black Otter rich man."

"Did you catch up with 'em?" Finn asked.

"One of 'em," Adam replied. "One of 'em got away." He glanced at the coffeepot seated in the coals of the fire. "Any coffee left in that pot?"

"A little," Bonnie answered. "I'll get it for you." She filled the cup she had been using and brought it to Adam. "I'll bet this is the only reason you came back here," she chided, knowing the big man's love for the bitter black brew.

"It's one of 'em," he admitted, "that's a fact."

Accustomed to Adam's inclination to save words, Finn pressed him for more details. With an indifferent shrug of his shoulders, Adam told them of his encounter with the two outlaws, resulting in the death of one of them while the other went free. "I'm goin' after him. I think I know where I can find him. His name's Bailey Cruz."

This immediately sparked Bonnie's interest. "Bailey Cruz," she echoed. "I know him. I saw him several times in O'Grady's Saloon." She shook her head in warning. "You'd best be careful if you're going after Cruz. I've heard he's put a lot of men in the ground." Her comment was not enough to dispel the expression of indifference on Adam's face, causing her to wonder if the man was devoid of feeling, or was it a lack of sense?

Finn's concern was for a different matter. "You're still goin' after this fellow, Cruz?"

The obvious distress in Finn's question prompted Adam to reassure him. "I'll see you and Bonnie outta here first. Then I'm goin' after Cruz." His statement brought another sigh of relief from Finn, and a smile to Bonnie's face.

Chapter 13

With Black Otter as their guide, the belabored party of fugitives from Henry Plummer's army of road agents crossed through the towering mountains that guarded the lone Bannock warrior's camp. When they finally left the eastern slopes, they found themselves in the broad Madison River Valley, approximately a day and a half below Three Forks. There they said good-bye to Black Otter, after expressing their appreciation for his help.

"Big Hunter good friend," Black Otter told Adam before turning back toward the mountains.

"Maybe I'll come back to visit with you sometime," Adam said while shaking the Indian's hand.

"Maybe," Black Otter said. "Have to look hard. Move camp now." He had already told Little Flower to prepare to take the tipi down in preparation for the move to a new location. His camp had been discovered by white men, so he could not risk staying there another season. He had gained much from his friend, but as

Little Flower had repeatedly warned him, "Big Hunter brings death with him." He said farewell to Finn and smiled at Bonnie. "Woman shoot gun like man." Then the Bannock warrior turned his newly acquired horse back toward the mountains. Sitting a single-rigged saddle, a rifle in the scabbard, and his bow slung on his back, he disappeared into the trees.

"We can ride down the river to Three Forks," Adam said, giving them an option, in case they had decided what they were going to do. "Or we can cross over and head toward my pa's place. It's a little farther, about three days, I expect, but you might feel a whole lot safer there."

There was no hesitation on the part of either Finn or Bonnie. "I'd prefer to go to your pa's place," Finn said.

"I'll go with the gold," Bonnie said, and winked at Finn.

They had approximately fifteen miles to reach the Madison, with enough daylight left to make it before dark, so Adam set out to the east across the valley. He figured they were far enough north of Virginia City to avoid trouble from Plummer's road agents, thanks to Black Otter leading them through the mountains. But he knew it would be difficult for Finn and Bonnie to find the Triple-B without him. It was difficult to get Bailey Cruz out of his mind, however. It was something he felt he had to do, and the sooner he had settled the issue, the sooner he would feel that he had done all he could to punish those who had murdered Jake and Lacey. His impatience did not go unnoticed by his two companions.

"You know, it ain't your fault Lacey got killed," Bonnie told him as they sat by their campfire on the east bank of the Madison. "She was just unlucky enough to be walking by the fire when those murderers sneaked up on us."

"I reckon I know that," Adam replied stoically, although not convincingly to Bonnie.

"Well, it's time you stopped blaming yourself," she said.

"I ain't blamin' nobody," he insisted, "but things won't be right as long as Bailey Cruz goes free." He knew that he couldn't explain to her the feeling of failure that hovered over him. His father had sent him to Bannack to bring his brother home. He had not only failed to do that, but he had also failed to bring the girl Lacey back, as Jake had intended to do. He was dreading the moment when he had to admit his failures to his father. He didn't know if killing Cruz would alleviate his feeling of defeat, but it would rid the world of an evil presence. That much he was certain of, so there was no use for Bonnie, or anyone else, to try to talk him out of going back to finish that piece of business.

All was peaceful during the night, but Adam awoke early, unable to sleep any longer, so he got up to revive the fire. As he moved quietly in the dark pocket of firs that surrounded their camp, he paused for a moment, unsure. At first glance, he thought someone was missing, for he saw only one blanket other than his own. Maybe, he thought, his eyes were playing tricks on him in the dark. With his hand on his revolver, he moved closer to the remaining blanket, thinking it belonged to Finn. He stopped short when he discovered two bodies wrapped inside two blankets and Bonnie snuggled up to Finn, her head nestled against his neck. Astonished, he could not suppress a grin. *Damned if she didn't do it. I never thought it was possible.*

Afraid he was going to laugh out loud, he stepped back and returned to the fire. Still grinning, he grabbed the coffeepot and went down the bank to fill it.

The coffee was boiling nosily when Adam heard a rustle of blankets. He glanced over in their direction. Although the light was still poor under the canopy of fir limbs, he could make out the one form suddenly separating into two. A few minutes later, Finn walked up closer to the fire. "Mornin'," he said.

"Mornin'," Adam returned. "Kinda cold last night. You sleep okay?"

"Well, I can't complain. It was a wee bit chilly, though."

"Maybe you oughta sleep a little closer to the fire," Adam said, enjoying the game. "I wonder how Bonnie slept."

"All right, I suppose. The woman can sleep with no trouble a'tall." Anxious to change the subject, he blurted, "Is that coffee done yet? I've a strong need for it this mornin'."

"I reckon," Adam said. "Yeah, it's about ready."

Bonnie was up a few minutes after that, but she walked up the river for a ways before joining the men at the fire. "I could eat a horse," she exclaimed when she knelt by the fire.

"Will some deer meat do?" Adam asked. "We're gonna need the horses." She cocked a wary eye at him, then favored him with a wicked grin. He knew. She could tell by his unusually cheerful demeanor. She shrugged her shoulders and helped herself to coffee. *She kept telling us she was going with the gold*, Adam thought.

Mose Stebbins leaned his pitchfork against the barn door and walked out to see if he recognized the riders approaching from the south. His eyes weren't as strong as they used to be, but the man sitting tall in the saddle looked like Adam. *By God,* he thought, *it's time you were getting home.* He started to hurry to the house to get Nathan, but decided to wait a moment longer, squinting in an effort to see Jake. "What the hell?" he blurted to himself. "Who the hell is that with him?" Mose could clearly see them now. There was a man with Adam, but it sure as hell wasn't Jake—and a woman—and they were leading horses and a string of mules! "Uh-oh," he whistled. This could only mean bad news. Shaken to action then, he ran toward the house, yelling, "Nathan, Nathan! Adam's come home!"

In a few short seconds, Nathan Blaine came out on the porch, at once searching in the direction Mose was frantically pointing. Like Mose, he was stopped for a moment when he saw the man and woman with his son, at once overtaken by a feeling of dread to hear what Adam was surely going to tell him. He remained standing at the top of the porch steps and waited until Adam reined his horse up just short of the steps.

"Pa," Adam said, greeting his father solemnly.

"Adam," was his father's simple return. It was unnecessary to ask, for Nathan could read the regret in his son's face.

Mose was not as adept at reading expressions. He required verbal explanations. "Did you find Jake?" he interrupted. "Who are these folks you brung with you?" He looked Finn and Bonnie over with a curious eye, taking special interest in the three mules on a line behind Finn's horse.

"Jake ain't comin' home," Adam stated simply. Nathan remained calm, his reaction only a slight twitch of his eye as he fought the emotion that Adam knew was tearing at his insides. He turned his head toward Finn and Bonnie, who had pulled their horses up short to wait for Adam to greet his father. "This is Bonnie and Finn . . ." He paused then, trying to recall. "I can't remember your whole name, Finn." He couldn't remember Bonnie's last name, either, but let it go at that.

"It's Michael," Finn quickly replied, "Michael Finn, and I'm pleased to meet you, sir."

"Right," Adam continued. "Anyway, Jake was prospectin' with Finn for a while before he was killed."

"Lord have mercy," Mose uttered sorrowfully, "Jake dead?"

Nathan ignored Mose's lament and turned his attention to the strangers his son had brought to his home. "You folks must be tired. Looks like you've been ridin' awhile. Adam, maybe you can help Mose take care of the horses, and I'll see if Pearl can't rustle up somethin' to eat for Mr. and Mrs. Finn. Then you can tell me about your brother." He didn't notice the quick smiles on Adam's and Bonnie's faces that his gracious invitation caused. They made no effort to correct his assumption, but Finn was quick to respond.

"She's not my wife," he blurted. "She's just ridin' with us."

"I beg your pardon," Nathan said, then stood aside and motioned for them to come in. He was playing the part of the perfect host, but Adam knew he would take his grief to a private place later, when he could be alone.

Bonnie beamed her thanks for the invitation and headed for the door, but Finn held back, reluctant to take his eyes off his packs. Adam assured him that his mules, and the load on their backs, would be fine. So

Finn followed Bonnie into the house, still with some reluctance.

When they had gone into the house, Mose stepped up beside Adam and whispered, "Where'd you pick up the horses? What's in them bags on them mules?"

"Somethin' Finn don't wanna lose," Adam replied. "We'd best unload 'em and lock 'em in the tack room."

"I knew it!" Mose said. "I knew right off there was pay dirt in them bags—had to be. Is part of it yours?"

"Nope, but we'd best protect it like it was."

After the livestock were taken care of, Adam went back to the house to join his friends in a quick supper that Pearl, Nathan's half-Shoshoni cook, prepared. Mose would eat with Doc and the rest of the hands in the bunkhouse when the crew returned for supper. Ordinarily, Nathan and Adam would have eaten with the men in the bunkhouse as well.

During their supper, his guests related their hazardous journey to reach Nathan's ranch, and the fact that Adam had been kind enough to see them through. The details of the many killings, and Adam's finding of the mutilated body of his brother, were left to Adam and his father after the others had retired for the night—Bonnie to the front bedroom, and Finn to the barn to sleep in the tack room. Adam assured him that his packs would be safe there, but he understood why Finn was reluctant to have them out of his sight.

Father and son talked late into the night, and Adam tried to explain why he had to go back to Alder Gulch. "I know you say it ain't my fault about Jake, but I won't ever feel like I've done him justice if I let that one murderin' bastard get away with what he done—not only for Jake, but for the girl Jake was plannin' to bring here to live."

Finally, when Nathan was convinced that nothing he could say was going to change Adam's mind, he gave up trying. "What about the folks you brought home with you?" Nathan asked.

"I'm hopin' it'll be all right with you if they stay here for a spell till they decide what they're gonna do."

"Sure," Nathan said. "We've got plenty of room. They're welcome to stay." He stroked his chin thoughtfully, then said, "If that Finn has as much gold dust as you say, I expect he won't be here long before he heads to Butte or Helena, or someplace else where he can spend it."

"I wouldn't be surprised myself," Adam agreed. "And I doubt if Bonnie will let him out of her sight."

Nathan smiled. Then his expression turned serious again. "When are you plannin' to go back?"

"Tomorrow—don't see any sense in waitin'. Cruz might decide to take off somewhere."

His father nodded solemnly as he studied his son's face. Adam had been a man since he was fourteen, and Nathan had trusted him to do the right thing. No one but Adam was qualified to say if one more killing was justified. Nathan only hoped it would be enough to eliminate the guilt his son harbored and bring him peace of mind. "Adam," he finally said, "I've lost one son already. I can't afford to lose another one. You be sure you come back home."

"I will, Pa."

"I noticed you rode in on a new horse," Mose called out as he came out to the corral where Adam was examining Bucky's left front hoof. "What happened to Brownie?" Adam explained that he had been forced to put Brownie down after he broke his leg in a badger hole. "That'un you rode back looks a lot like Bucky," Mose said.

"I reckon that's one of the reasons I picked him," Adam said as he slipped a bridle on the bay gelding and led him to the gate. "Looks like I was worried about Bucky's hoof for nothin'. It looks all right now."

"Your pa said you was headin' out again," Mose said. He pulled the bar on the gate and held it open for him. "You takin' a packhorse?"

"Nope. I ain't takin' nothin' but what I can carry on Bucky. I don't plan to be gone long."

Mose's demeanor turned to serious for a moment. "Damn it, boy. Don't go gettin' yourself killed. Your pa may act like the toughest son of a bitch north of the Yellowstone, but I don't see how he could hold up if somethin' happens to you. You know, maybe it ain't up to you to right all the wrongs that happen in this territory."

"Only the ones close to the family," Adam responded as he pulled his saddle off the top pole of the corral and approached the bay. Bucky sidestepped a couple of times before he stood still to accept the saddle.

"He ain't been rode since you been gone," Doc said as he walked out of the barn and came over to join them.

"I can see that," Adam remarked. "He always gets a little spooked when he ain't seen a saddle in a while."

He was almost ready to leave when Finn and Bonnie walked down from the house to see him off. "I wanna thank you for seein' me through," Finn said. "You're walkin' right into the devil's den if you go in Virginia City lookin' for Cruz. I don't suppose you'd reconsider?"

"If I have one more person tell me . . . ," Adam started, then stopped. "I'll be comin' back."

"I meant what I said before we left Bannack," Finn said, lowering his voice so only Adam could hear. "I'll be payin' you for actin' as my guide and protection."

Adam smiled at the earnest little man. "I told you, Finn, you don't need to pay me. I was coming here anyway." He stepped up in the saddle when Finn started to protest. "We'll talk about it when I get back."

Bonnie stepped up quickly when Finn moved away to give Bucky room to turn, and motioned for Adam to bend low so that she could tell him something. "You take care of yourself, big boy," she whispered. She paused a moment before saying, "Thank you for not telling your father I was a prostitute." It had been a while since anyone had treated her like a lady.

"I don't see any reason to bring it up," he told her. She favored him with a grateful smile and stepped back from his stirrup. He wheeled the big bay and prepared to give him his heels. Looking back toward the house, he saw his father step out on the porch and stand to watch him depart. Adam saluted with a touch of his hat brim with one finger. His father acknowledged the gesture with a single nod of his head, then turned and went back inside. Once Adam set something in his mind, there was very little that could dissuade him. *I guess he got it from me*, his father thought, *because I'd do the same thing in his shoes.*

"What the hell do you mean, showing up here with your tail between your legs, and that old man and his gold wandering out there somewhere in the mountains? Hell, you just let a fortune in gold ride right outta the territory to who knows where."

Cruz cringed from the stinging rebuke from Henry

Plummer, his swagger properly deflated by Plummer's wrath. He did his best to defend his defeat at the hands of one old miner and an alleged hired gun hand. "That feller with old Finn ain't human—" he started, but Plummer cut him off.

"He ain't human?" Plummer roared. "Are you trying to tell me he's a ghost or something?" He slammed his hand down hard on the desk, making no attempt to control his anger. "Five of you went after him and four of you don't come back? Obviously, I picked the wrong five stumblebums to do a simple job of taking care of one man with a rifle." His patience gone, he yelled, "Get out of my office before I decide to shoot you myself!"

"Yessir," Cruz replied, humbly, his bull-like shoulders slumping as a result of the vocal whipping. He wasted little time going out the door, knowing that the only reason he didn't get a bullet in the back was due to the fact that it was broad daylight and he was at Plummer's office on Wallace Street. At the hitching rail in front of the building, he met Joe French, just then dismounting.

"Heard you was back," French said. "Heard you came back by yourself. What the hell happened?"

Cruz had already had his fill of explaining why he failed to carry out Plummer's orders. "Ran into some bad luck," was all he offered.

French cocked his head to one side and grinned. "Big feller, totin' a Henry rifle?" The smile vanished as suddenly as it had appeared and French became serious. "I've knowed you for a good while, Cruz, and that's the only reason I'm tellin' you this. You'd best make yourself scarce around Virginia City. Bannack, too. You know Plummer don't have much use for anybody who don't do the job for him. I'm just tellin' you, that's all."

Cruz was not in a mood to appreciate the advice. "Is that so? Anybody comin' after me is gonna regret it." He glowered at French defiantly for a long moment before turning toward his horse.

"Like I said," French remarked, "I was just offerin' you some friendly advice." He turned then and went inside the sheriff's office.

"Where've you been?" Plummer demanded gruffly. Without waiting for an answer, he said, "I think Cruz's worn out his usefulness to us. I want you to take care of him. I can't tolerate a man working for me who ain't got the spine to do a simple killing. Maybe it'll send a message to everybody else that they'd damn sure be ready to do whatever I tell them." French shrugged indifferently and started toward the door, but Plummer stopped him. "Do it out of town somewhere. No sense in getting the people in town more fodder to chew on." He was thinking about some recent developments that had given him cause for serious concern. The vigilantes had gotten a tip-off on the whereabouts of eight members of his network of road agents and arrested five of them—caught them in their camp. Instead of bringing them back to Virginia City or Bannack, where Plummer's judges could have found them not guilty, they took them instead to trial in Nevada City. It was the first real threat to Plummer's control over the concept of law and order. Especially of concern to him was the fact that these people had acted without making their intention known to him. He had joined the vigilance committee when it was first proposed, so as to know what their plans were, and thus be able to warn his gang members. The fact that it was obvious to at least some members of the vigilantes not to inform the entire committee of arrests like this recent one led him to believe that it might be approaching the time when he should be moving on to another town. He was reluctant to leave. He had established himself well here, and it had made him a very wealthy and powerful man.

"When did you get back in town?" O'Grady asked when Cruz walked in the front door of his saloon. "Where's the rest of your friends?" The sight of the brooding bully was not a welcome one to O'Grady. He had hoped he had seen the last of Cruz and his troublesome gang.

"In hell by now, I expect," Cruz answered. "Gimme a beer."

"Somethin' happen to 'em?"

"I guess you could say that," Cruz replied, and paused while O'Grady set a glass of beer before him. He tipped the glass back and drained half of it before continuing. "*Somebody* happened to 'em would be better said."

O'Grady was curious, but as usual, deemed it better not to know what Cruz and his friends had been up to, so he tried to steer the conversation away from the subject. "You stayin' in town long, or just passin' through?"

"Hell no," Cruz replied. "I ain't stayin' around this damn town. I'm on my way now as soon as I have me another glass of beer. Folks are more friendly in Bannack." He said it before he took time to think about it, so he warned O'Grady, "I expect you'd best keep that under your hat. Ain't nobody's business where I'm goin'. You catch my drift?"

"Oh, hell yeah, Cruz. You know me," O'Grady was quick to reply.

"Right," Cruz grunted, and fixed O'Grady with a cold eye. "I know you." He finished off his second glass of beer, wiped his mouth with the back of his hand, and turned to leave without any gesture of paying.

"Beer's on the house," O'Grady called after him with a hint of sarcasm. Although annoyed by the somber brute's indifference to an obligation to pay for his beer, he was far too afraid to make a demand.

O'Grady wiped the bar where Cruz's glass had left a ring, then plunged the glass in a bucket of water behind the counter and set it on a towel to dry. No more than fifteen minutes later, he turned to see Joe French come in the front door. "How do, Joe?"

"I'm lookin' for Bailey Cruz," Joe said, "thought he mighta come in here."

"You just missed him," O'Grady replied. "Couldn'ta been more'n a quarter of an hour, maybe less."

"He say where he was goin'?"

O'Grady hesitated for a brief moment, thinking about Cruz's warning, but Joe French was probably one of the few friends Cruz had. "I think he might be headin' for Bannack, but I don't know for sure."

"Bannack, huh? I expect he might be at that." French turned and left without further comment. One of Cruz's favorite hangouts was the Miner's Friend in Bannack, a saloon near the end of the short main street, with several rooms upstairs to let. It was a good bet he could be found there if French failed to overtake him on the road to Bannack.

Feeling the familiar weight of his master on his back, Bucky settled into a comfortable gait that would be easy for him to maintain for as long as Adam felt reasonable.

The partners knew each other well. Retracing his previous journey to find Jake, he reached the camp where he had met Rob Hawkins and Jim Highsmith, making the ride in three days, a full half day better than the first time. Remembering the two as pleasant men to share a camp with, he found it ironic that he was now sitting by the fire sipping his coffee, knowing that he had killed them both. *They chose the path to follow*, he reminded himself.

From this camp, it was no more than a half day's ride to Virginia City, but he decided not to start out early the next morning, thinking it better to arrive after dark for a couple of reasons. It was a pretty good bet that there might be a lot of Plummer's men looking for him, so it made sense to hit town under the cover of darkness. And, too, it was more than likely that Cruz might be easier to find, in O'Grady's, or one of the other saloons, at night.

With a cautious eye to either side of him, Adam rode along Wallace Street at a slow walk. As usual, Virginia City was noisy after dark, with saloons and bawdy houses in full swing. There appeared to be no one in the sheriff's office when he passed it on his way toward the end of the street and O'Grady's saloon. No doubt Plummer's deputy was making the rounds of the town, so Adam warned himself to be extra careful. There was no way he could identify a deputy from any other man on the crowded boardwalk unless the deputy wore a badge. He was counting on the possibility that no one of the sheriff's *deputies* could really identify him as well. If events occurred as he hoped, he would find Cruz, take care of business, and be on his way before

Plummer could react. Being the realist that he was, however, he doubted things would happen in that orderly fashion.

Unlike the other saloons in town, O'Grady's seemed to be doing a less than lively business when he reined the bay up by the hitching rail and dismounted. He drew his rifle from the saddle scabbard, took a quick look up and down the street, then stepped up on the boardwalk. Inside, he paused to look the room over, his gaze skipping from table to table, searching for someone that might match the description Seeger had given him, but none fit the picture he carried in his mind. His gaze shifted to the bar, and he recognized the bartender from the time before when he had come in for a drink and had an altercation with two of Plummer's boys.

When he walked up to the bar, O'Grady glanced up and immediately recognized him. He started to say so, but decided to hold his tongue. He had overheard enough of the talk between Cruz and Seeger to know that Adam had been targeted for death, along with the confiscation of Michael Finn's fortune. He was not sure what the unexpected presence of the big man with the Henry rifle meant, but he had a feeling it promised trouble for someone. "What's your pleasure?" O'Grady managed to ask.

"You remember me?" Adam asked.

"Yes, sir, I do."

"I'm lookin' for a fellow named Cruz. Is he in here?"

"No, sir, he ain't," O'Grady replied. That was all he intended to say, but reflecting for a moment on how much he resented Cruz's presence in his bar, and the effect it had been upon his patronage with the town's honest citizens, he changed his mind. "He was here, but I think he's on his way to Bannack. I might oughta tell you that one of the sheriff's deputies, Joe French, is lookin' for him, too."

Adam could not be sure. "You ain't just tellin' me that to send me off on a wild-goose chase, are you?"

"Mister—" O'Grady looked up at the formidable figure towering above him and answered frankly, "I'm afraid to lie to you, and that's the God's honest truth. Cruz's been gone since this afternoon."

"Much obliged," Adam said, then promptly left the saloon. Outside, he replaced his rifle in the scabbard and stepped up in the saddle. Turning Bucky's head toward the road to Bannack, he decided not to take the shortcut, as he did the last time, still remembering Brownie's untimely demise caused by a badger hole. There was a three-quarter moon hanging over the hills surrounding the gulch, so he figured he wouldn't wait for daylight to get started.

Chapter 14

Close to the time Adam started out along the moonlit road to Bannack, a lone rider thirty miles west of Virginia City guided his horse cautiously up a wooded ravine toward a soft glow near the top of a bald ridge. When within about fifty yards of the campfire, Joe French dismounted and tied his horse to a pine limb, planning to go the rest of the way on foot. The trees that lined the ravine provided ample cover, although the darkness might have been protection enough, but French was not inclined to take any chances on being seen. Never one to complicate things, he sought only a clear line of sight where he could let his rifle take care of the business he was about. Cruz would be scratched off the list. He had no particularly hard feelings toward Cruz. The man was an especially crude brute, but French had never had any trouble getting along with him. He'd even spent a few nights drinking with Cruz and his late companion, Tom Seeger. French was just carrying out his boss's orders.

It had been a stroke of pure luck that he had noticed the small glow of a campfire far up on a ridge; otherwise he would have passed Cruz by. It was well off the road, but since he did see it, his job might be finished a whole lot sooner, and he could start back to Virginia City in the morning. *I wonder if ol' Cruz has anything to eat*, he thought as he moved to within forty yards. The trees ended about five yards in front of him, so he crept up to the last of them and knelt on one knee. Pulling a pine branch aside, he now had a clear view of the camp. He saw the fire, and Cruz's horse, as well as his saddle and blanket on the ground, but there was no sign of Cruz. *Now, where the hell can he be?* he wondered.

"You lookin' for me?"

"Jesus!" French yelped in alarm. "You scared the hell outta me!"

"Is that so?" Cruz replied. He was kneeling beside a wagon-sized rock, his rifle cradled before him. "I was wonderin' what would cause a man to come sneakin' up on another man's camp."

French tried to think fast. "Oh, hell," he blustered, hoping to convey a feeling of relief. "Is that you, Cruz? I thought I'd run up on a miner or somethin'; thought I'd best be sure before I went ridin' in on who knows what. I reckon it's a lucky thing for me it's just you."

"Yeah," Cruz replied drily, "it's your lucky day. It's just me. How'd you know there was a camp up this far on the ridge?"

"What?" French stumbled. "Uh, I didn't. I was lookin' for a place to camp myself. I didn't have no idea there was anybody up here. Boy, I'm glad it's you."

"What are you doin' out this way?" Cruz asked, still very deliberate in his speech, and still holding his rifle in position to fire in an instant. He was enjoying the position he had French in.

"On my way to Bannack," French said. "Runnin' an errand for Plummer."

"You coulda told me this mornin', and we coulda rode together."

"I didn't know this mornin'," French said, "else I sure woulda rode with you. I reckon we can ride on in the rest of the way."

Cruz casually shifted his rifle around to point at French. "Nah," he said, "I don't think so. I don't much like to ride with no lying, back-shootin' son of a bitch."

"Now, wait a minute, Cruz!" French pleaded frantically. "You got no call to talk thataway. I'm your friend! Ain't I the one that warned you this mornin' that you oughta get outta Virginia City? Didn't I tell you you need to be careful?"

"Yeah, you did," Cruz allowed. "You surely did tell me I'd better be careful. That's why I'm settin' here by this rock with a rifle aimed at your head, knowin' Plummer was gonna send some low-down bastard after me."

French knew his ticket to hell was all but punched. No amount of talking was going to get him out of the fix he was in. He had no choice but to make a move. It was a useless attempt, for as soon as he tried to raise his rifle, Cruz pulled the trigger, sending a bullet into the side of his head. "Glad you could come to call," Cruz said. There was no need to check to make sure French was dead. There was only a small black hole in his temple, but a sizable part of his brain was protruding from the other side of his head. "I ain't as dumb as you thought I was," he said to the corpse. "I knew Plummer would send somebody after me, either you or that

damn ghost, Briscoe. It's your tough luck he sent you."
He tried not to admit that it was his good luck that Briscoe had not been sent, at the same time wondering if
that would be next. He made up his mind that he was
going to hole up in Bannack, in the midst of plenty of
witnesses, until he felt sure no one was waiting for him
to leave town. Then he was heading for Salt Lake City,
or maybe beyond. That decided, he emptied French's
pockets, took his watch and chain, a pocketknife, a
hand-tooled belt with a silver buckle, and the little bit of
money he found. Then he walked back down the ravine
to fetch his horse. It was there in French's saddlebags
that he found a small sack that he estimated to contain
at least a pound of gold dust. That would be the equi-
valent of over three hundred dollars. "Looks like ol'
Plummer was payin' some of you boys better'n the rest
of us," he said with a smirk. "Yessir, glad you could
come to call." French's saddle would bring a fair price
to boot. When he had taken all from the late Joe French
that he would have use for, he sent the corpse rolling
over and over for a few yards down the slope of the
ravine with a kick of his foot.

Down at the end of the bar, Big John Tyson, the owner
of the Miner's Friend Saloon, was involved in a serious
conversation with his bartender, Fred Smith. The topic
of their conversation was at the moment seated at the
last table in the far corner of the barroom, a half-empty
whiskey bottle and one glass on the table before him.
"How long's he been there?" Tyson asked.

    "He came in this mornin' about ten o'clock and he's
been there ever since," Fred replied. "He don't even
leave to go eat—has Loretta bring him his food right

where he's settin'. The only time he leaves that table is
to go out back to the outhouse. Then he's right back
there in the corner."

"Well, we can't have him settin' up camp at one of
my tables," Tyson said. "I'm payin' that damn worth-
less sheriff to keep control of his gang of riffraff. I'll go
see Ainsworth and tell him to get the brute outta here."

"Are you sure you wanna do that?" Fred asked. "It
ain't like he's runnin' up a bill. He's payin' all along.
He's even paid in advance for a room upstairs, and it
looks like he ain't fixin' to run outta money no time
soon. He don't say nothin' to nobody, just sets there
starin' like he's expectin' somebody to walk in the door.
So he ain't really causin' no trouble, just maybe makin'
the other customers a little nervous."

This caused Tyson to look at the problem from a different perspective. He had assumed that Cruz intended
to drink all the whiskey he wanted, eat food from the
kitchen, sleep upstairs for as long as it suited him, then
walk out without paying for any of it. It was typical of
the band of robbers and murderers that had taken over
the town, free of concern for their lawlessness. He had
seen Cruz before. The man had a reputation for vio-
lence, but he had never experienced Cruz as a paying
customer. "Well, I guess he ain't doin' much harm just
sittin' in the corner. As long as he doesn't start causin'
trouble, let him be, at least till his money runs out.
Then we'll go get Ainsworth to throw him out."

Cruz's gold dust was not even close to running out
when he finally got up from his corner table and, with
another full bottle of whiskey, went upstairs to the
room he had rented for the night. His plan was to leave
for Salt Lake City in the morning, but when morning

came, it found him sick in the stomach and head, the
result of the previous day and night's ingestion of food
and spirits while waiting for the next assassin that he
was certain Plummer would send.

Knowing he had to pull himself together, lest he be
taken by surprise, he staggered to his feet after empty-
ing the contents of his stomach in the slop jar beside
the bed. Feeling drained then, as if part of what he had
just vomited was supposed to be a permanent part of
his insides, he decided that he needed to put food
in his belly again, as well as a glass of the "dog that bit
him." On unsteady feet, he strapped on his gun belt,
picked up his rifle, and headed for the stairs. Halfway
down the steps, he stopped to look the barroom over
before descending the rest of the way. He was relieved
to see no one who could possibly be a threat, only a
couple of the saloon's usual early-morning drunks.
From the foot of the stairs, the kitchen door was only a
few feet away, so he stuck his head in and yelled to
Loretta to cook him some breakfast.

Johnny Pitt sat at the back corner table eating his
breakfast of ham and biscuits smothered with sawmill
gravy, with a steaming hot cup of Loretta's coffee. It
was a morning ritual that had endured for over a year,
before going to his blacksmith shop at the stable. He
always sat at the back corner table, facing the door, so
anyone needing some early work at his forge could easily find him. He glanced up when Cruz yelled in the
kitchen door for Loretta, but paid him no further mind.
That is, until he looked up again to find the notorious
bully standing before him, glaring at him through dark
bloodshot eyes, causing him to stop chewing.

"Find yourself another table," Cruz ordered.

Without thinking, Johnny glanced around the empty tables and asked, "Why?"

"'Cause this'un's mine," Cruz replied, his heavy brows glowering menacingly.

Johnny looked down at his half-eaten breakfast, then back at Cruz. "Hell," he said, trying to show some measure of backbone. "All the other tables are empty. Why don't you just take one of them?"

"'Cause I'm fixin' to put a hole right through that dumb skull of yours if you ain't outta my chair by the time I count to three." He leveled his rifle, with the muzzle about four inches from Johnny's forehead, and started counting. "One . . ." Johnny was on his feet before hearing the word *two*, knocking his chair over backward in the process.

Seeing the disturbance in the back corner, Fred hurried from the bar to try to prevent bloodshed. "Here, Johnny, let me help you move your stuff over to another table." He grabbed Johnny's plate and cup as quickly as he could and removed them. "Cruz *has* been using this table, and one's just as good as another." Cruz said nothing, but continued to glower while Fred picked up Johnny's knife and fork.

When the table was cleared to his satisfaction, and Johnny was settled quietly at a table close to the bar, Cruz yelled, "Bring me a bottle." He sat down at the table then, laid his rifle on it before him, and waited for his breakfast while trying to calm his uneasy stomach, still with a notion to shoot the blacksmith. He had a strong desire to punish someone for the rotten way he was feeling. *Or maybe*, he thought, *I ought to shoot Fred for selling me that damn rotgut whiskey.* It occurred to him that the whiskey had to be bad to make him feel that sick. His condition was worsened, however, when Loretta brought his breakfast and placed it before him. The greasy odor that wafted up from the plate of ham and potatoes, drowning under a blanket of thick gravy, triggered a response from Cruz's gut that would not be denied. He jumped to his feet, grabbed his rifle, and headed out the back door to the outhouse.

No more than a second or two had elapsed when the front door of the saloon was filled by a tall, broad-shouldered man carrying a Henry rifle in one hand. Fred remembered the stranger. He would be hard to forget. No one spoke for a moment while Adam looked around the almost empty saloon. Turning to Fred then, he said, "I'm lookin' for Bailey Cruz. Somebody told me I might find him here."

Not certain if he should say anything, Fred hesitated. Johnny Pitt, struck dumb for a few moments, his fork suspended halfway between plate and mouth, eagerly volunteered. "He just stepped out to the outhouse." Then he pointed toward the back door with his fork, still with a wad of ham speared on it.

Without hesitation, Adam went deliberately to the door and stepped outside. About sixty feet behind the building stood the five-by-eight-foot privy. Adam halted to stand squarely facing the board structure, his rifle raised to fire. The thought flashed through his mind that he should make sure that Cruz was in there, and not someone else. "Cruz!" he called out. "It's time for you to settle up for your murderin' ways. If it ain't Cruz in there, you'd best step out right now, so I can see you." There was no reply from the little shack, so Adam was about to repeat the demand when the door of the outhouse opened slightly and a rifle barrel protruded several inches. Adam saw it in time to jump to the side and kneel to avoid the bullet that whistled wildly by the side of the saloon. From his position at the corner of the building, Adam laid down a continuous wave of fire, intent upon shooting the outhouse to pieces.

Inside the besieged outhouse, a snarling Bailey Cruz sat on one hole of the two-seater toilet, trying to see something through the boards to shoot at. With the flimsy structure coming to pieces, as the hail of .44 slugs continued to tear holes all around him, it was only a matter of time before one of them found him. When a bullet finally tore into his arm, he yelped with pain, and all thoughts of his upset stomach were completely forgotten, replaced by the realization that the next bullet might be the fatal one. There was no thought of surrendering, for he was certain that this was an execution, pure and simple. In a panic to find cover from the relentless blistering that was knocking huge chunks from the walls, he found only one possible escape. Howling in agony when a second bullet found purchase in his shoulder, he gripped the back of the box that formed the seats of the toilet and jerked it free of its base. Without hesitating, he then dropped down into the pit of the toilet to find refuge amid the putrid mess on the bottom. Short in stature, Cruz found that he could just barely see over the top of the foul hole he had been forced to occupy. At least it afforded protection from the constant rifle fire that now went over his head.

Almost certain he had heard at least two cries of pain, Adam paused to reload the magazine of his rifle. Already, the under barrel of the weapon was too hot to handle because of the repeated firing, so he wrapped his bandanna around it to hold on to while he loaded in fifteen more shots. Then he waited for a couple of minutes. There were no more shots coming from the outhouse, so the question now was had he landed a fatal shot, or was Cruz trying to lure him in?

Cruz had stopped shooting for the simple reason he was too short to fire over the edge of the hole he was in. His only option for defense was to lean back in the corner of the pit to give him an angle to fire at Adam if he came in the door. The situation resulted in a stalemate between the two, with another worry to confront Adam. How long had he been there, pumping bullets into that toilet? Surely the sheriff, or some of Cruz's friends, might show up at any minute, but he wanted to make sure he finished the job before taking to the hills. *Maybe he's dead*, he thought, knowing that he had to be certain. *But if I walk up and open that door, and he ain't dead, then I'm as good as.* "Hell," he exclaimed in frustration, "I can't just sit here wonderin'."

He got to his feet and ran back along the side of the saloon, looking back frequently to make sure Cruz didn't come out of his hole. At the front of the building, he quickly untied Bucky's reins, jumped in the saddle, and raced back to the outhouse, shaking out a loop in the rope on his saddle. With no regard for the possibility of a shot coming from inside the cramped privy, he looped the noose over a corner of the roof, took a couple of turns around his saddle horn to pull it taut, then gave Bucky his heels. The big bay jumped to the task and lunged, pulling the outhouse over on its side and revealing the trapped murderer huddled in the corner of his malodorous grave. The fatal bullet came as Cruz tried to turn for a better angle to fire. Adam's slug caught him square in the chest, and he immediately sank to his knees in the filthy slime before falling over on his side.

Adam took only a few moments to gaze down at the corpse lying in the muck of the toilet to make sure another bullet wasn't necessary. It seemed a fitting ending for the conscienceless killer. He shook his rope loose from the roof corner and coiled it. Back in the saddle, he could hear the clamor of voices in front of the saloon. No one had dared to venture around to the back while the shooting was going on, but Adam knew it would only be a matter of minutes before they did, now that it had stopped. With no desire to get into it with the sheriff or any of Cruz's friends, he gave Bucky a firm heel and galloped away behind the buildings.

As he approached the rear of the assay office, beside one of the stables in town, a man ran out in the alley, waving his arms, trying to flag him down. Adam pulled his rifle, but the man appeared to be unarmed. "Hold on!" the man pleaded, and moved from side to side, trying to block Adam's path.

Adam pulled Bucky up to keep from running the man down, but he was in no mood to waste time with him. "Mister, I don't wanna run over you, but I damn sure will."

"Wait! I'm a friend of Bonnie Wells! My name's Clyde Allen."

"Well, whaddaya want, Clyde Allen? I'm kinda in a hurry."

"I wanna warn you, mister. One of Ainsworth's men saw you ride into town, and they've set up ambushes on both ends of town, just waitin' for you."

Adam was at once alarmed. He had counted on riding in unnoticed, completing his mission, and riding out before the outlaw sheriff knew what had happened. He peered at Clyde Allen in an effort to make a quick judgment. Maybe he was just part of another trap to stop him, but he seemed genuine in his concern for Adam's safety. And if what he said was true, it would explain why it took so long for the sheriff to respond to the shooting behind the saloon. Before deciding, he looked out across the open ground between the buildings and the ridge bordering the gulch with a thought to simply hightail it toward the slope, avoiding both ends of the town.

Reading his thoughts, Clyde said, "That's a long ride without a tree for cover. You'd be an easy target."

Adam tended to agree. "All right, what have you got in mind?"

"Follow me," Clyde said, and motioned toward the stable behind him. "Nobody's gonna look for you there, but we need to be quick about it." Without waiting for Adam's response, he turned and trotted toward the open door.

Aware that his options were few, Adam decided to put his faith in the man's honesty, and followed him through the door of the stable. Coming from the bright sunny morning, he needed a few seconds for his eyes to adjust to the dark interior of the stable. When they did, he was startled to find himself confronting a semicircle of perhaps a dozen men. His initial reaction was to draw back hard on Bucky's reins while reaching for his rifle. "Hold on, Adam!" a voice bellowed. "We're friends!" Since no one of them raised a weapon against him, he hesitated, still unsure. The man who had called out to him stepped up beside his stirrup. His eyes now fully adjusted to the darkness of the stable, Adam recognized Mutt Jeffries, the stage driver.

"Mutt? What the hell?" was all Adam could say. He noticed then that all of the men were heavily armed, although none of them appeared to be other than store clerks and businessmen.

"You got here at a pretty good time," Mutt said. "This is the vigilance committee of Grasshopper Creek, and we're fixin' to clean out this town of all the outlaws that have been robbin' and murderin' all over this valley. We've got the names of ever' one of the bastards that have been ridin' for Ainsworth and his outlaws. We was plannin' on goin' to get that murderin' son of a bitch that's been sittin' in the back corner of the Miner's Friend since yesterday, but you kinda beat us to it." He paused to grin at the men behind him. "Matter of fact, you've cut down on the amount of work we had to do, ever since you landed in town a while back. Now we feel like we got enough men to finish the job you started."

Astonished to hear that he had played a significant part in the vigilante effort to clean up the town, Adam was not sure if they expected more from him. "I told you from the first why I came to Bannack. I wasn't successful in finding my brother alive, but I did find the men responsible for his death. They're all taken care of. That fellow, Cruz, was the last on my list, so I'm done with what I set out to do. All I want now is to get on back home."

"Adam," Mutt implored, "this business is bigger'n

just Grasshopper Creek. We've been workin' with the committee in Alder Gulch and Daylight Gulch, too. We're takin' our towns back from the outlaws that have been makin' a livin' robbin' honest folks. They're all comin' down, and I'm talkin' about Henry Plummer, too. A citizens group arrested him yesterday in Virginia City, gave him a short trial, and hung him— said he cried like a baby." His remark caused a muttered wave of approval from the men gathered around him. "Last week a citizens group arrested five outlaws and took 'em to Nevada City for trial where Plummer couldn't get to 'em. They hung 'em, but before he died, Red Yager confessed and named Plummer as the boss of the whole thing. A lot of us knew Plummer was behind it all, but we couldn't prove it."

"So now you're wantin' me to join you fellers. Is that it?" Adam asked.

"Well," Mutt said, "we'd sure welcome it, but like you said, you've done your part, and you're ready to get the hell outta here. Can't blame you for that. To tell you the truth, we've got things under control now. Some of the outlaws got wind of what was goin' on and turned tail and cleared out. We've got enough of us to handle those waitin' in ambush for you at each end of town." He grinned confidently. "No, we didn't stop you for that. We just wanted to keep you from ridin' right into an ambush. You just give us a head start and we'll take care of that situation."

Although surprised by Mutt's statement, Adam was glad to hear that they weren't looking to him to participate. He had had enough of killing to last him the rest of his life, something he was going to have to carry on his conscience, even allowing the fact that every life he had taken would be justified by most men. "I appreciate it, Mutt," he said. "I expect it is time that I got back home to help my pa with the stock. I wish you men good huntin'."

"There's somethin' more you need to be worryin' about," Mutt said. "Red Yager also told 'em that Plummer had already sent word to that damn professional killer of his to track you down and kill you. Yager said you had killed off too many of Plummer's gang. They was all sure that you was a hired gun that the citizens here had called in to clean 'em out. And since nobody he sent after you came back alive, he decided to call in some high-priced help."

Adam didn't respond right away. Mutt had given him something to think about, something he hadn't considered, and something he could certainly do without. "Who is this professional killer?" he asked.

"I don't know," Mutt replied. "There ain't much I can tell you about him. I don't believe he's ever been around here. If he has, nobody's ever seen him."

"I heard Fred Smith talkin' to Big John Tyson about him," Clyde Allen offered. "He said his name is Briscoe. That's all he goes by. When I asked Big John about him, he told me to mind my own business."

"Sorry we can't tell you more about him," Mutt said. "You just be sure you're careful, and don't leave a trail for anybody to follow."

"Yeah, I will," Adam said. "You mind you be careful, too, and good luck to you." He grabbed Mutt's hand when it was offered to him, and they shook. "Briscoe, huh? Well, I don't plan to wait around for Mr. Briscoe. I'm headin' back to the Yellowstone. He's gonna have to be part Indian to catch me."

He stood there, holding Bucky's reins, while the solemn group of men filed out of the stable on their way to the site of the ambush at the upper end of town. He waited nearly twenty minutes before stepping up in the saddle again. Walking Bucky to the doorway, he paused to search up and down the alley before venturing out again. A sudden eruption of shotgun and rifle fire from the upper end of town, past the hotel, told him that the vigilantes had confronted the outlaws waiting in ambush. And from the sound of it, Adam guessed that the outlaws were on the run. *I guess Mutt wasn't lying when he said they could handle it*, he thought. He nudged Bucky into an easy lope, pleased for the honest people of the town that they were ridding themselves of the vermin that had preyed upon them for over two years.

Kneeling between two lone fir trees near the top of the very hill that Adam had first considered heading for, an interested observer watched the developments taking place in the small mining town. While looking the town over earlier, he had spotted the miners' hired gunman when he rode up to the saloon. At least, he was about seventy-five percent certain that it was the man he had been sent to eliminate. He wasn't able to tell much about the man at that distance. He had simply been told that he was a big man, riding a bay horse. When, a few minutes later, the gun battle behind the saloon took place, he became more convinced that he was the right man. It was obvious that the gunman had come looking for his victim, and when he had done the job, he rode away behind the buildings. At that point, he lost track of him until the group of men emerged from the stable and headed for a confrontation with three bushwhackers hiding at the head of the trail out of town. Then his target appeared again, riding away toward the far hills. Briscoe was a hundred percent certain then that he had the right man.

He had the feeling that something on a large scale was occurring in the mining towns. What he witnessed here in Bannack on this day was something he never expected to see any time soon—a citizens' committee moving against the outlaws. Perhaps had he been in constant contact with Henry Plummer, he might have seen this coming. But it was not his style to stay close to the rabble that Plummer employed. In fact, he preferred to remain apart until summoned for a specific job, as in this case. He suspected that Plummer's days were numbered, but he had been paid a handsome fee to eliminate this so-called professional gunman, and he had always earned his money. And now he had a hot trail to follow. Mr. Professional Gunman was on a short string, because once Briscoe had a trail, the execution was as good as done. He stepped up in the saddle, guided his horse down the hill, and angled across the broad valley in the direction the big man on the bay had taken.

He struck his trail just west of the town, fresh tracks in the soft dirt beside a trickle of a spring, and he dismounted to study them. He wanted to familiarize himself with that particular set of tracks. Satisfied, he mounted again and followed the trail until it led to the road to Virginia City. *He's going to make it pretty easy for me if he stays on the road*, he thought. *It'll just be a matter of catching up with him.* Pausing to look for signs that the tracks departed from the many other tracks on the road, he studied both sides of the road for a distance of about a hundred yards. Satisfied then that his target was intent upon taking the road to Virginia City, and not concerned about being followed, Briscoe urged his horse into a lope.

Chapter 15

It was Adam's plan to leave the main road when he came to the Beaverhead, then follow that river north to bypass Virginia City before cutting across to the Madison. This was what he had attempted to do before with Finn and the two women, only to be driven into the mountains to hide. Recalling that journey caused him to think about the young girl, Lacey, and the sorrow he felt for not seeing her safely home. He had no idea if it would have been a good idea to take Lacey to the Triple-B, but he felt that his father would have taken her in, especially if Adam told him that Jake had planned to marry her. No one would have to know her past. Adam was convinced that she deserved a second chance. *But I reckon it just wasn't in the cards*, he thought.

Eager to take his mind off Lacey, he thought about the warning he had gotten from Mutt. There was a hired killer searching for him. The thought did not frighten him. He viewed it more as an irritation than anything else. The part of the story that he found ironic was the outlaws' belief that he himself was a hired assassin for the miners. *Well*, he considered, *maybe I was an assassin, but I'm not one anymore and I sure as hell didn't kill for money.* Still, he had to deal with the fact that there was someone somewhere in these mountains who was out to kill him—and he had no idea what he looked like. So that meant that all strangers had to be held in suspicion.

He struck the Beaverhead just before dark, just short of its confluence with Blacktail Deer Creek. The wide, grassy valley was almost devoid of trees, offering very little concealment for a camp. He looked across the valley at the mountains in the distance and decided they were too far, so he decided to follow the river north until he came upon a spot with thick brushy banks and a handful of willow trees. "This will have to do, Bucky," he finally announced, and dismounted.

Briscoe considered himself as good a tracker as any man, but he had to admit that it was pure luck, or maybe instinct, that caused him to turn around and go back to take a closer look at the road where it crossed a small trickle of a stream. Something told him that it would be an ideal place to leave the road if a man wanted to without leaving sign for someone following. At first, there appeared to be no evidence that his target had done so, but after careful examination, he was able to form a picture in his mind of a horse being led up the tiny stream. He smiled to himself as he knelt to touch a sizable pebble that had recently been dislodged. He and his prey thought very much alike, and he wondered if the man knew he was tracking him. It didn't matter, Briscoe thought, because he knew who was going to win in the end. Meanwhile, it would make the hunt more enjoyable.

The man he had come to kill had walked his horse for almost two hundred yards up the stream before leaving it and remounting. There had been barely enough light for Briscoe to see the tracks where he had exited the water. They told him that the man had continued to follow the general course of the stream as it made its way to the Beaverhead. A full moon had peeked over the mountains to the east by the time Briscoe reached the banks of the river. He paused on the grassy bank to consider what he would do, if he were in his target's shoes. The answer was obvious, so he started out along the bank, looking for a suitable place to set up a camp.

The moon was fully on top of the mountains, spreading its light across the valley, when Briscoe saw what he was looking for. A thicket of willows and brush stood a couple of hundred yards ahead on the opposite bank. He waited for several long minutes, watching the trees, before he turned his horse toward the water and crossed over to the other side. Finding a sizable berry bush, he tied his horse there, not willing to chance a whinny from the blue roan as he neared the camp. Then, readying his rifle, he started forward on foot to see if, in fact, there was a camp in the willows. After he'd advanced to within fifty yards, his instincts were confirmed by the sight of a flicker of flame amid the trees. He carefully began to move in closer, but he did not hurry. It made little sense to take unnecessary chances. His prey was supposedly a professional killer. So he decided to bide his time and wait for him to bed down, then walk in and shoot him while he was in his blanket, swift and simple. It would even be easier on the victim.

Adam knelt by the river where a large clump of berry bushes hung over the water. He took a last swallow of coffee and dumped the dregs from his cup, then rinsed it. He had an uneasy feeling that he could not explain. Maybe it was the full moon, he thought, for he was not really worried about the man who was supposed to be stalking him. It was unlikely that anyone had any idea where he was. *It would sure make sense to be a little more careful, though,* he thought. So he went back to his campfire and pulled his saddle and blanket closer to the edge of the tiny clearing, where they would not be so easily seen.

The night wore on as the moon continued its journey across the sky, moving closer to the western mountains, and the firelight flickering through the trees had almost faded away, when Briscoe got to his feet and stretched. *Time to earn your money,* he thought. He was not a man entirely without conscience, but he felt no compassion for his victims. They were all outlaws, robbers and murderers, so in effect, he was doing the world a favor every time he eliminated one of them. He started to move in.

Making his way carefully and quietly, he moved slowly through the outer fringe of the trees until he could see a small clearing in the center. Dropping to his hands and knees then, he edged even closer until he could see the entire camp: the bay horse down close to the water's edge, the dying campfire, and off to the side, the sleeping figure of the man he had come to kill.

Still with no cause to rush the execution, he slowly rose to his feet and stepped into the clearing, his rifle aimed at the sleeping form by the saddle. Taking careful aim, so as not to waste cartridges, he took a few more steps closer to his unsuspecting target and stopped.

The next few seconds were shattered by gunfire when Briscoe pulled the trigger and sent a .44 slug ripping into Adam's blanket, only to feel the burning impact of a bullet almost immediately after slamming into his back. With animal-like reflexes, he spun around to fire at the man standing in the deep shadows across the clearing, but his shot was wide of the mark. Already dying, he nevertheless cocked his rifle again while fighting to stay on his feet, for he knew, if he went down, he would never get up again.

Adam stepped out of the shadows just as the moon slipped from behind a cloud, illuminating the tiny clearing. He raised his rifle to deliver the final shot, but suddenly he could not pull the trigger. His whole body froze, unnerved by the face he saw in the moonlight. "Jake!" He gasped as the rifle dropped from his brother's hand and he slowly sank to the ground. "Jake!" Adam cried out again in horrified realization that he had just killed his brother. He dropped his rifle and ran to his brother's side. Dropping to his knees, he started to lift Jake up to hold him in his arms, but Jake gasped in pain and begged him to let him lie.

"Adam?" Jake forced the words through teeth clenched in pain. "What are you doin' here?"

"I'm gonna take you home," Adam said, his words halting and trembling with the crushing realization of what he had done. "You'll be all right. I'll take care of you. Just lie still now and don't try to talk." He was trying hard not to panic. His shot had been a kill shot, and it was obvious to him that Jake was fading fast. And he didn't know what to do to save him.

"I reckon he outsmarted me," Jake gasped, then tried to cough up the blood that was now filling his lungs. He was still unaware that it was Adam who had fired the fatal shot. "I didn't kill any innocent folks." He closed his eyes then and seemed to relax.

Alarmed, Adam took him by the shoulders and begged, "Jake, hold on, hold on. Don't give up. Oh God, I'm so sorry! I didn't know it was you!"

Jake opened his eyes one last time and smiled faintly. "Big brother," he whispered, "you always come to take care of me. I was comin' home after this last strike." Then his eyelids fluttered briefly and he was gone.

Overcome with the tragic grief that now consumed him, Adam pulled Jake's lifeless body up in his arms, pressing him close to his chest until he could contain his anguish no longer, and he roared out his pain into the indifferent night. He remained there on his knees, holding his brother for a long time, tears streaming down his rugged face, until he at last was able to gather his emotions and take control again.

He buried his brother near the bank of the Beaverhead River, digging the grave with a short hand axe and his hunting knife. With only those tools available to him, it took him the rest of the night to dig the grave deep enough to suit him, for he could not abide the thought of leaving Jake in a shallow grave to be torn apart by scavengers. When it was done, he sat down in the early-morning sunshine to think about what had happened. Although still emotionally drained, and physically spent from his nightlong labor, he was able to try to make some sense of it all. He had been so convinced that the body he had discovered in the gully near Finn's camp was Jake, because Jake had disappeared completely. It was difficult to believe, knowing his brother, that Jake could turn to murder to make his fortune, even though he might have thought he was doing the world a favor. He had said as much before he died. *It's my fault*, Adam thought. *I should have been there to talk some sense into him*. Then he paused to consider the name Jake had chosen, and it occurred to him then where it had come from—Briscoe. It had come from their home in Briscoe County, Texas.

It was not going to be easy for him to live with the horrible sin he now carried on his conscience. There was no forgiving a man who had killed his brother. Of that he felt certain. He would go home to the Triple-B now, but he was not sure he could ever tell anyone of the real circumstances that had led to his brother's death. When he thought about it, he decided that it would be best to let his father go on believing Jake was killed by outlaws near Bannack. He had already resigned himself to his son's death. Why open up a new source of grief? Smoothing over the grave as best he could, he spread dead limbs from the willows over it in an effort to disguise it.

He found Jake's horse about two hundred yards short of the camp, tied to a berry bush. At first, he had thoughts of setting the horse free, thinking it would only remind him of what had happened here. But there was the matter of the saddle and bridle, and the rest of Jake's belongings. He couldn't carry them on Bucky, and he was afraid if he left them here, it would cause someone to nose around and stumble upon the grave. So he tied the blue roan on behind his horse and set out on the sorrowful journey home.

He rode back into the Triple-B almost unnoticed. Had it not been for Doc, who was cleaning out one of the stalls in the barn, he would have been. "Well, damn!" Doc exclaimed when he turned to see Adam opening the corral gate. "Howdy, Adam. How'd you slip in here?" He leaned his pitchfork against the side of the stall. "Here, lemme give you a hand," he said, and hurried out to pick up one of the saddles. "You back to stay for a while now?"

"I reckon so," Adam said as he picked up the other saddle and followed Doc into the tack room. "Where is everybody?"

"Well, your pa's in the house," Doc said. "Mose went up to the north range, where them cows are always bunchin' up. Just to aggravate the boys trying to head 'em back from the river, I s'pose. Finn and Bonnie rode into town for somethin'."

The last comment served to amuse Adam slightly, and the first hint of a smile touched the corners of his mouth since he had left the Beaverhead. "Finn and Bonnie, huh?"

"Yeah," Doc answered in his simple way. "I believe they're thinkin' 'bout gettin' hitched." This brought a genuine look of surprise to the somber man's face. He didn't express it aloud, however, as he finished putting away his gear. "Where'd you pick up the extra horse and saddle? That looks like that black horse Jake used to ride."

"It's Jake's," Adam replied. "I picked him up in Virginia City." He left then and went to the house to find his father.

Caught by surprise, Nathan Blaine almost dropped his cup when his eldest son walked into the kitchen. "I hope that pot ain't empty," Adam said. "I've been out for a while."

"Good gracious alive, boy!" Nathan exclaimed. "You almost made me spill my coffee. Yeah, hell, grab you a cup. If it's empty, I'll call Pearl in here to make us another pot." The joyous relief to see Adam would have been difficult to disguise, even had he tried.

For the next hour, father and son discussed all that had taken place to change everyone's life on the Triple-B. Adam told him that the ledger was balanced as far as he was concerned in regard to Bailey Cruz, and he hoped that his days as a hunter of men were past him forever. When the conversation got around to Finn and Bonnie, it drew an amused chuckle from Nathan. "That's one helluva spunky woman," he allowed.

"Doc said they were talkin' about marryin'."

"That's a fact," his father said, still smiling broadly. "They are, indeed. We're plannin' to throw a big weddin' party for 'em—gonna get the preacher in the settlement to come out and tie the knot—do it up right. And that ain't all the news I've got for you. Looks like we've got a new partner. Finn's decided he wants to get into the cattle business—wants to use some of that gold to buy new stock and land. He says he's wantin' to build him and Bonnie a big house over there by the creek and then build a bigger barn and bunkhouse. Whaddaya think of that?"

Adam shook his head, truly amazed. "What do *you* think of it?" he came back.

"Hell, how can we lose? I ain't lookin' a gift horse in the mouth. It'll give us the money to do a lot of things I've wished we could do."

Nathan and Adam were eating supper in the bunk-house with the rest of the crew when Finn and Bonnie came back from town. Mose heard them come in, so he went to the barn to unhitch the buckboard and put the horse in the corral. "Adam's back," was the simple announcement he made before returning to the bunk-house and his supper.

"Well, I see the prodigal son has returned," Finn joked upon seeing Adam at the table. The joy in find-ing his friend back where he belonged was evident in his face as he fairly beamed his pleasure, a look that was reflected in Bonnie's face as well.

Only Adam could appreciate the irony in Finn's greeting. And although he did not show it, the remark created a picture in his mind of the last moments of his brother as he had held him in his arms. *In time*, he thought, but he feared he would never be at peace with himself. For now, however, he forced himself to rise to the occasion. "I hear there's gonna be a weddin' at the Triple-B," he said cheerfully.

A ragged cheer went up from the table of rough cowhands, but Finn quickly put up his hands to stifle it. "There'll be no weddin' at the Triple-B," he said, bringing a stunned silence to the room.

"We tied the knot in town today," Bonnie announced, causing another cheer. She looked at Adam and winked.

He nodded. *Damned if you didn't marry the gold*, he

thought, *just like you said you would.* He had to admit, it was probably the best thing that could happen to both of them.

Mose pounded Finn on the back and exclaimed, "You old dog, you!"

"Yep," Finn replied, beaming, "I'm an old dog, all right, and I need a feisty little bitch to take care of me." He looked at Bonnie and grinned.

Please read on for an excerpt from
the next exciting historical novel
from Charles G. West,

DEATH IS THE HUNTER

Available now from Berkley!

Little Bit Morgan pulled his gray gelding to a halt at the top of a gentle rise, took off his hat and waved it in the air to signal the six riders following a short distance behind. "There's a farmhouse up ahead," he said when they caught up to him. He put his hat back on, carefully cocking it just so. The black wide-brim hat with a silver chain around the flat crown was his pride and joy.

"Good," Webb Jarrett said to Bevo Rooks, who was riding beside him on the dusty Texas trail. "We'll stop and get some of this grit outta our throats."

"These horses is plum wore out," Bevo said. "If we don't rest 'em pretty soon, we'll be walkin' to Injun Territory." The horses had been ridden hard in the gang's race to beat a sheriff's posse to the Red River. At nine o'clock that morning they had held up the new bank in the little town of Sherman, leaving a teller dead, shot down when he attempted to run out the back door. It appeared that they had successfully lost the posse, but even if it persisted in trying to get on their trail, they were confident that a posse of Sherman citizens would be reluctant to stay after them once they were across the river into Oklahoma Territory. Once there, they wouldn't worry about any Texas Rangers coming to look for them.

When they caught up to Morgan, who was referred to as Little Bit due to his short stature—and more so because of a short fuse when his temper was riled—he said, "Looks like a nice little nest somebody's built right next to the river.

"Might be we could stop and visit a spell. That looks like a smokehouse behind the house. This time of year there oughta be some hams hangin' up in there. That'd be all right, wouldn't it, Webb?"

Webb Jarrett grinned. "It'd sure be to my taste right now. I swear, robbin' banks makes a man hungry." He paused to look the place over while the rest of his men pulled up beside him to have a look as well. "A right smart little farm that feller's got for himself." Off the corner of the house, opposite the smokehouse, was a modest-sized barn that looked to accommodate maybe two horses or mules. The house had a nice front porch, which indicated that the woman of the house had a say in the decisions. "Yes, sir," he continued, "a right smart little farm. I expect we wouldn't be polite if we was to ride on by without stoppin' to visit." His comment brought forth the malicious grins he expected. "Let's ride on in and pay our respects. Jake, you ride on back to that hill yonder and keep your eyes peeled. I think we most likely lost that posse, but you hightail it back here if you catch sight of 'em—give us enough time to slip across the river."

"Hell, Webb," Jake complained, "why me? Why can't somebody else do it? Besides, we ain't seen hide nor hair of 'em in the last hour."

"'Cause you're the one that shot that teller, and

most likely stirred the folks there into comin' after us," Webb said. "I'll send somebody to spell you. You ain't gonna miss much."

Franklin Chapel walked out of his barn in time to see the six riders descending the low ridge that bordered the river on the south side. He paused and shielded his eyes with his hand as he tried to see who they might be. His first impulse was to go back in the barn and dig into the corn bin for the .44 Colt hidden there, but there had been no trouble from Indians or outlaws on this stretch of the river for quite a long time, so he decided he was being too cautious. It wouldn't be a very neighborly reception to meet a group of visitors with a gun in his hand. Still, he studied the riders intently as they approached, as they obviously were not planning to bypass his house. When they reached the end of the corral where the cow was penned, Franklin called over his shoulder toward the house, "Ruth, there's company comin'." Not waiting to see if she had heard him or not, he walked forward to meet the strangers. "Afternoon," he said in greeting.

"Afternoon, sir," Webb returned politely. "We're a company of Texas Rangers on the trail of some bank robbers. Wonder if you'd mind if we watered and rested out horses here for a short spell?"

Franklin replied, "Why, no, I wouldn't mind. You're welcome to rest here, and I expect my wife could rustle you fellows up somethin' to eat as well." He was relieved to hear they were Rangers, for he had decided that they were a rough-looking group of men. Even though this area along the river had been trouble-free with the Civil War having just ended, there were a lot of outlaw gangs roaming the northeastern part of Texas. "You fellows step down and I'll tell my wife to get somethin' goin' on the stove."

"That's mighty neighborly of you, friend," Jarrett

said. "Me and the boys have been ridin' hard for a few hours, and that's a fact."

"Well, there's good water at the well, there, and if you want to take the saddles off, you can turn your horses in with the cow. I'll go in and get Ruth started." He paused to consider the six rough men before suggesting, "I expect it'd be best for you fellows to come on up on the front porch when you're ready."

"We're much obliged," Jarrett said. He waited until Franklin disappeared through the kitchen door, then turned to remark, "Did you hear that, boys? He's gonna go in and get Ruth started. She's gonna fix us Rangers a big meal."

After the horses were watered and turned out with the cow in the corral, the outlaws strolled over to the front porch. Webb took one of the two rockers there and Bevo took the other, while the rest of the gang sat down on the edge of the porch to await their supper. Franklin Chapel returned to make conversation with his guests while they waited for Ruth to fry some bacon and boil some beans that she had planned to cook later for supper. "You fellows say you're chasin' some bank robbers?" Franklin asked.

"That's right," Little Bit answered. "We're chasin' some dangerous outlaws."

"Where'd they rob a bank?" Franklin asked.

"Down in Sherman," Webb replied. "It's a new bank. First Bank of Sherman, I think was the name of it."

"Did they get away with much?"

Bevo grunted and said, "Not as much as they thought they was gonna get."

"You said they robbed it this mornin'," Franklin said. "You fellows got onto 'em pretty quick. I never knew there was a Ranger station anywhere near Sherman."

Webb smiled patiently. "There's a new Ranger headquarters just a few miles south of Sherman, so it didn't take long to get on their trail." He glanced at Bevo in the rocker beside him and winked.

"That's right," Bevo said. "We were in the saddle almost as soon as the bank robbers." His comment drew a chuckle from the other three sitting on the edge of the porch.

The response caused Franklin to become a little nervous, unable to see the humor in Bevo's remark. News of a recently established Ranger station as close as a day's ride from his farm would ordinarily have spread rapidly throughout the small community of farmers just across the river from the Indian Nations—but he had heard nothing at all, not even a rumor. "Well, I reckon it's lucky you boys were that handy." Feeling a bit uncomfortable then, he was glad when the door opened and his wife came out on the porch carrying a huge pot of coffee fresh off the stove and an armload of cups. *Best to get them fed and back in the saddle,* he thought.

"I'm Ruth Chapel," his wife announced as all six outlaws scrambled to grab a cup from her. "You gentlemen caught me without much food prepared, but in a few minutes I can at least feed you some bacon and beans. I'm sorry I don't have time to bake any bread." Ignoring the fact that every eye was locked upon her, she went along the line, filling each cup. "How about you, Franklin? Do you want coffee?"

"I reckon not," he replied. His discomfort was gradually becoming more intense, and he wondered if he had made a mistake in not fetching his .44 when he first had the notion. When Ruth had filled each cup, he stated, "I'll go in and give you a hand." Then he followed her into the house.

"Ol' Franklin looked like he all of a sudden got sick in the stomach," Little Bit remarked. "You reckon he's startin' to smell a skunk?"

"Don't make a whole lotta difference if he did," Bevo

said. "There ain't a helluva lot he can do about it, is there?" He took a gulp of the hot coffee and smacked his lips in appreciation. "That wife of his ain't a bad looker. How old a woman you reckon she is?" he asked Webb.

"Hell, I don't know," Webb answered. "Old enough, but not too old, I reckon." Bevo's question sparked an enthusiastic interest in the rest of the men.

"I swear, Bevo," Little Bit taunted, "you ain't been married but about a year, and you're already eyeballin' women older'n you are."

Bevo grunted stoically. "I got married," he said. "I didn't go blind."

Little Bit chuckled. "I bet you don't tell Pearl Mae that. She's damn-near as big as you, and she looks like she might be a little tougher."

"One of these days that mouth of yours is gonna open a door you ain't wanna go through," Bevo warned.

"Is that a fact?" Little Bit replied. "I ain't worried about openin' no door. My style is to kick the damn door down and kick whoever's ass is on the other side." His taunting grin invited Bevo to take the next step as his hand dropped to rest on the skinning knife he wore.

"You two just simmer down," Webb ordered, "before they come back."

The incident advanced no further because the door opened just then and Ruth informed them that their food was ready. "You can come on in the kitchen and get your plates," she said. "The food's on the table, such as it is. You can help yourselves." She stood aside as the rough crew filed inside, each one eyeing her openly. She sent a worried glance her husband's way as he stood near the pantry door. He had held a hurried conversation with her in the short time they were alone in the kitchen, and she was in agreement that there was something awry in the manner of these self-professed Texas Rangers. As a precaution, he had loaded his shotgun and stood it up just inside the pantry door. She hoped with all her heart that there would be no occasion for him to use it. She not only feared for hers and her husband's safety. Their son, John, was somewhere down the river hunting, and had been gone since early morning. She was in a quandary over whether she wished he would show up, or if she should pray that he didn't. John was only thirteen, but he seemed older than his years, and was unacquainted with fear in any form. If these men were evil, as she now suspected, he would not hesitate to attack them with no thought of the consequences.

Ruth and Franklin stood back and watched while the six men attacked the pot of beans and the plate laden with most of a side of lean. Like a pack of hungry wolves around the carcass of a cow, they set upon the modest fare until there was nothing left. One of the men, a tall, lanky bean pole of a man named Earl set his empty plate on the table and wondered aloud, "You reckon we oughta saved some for Jake?"

"We might have at that," Webb replied. "Tell you the truth, I plum forgot about him."

"There's another one of you?" Ruth asked.

"Yeah, there's one more," Webb said, "but he don't need nothin' to eat." He looked at Earl then and said, "I reckon you oughta go on back there and tell him to come on."

"Ain't he gonna be hot when he finds out we been settin' around the table eatin'?" Little Bit remarked, amused by the prospect. "I can't wait to see his face." His remarks drew a round of chuckles from them all.

Growing more fearful by the minute, Ruth made a

subtle attempt to verify their claim that they were Rangers. "You know," she said, "I don't believe I've ever seen a Texas Ranger's badge."

Bevo Rooks cocked a wary eye in her direction. "Looks like any other badge," he said. "Nothin' fancy about it."

"May I see yours?" She said it before she gave herself time to reconsider.

"My what?" he responded with an impish grin, causing Little Bit to snicker.

"Your badge," she said, flushing with embarrassment.

"We don't always wear our badges," Webb interjected, "so the outlaws don't run off when they see us comin'."

"Oh," she responded fearfully. She knew then that her suspicions had been confirmed. Meeting her husband's worried gaze, it was obvious that he had reached the same conclusion. Her foremost hope now was that they would leave, since they had been fed and their horses watered and rested. Seeing Franklin inching his way closer to the pantry door, she frowned at him, trying to discourage him from making any suicidal attempts for the shotgun. He paused with his hand almost touching the doorknob.

"Well, I reckon you fellows are anxious to get on your way," Franklin said. "I'll help you saddle up." He walked to the kitchen door and opened it. None of the men made a move toward it.

"Why, we ain't in no hurry a'tall," Bevo said, leering at Ruth. "Are we, boys? We got time to get better acquainted. Now, me, I been wonderin' how an ugly son of a bitch like ol' Franklin got himself a spunky-lookin' woman like you. Hell, I'm as handsome as he is. My wife says I'm like a bull in season when I get to goin' good. If you ask me real polite-like, I'll be glad to show you." He cocked his head to sneer at her husband. "Ol' Franklin won't mind. Will you, Franklin?" Bevo's friends stood there grinning, enjoying the show and anticipating their participation.

"All right, fellows," Franklin spoke up. "This has gone far enough. We welcomed you and fed you. Now I'm tellin' you it's time you got on your horses and left." He looked at Ruth and said, "You go on back in the parlor till they've gone."

She hurried toward the door, but was not quick enough to evade the lecherous grasp of Bevo Rooks. She uttered a frightened squeal when he grabbed her arm. It seemed to please him. "Sounds like a rabbit when a hawk catches him," he said with a chuckle. "Let's me and you go in the bedroom. You got a few gray hairs on ya, but I bet you can still buck. Can't ya, honey?" He started pulling her toward one of the two bedroom doors.

It was too much for Franklin to endure. "Get your filthy hands off her!" He roared and ran to the pantry, where he managed to get to his shotgun—but that was as far as he got before Webb Jarrett calmly shot him down. Horrified, Ruth cried out once more before her legs collapsed beneath her and she fainted.

Ready to find
your next great read?

Let us help.

Visit prh.com/nextread

Penguin
Random
House